Festus knew the game was up.

He yanked his six-gun out of its holster and stood up just in time to see Waco jump behind Bessy and put a stranglehold around her neck as he drew his own. "Deputy, throw down your gun and get out here or I shoot everyone right now!" Festus knew he had no choice or Waco would turn the bank lobby into a slaughterhouse.

"Yes, sir," Festus said, hurrying back into the lobby and wondering how they were going to get out of this mess alive.

"Deputy, you get down on the floor. Bank teller, empty the drawers of cash, then empty the vault, too!"

Nash reached inside for his derringer. While he was trying to get a shot, Waco shot the retired riverboat gambler in the chest. That was when Festus attacked. He threw himself into Bessy, ramming her so hard that both she and Waco crashed into the wall. Before the Texan could recover, Festus scooped up Nash's spilled derringer, raised it, and fired both barrels point-blank into Waco's upper body.

GUNSMOKE™

A NOVEL BY
GARY McCARTHY

*Based on the radio and television series
created by John Meston*

BERKLEY BOULEVARD BOOKS, NEW YORK

GUNSMOKE

A Berkley Boulevard Book / published by arrangement with
Viacom Consumer Products, Inc.

PRINTING HISTORY
Berkley Boulevard edition / December 1998

The Penguin Putnam Inc. World Wide Web site address is
http://www.penguinputnam.com

ISBN: 0-425-16518-3

BERKLEY BOULEVARD
Berkley Boulevard Books are published by The Berkley Publishing Group,
a member of Penguin Putnam Inc., 375 Hudson Street,
New York, New York 10014.
BERKLEY BOULEVARD and its logo
are trademarks belonging to Berkley Publishing Corporation.

PRINTED IN THE UNITED STATES OF AMERICA

10 9 8 7 6 5 4 3 2 1

CHAPTER

1

Marshal Matt Dillon stood beside the bar sipping his beer and only half listening as his friends Kitty, Doc, and Festus talked about the change in the weather and how the Texas cowboys would soon be arriving with their herds of Longhorns. The cowboys would be young and wild, mostly good, but some bad. Still, as far as Matt was concerned, this was just another spring and the cowboys would be dealt with fairly and with as much tolerance as usual, provided they obeyed the town's laws and acted at least half-civilized. Their annual arrival always created problems and long hours on the streets and in the town's rougher saloons for Matt and Festus.

"Doc, the thing of it is," Festus was complaining, "I never really had a chance to rest up this winter and now here comes trouble again."

"Oh?" Doc asked, raising his bushy eyebrows and peering over the reading glasses balanced precariously on the tip of his nose. "Then, Festus, why is it that I had the impression that you slept through all of January and February?"

"Doc!" Festus whined. "How can you say that! I been awoken like a dog all winter."

"Hmmph," Doc grunted just as a large and disheveled young homesteader barged into the saloon, squinted, and looked around with a pair of bloodshot eyes. Suddenly he spotted Doc and charged. Before either Matt or Festus could grab him, the stranger slammed Doc to the floor and was choking his neck in a fit of rage.

Matt grabbed Doc's attacker and hurled him spinning across the room to crash into an empty poker table. Then he collected him by the shirtfront and yanked him erect, shouting, "What's the matter with you!"

The homesteader's eyes rolled and his breath reeked of whiskey when he spat, "That old weasel murdered my wife and now he's going to pay with his life!"

Matt whirled around and shouted, "Festus, how is Doc?"

"Not so good!" Festus's expression was grim. "He's havin' trouble a-breathin'!"

Kitty was also at Doc's side and the two of them managed to get him to his feet, but Doc looked bad. Choking and wheezing, his complexion was pale and he was in obvious pain.

"Doc!" Kitty shouted.

"We'd better get him outside in the fresh air," Festus suggested, looking as worried as Matt felt. "The doc, he don't look so good, Matthew!"

"He'll probably be all right," Matt said with far more assurance than he felt. "You help Doc while I arrest this man."

"Is he crazy!" Festus yelled.

"I don't know," Matt answered. "After we make sure that Doc is all right, we can get to the bottom of this."

"I'd toss him in jail and then throw the cell key away," Kitty said, helping Festus escort Doc outside. "All Doc ever done was save lives. What was he raving about!"

"I'm talking about my *wife,* Lady! That so-called doctor you're so worried about murdered my wife!"

Kitty shot the drunken homesteader a look that would have killed had it been swallowed as poison, then said, "Mister, you're either crazy or a liar. And if I carried a derringer, I'd shoot you for this!"

Matt watched them take Doc outside and then he shoved the wild young stranger toward the door. "You're under arrest. What's your name?"

"George. George Bates. My wife's name was Polly."

Now Matt recalled the connection. "Doc told me about Mrs. Bates. He'd raced out of town late one night on an emergency to save your wife."

"He *killed* her!"

"No, he didn't. Doc takes his profession as seriously as I do mine. And I remember how upset he was about your wife dying. He said that she was too small to deliver her baby, and by the time that he arrived, she'd lost way too much blood. He felt so bad that I remember that he got half-drunk the next night right here in the Long Branch, and Doc doesn't do that very often."

"He might as well have been drunk the day he came out to attend to my Polly," George said bitterly. "That man ain't qualified to practice medicine, not even to a dying dog!"

Matt's square jaw jutted out and he had to rein in his temper. "Listen, Bates, I wasn't there when your wife died in childbirth, so I don't exactly know the circumstances. But I can tell you this much—Doc is a fine man and an excellent physician. He's saved hundreds of lives in Dodge City and I've watched or even helped him save more than a few of them that had been shot, stabbed, or beaten. I know that he's a good doctor, and while I'm sorry about your wife dying—"

"Wasn't just my wife! I lost my unborn child as well. Polly was carrying our first *son*!"

Matt could hear the anguish in the stranger's voice and knew the poor man had been drowning his sorrow in cheap liquor. Maybe, just maybe his action could be excused. Matt had never had a wife or child, but he could well imag-

3

ine how losing either might drive an otherwise decent man to the edge of insanity.

"Look, Bates, I am sorry about your wife and son dying, but that doesn't give you the right to blame Doc. And it damn sure doesn't give you free rein to barge in here and attack him!"

"The next time I get my hands around his scrawny neck, I mean to break it!" George raged through clenched teeth.

Matt had heard enough. "Bates, you're under arrest and I'm hauling you off to jail. Try to resist and you'll only make things harder."

"Matthew!"

It was Festus shouting. Matt shoved George out the front door of the Long Branch and hurried over to see Doc collapsed in the street, still having trouble breathing. Worse yet, he was trembling and clutching his chest. Matt wasn't a doctor, but it didn't take one to realize that Doc was suffering a heart attack.

The man was trying to speak, and when Matt knelt in the dust by his side, he heard Doc whisper, "Medicine. Get . . . me . . . to my office!"

"Festus, I'm taking Doc to his office now!" Matt bellowed, scooping Doc up as easily as if he were a boy before hurrying away.

"Matthew, what about this fella that attacked him!"

"Lock him up!" Matt bellowed over his shoulder.

Kitty was right at Matt's side when he eased Doc down on his own examining table and found a blanket and a pillow to put under the physician's head.

"Medicine!" Doc wheezed. "In that glass cabinet. Nitroglycerin. Hurry!"

Kitty reached the cabinet first and quickly found the bottle of nitroglycerin and said, "How many?"

"One!"

Doc took the tablet, clamped his jaw shut, and closed his eyes. Matt heard the man's sigh of relief and looked up at Kitty, saying, "Do you think . . ."

"I don't know *what* to think," she whispered, brushing back a tendril of damp hair and then motioning Matt out of the examining room so they could speak in private.

"He had a heart attack, didn't he, Kitty."

It wasn't really a question. Matt had seen it happen before, once to an older prisoner in his own jail awaiting trial for murder. Doc had been summoned and had administered the same nitroglycerin he'd just taken, but it had been too late. What Matt most recalled was that the prisoner's color had been grayish white, like Doc's, and he'd also had severe chest pains and difficulty breathing.

"All we can do now is make Doc comfortable," Kitty said.

"We must be able to do more than that."

"What do you suggest?" Kitty asked. "The nearest doctor lives eighty miles away and he's usually drunk. I wouldn't trust Doc Payson as far as I could throw the man and neither would anyone else in Dodge City."

"You're right," Matt growled. "But I sure wish we had another doctor here in Dodge! We've needed one for years."

"The problem is that Doc is so good no one will risk going to a new man. We've both seen new doctors try to establish themselves here but fail and then move on."

"Yep, Doc's his own worst enemy," Matt said with a shake of his head. "And now, when he needs an assistant to take care of him, he's out of luck."

"We're just fortunate that Doc is conscious and can tell us what to do," Kitty said, heading back into the examining room.

"I'm feeling better already," Doc whispered. "What got into George Bates?"

"He blames you for the death of his wife and son."

Doc sighed. "Don't arrest him, Matt. The poor man is crazy with grief. I expect that George didn't even know what he was doing when he attacked me in Kitty's saloon."

"Oh yes he did," Matt countered. "And he vowed to finish the job next time."

5

Doc shook his head. "It's just a damn shame that George didn't bring that poor woman in earlier. Polly Bates was small in the hips and her husband is a large man. I would have ordered him to keep Polly in town and then I could have watched that girl and maybe made a difference. But, by the time that I got out to his homestead . . ."

"It wasn't your fault, Doc. You're a doctor—not God. And as for Bates, well, I'll let him sober up overnight in jail and then I'll have a stern talk with him. If he's willing to apologize and swear to me that he won't try a stunt like that again, then I'll probably let him go home. But, if I get any hint—any hint at all—that he still intends to attack you, then I'll keep him locked up and he'll stand trial for assault with intent to commit murder. Judge Brooker is your friend and he won't go lightly on Bates."

Doc closed his eyes. "I feel very tired," he said in a voice that sounded old. "Help me to my bed and then let me sleep. Tomorrow I'll be fine."

"Are you sure?" Kitty asked. "Maybe I should stay with you tonight or at least have one of my girls keep you company. You know you're a favorite among them."

Doc managed to wink. "Then they might try to attack me in my sleep and I'm not up to that, Kitty. I'll be fine. I just need sleep."

"You had heart trouble, didn't you?" Matt asked.

"Hell no!" Doc exclaimed. "What are you talking about!"

"I'm talking about how you were clutching your chest in pain," Matt said bluntly.

"Look," Doc said after a long silence, "maybe I did have a little pain in my chest. But who wouldn't with someone choking them? I tell you, I'll be fine."

"Doc," Matt said, "you need to slow down."

"Tell my patients that and see what they have to say about it."

"If we had another doctor in Dodge, you could cut back and not work so hard or be on call for emergencies every night and weekend."

"Other doctors have come and gone." Doc scowled. "Can we carry on this conversation some other time?"

"Sure," Matt agreed. "Let's get you to bed and hope that no one in town suddenly needs a doctor for the next few days while you recuperate."

"I'll be fine by tomorrow," Doc promised as they helped him off the examining table. "Provided, that is, that no one else attacks me."

"I feel bad about that," Matt said. "But both mine and Festus's backs were turned and Bates had you down before we knew what was happening."

"Hell, don't go feeling guilty," Doc told him. "I'm just glad that Bates decided to strangle and not shoot me. Otherwise, I'd be dead."

Matt looked to Kitty, knowing that Doc was right. It could have been worse—a whole lot worse.

Matt dropped in on Doc early the next morning and he was shocked by how tired his old friend appeared. "You just stay in bed for a couple of days," he ordered. "We've got everything under control."

"Oh? Does that mean that you're going to deliver the next baby, sew up the next knife wound, or dig out the next bullet?"

"We'll handle it."

That remark gave Doc a chuckle which was a good sign. He snorted, "Well, you and Festus may *think* you can handle it, but I sure wouldn't want my life to depend on your poor medical skills."

"You must be feeling better," Matt said, " 'cause you're getting ornery again."

"Get out of here before you give me a headache."

Matt went back to his office. Festus was seated at his desk reading the morning paper and George Bates was sitting on his bunk with his head bent down nearly to his knees.

"How's Doc?" Festus asked.

"He's doing as well as can be expected. I think he'll be all right if he gets some rest."

"You know he won't," Festus replied. "There will be patients lining up at his office by noon when they hear he is under the weather. They'll all claim that they just need a minute or two of Doc's time, but those minutes add up and—"

"I know. I know," Matt said, turning toward the cell and then marching over to confront Bates. "You sober now?"

The homesteader didn't look up, but he did manage to nod his head.

"Good," Matt said. "Come over here to look me in the eye while I'm talking to you."

Bates did as he was told. "Marshal," he said, looking almost as bad as Doc and smelling like a brewery, "I shouldn't have gotten so drunk last night."

"No," Matt replied, "you shouldn't. Do you even remember what happened in the Long Branch Saloon?"

"Sure. I grabbed Doc Adams by the neck and nearly killed him."

"That's right," Matt said, not bothering to keep the anger from rising in his voice. "And you made Doc have a heart attack. Bates, do you know what would have happened if he had died?"

"No."

"I'd have arrested you for murder and the judge would have sent you to prison for at least ten years of hard labor."

"Even if . . ."

"Yeah," Matt growled. "Even if you were drunk and hadn't really meant to kill Doc. Is that what Polly would have wanted?"

"No, Marshal Dillon, it surely is not."

"So what is going to happen the next time you get blind drunk and show up in my town?"

"It won't happen again, I swear to you it won't! In fact, I'm leaving Kansas because there are too many ghosts haunting me. I need a new start in a place where everything doesn't remind me of what I lost."

"What about that homestead you and Polly proved up on? You both put a lot of work into it."

"I already had a fair offer to sell. Up until just now, I didn't know whether to accept it or not, but now I will." Bates shook his head woefully. "Marshal, you have to believe me. I regret what I did last night. I'll apologize to Doc. I'll do whatever it takes to make things right."

"Fair enough," Matt decided. "I'll tell Doc that you are sorry and we'll leave it go at that. As far as selling out, it might be the best thing. But you're going to have to deal with your loss of Polly and your baby. Going someplace new isn't going to fix everything."

"I know that, but I do believe it will help." Bates looked over to Festus. "If I slugged you or said anything against you, Deputy Haggen, I also offer you my apology."

"You didn't," Festus said, closing one eye and pointing a forefinger at Bates, "but if you ever touch Doc again, I'll be all over you like ugly on an ape!"

"I know that. But I'll be on my way to California."

"Then good luck," Festus said, relaxing. "And you should know that all of us feel real sorry about your loss. But you were wrong when you said Doc was responsible for it. Doc is the best there is. It wasn't his fault what happened out at your place."

"That's your opinion and you're entitled to it," Bates said with a hard edge suddenly creeping into his voice. "Marshal Dillon, can I go now?"

"Yes," Matt said, "but don't let me ever see you near Doc again. Is that understood?"

"Yep."

"All right, then." Matt turned on his heel and went over to his desk and retrieved a cell key. He released George Bates and, at the door, even offered his hand and said, "Good luck to you in California."

Matt and Festus both watched the big man shuffle away in his bib overalls and run-down-at-the-heels work boots. Festus looked up at the marshal and said, "Can we trust him?"

"Just to be safe, why don't you tail Bates until he's left town. That way we won't have to wonder if he was telling the truth or not."

"I expect he is," Festus said, "but Doc's poor old ticker might not stand any more rough surprises."

"I agree. Follow Bates to the city limits and then stop by and see Doc on your way back. If there's anyone pestering him for attention, run them off."

"I'll do that," Festus promised, "unless they're bleeding to death or somethin'. If that they were, what'd I do then, Matt?"

"Use your best judgment."

"Well," Festus said, "we gotta figure out something 'til the doc heals. People are going to get sick and hurt and have babies same as always."

"I'll put my mind to it. Go on now, Festus."

Matt watched his deputy hurry after George Bates, confident that the grieving homesteader had told the truth and was headed for California, although Matt could not imagine why he'd chosen such a distant place to start over again. Matt's preference would have been Colorado, New Mexico, or Arizona. All closer and with opportunities aplenty.

"I've got to think about Doc now," Matt muttered to himself as he hunkered down behind his scarred old desk. He kicked his heels up on top of it and steepled his fingers under his chin, knowing that they needed a second doctor in Dodge City and they needed one soon. Otherwise, it was just a matter of time before Doc was back in harness and working himself into the grave.

After several minutes, Matt dropped his boots to the floor with a loud thud. He found a pencil and some paper and began to write:

WANTED: AMBITIOUS YOUNG DOCTOR TO SET UP A NEW PRACTICE IN DODGE CITY, KANSAS, OR ASSIST IN AN ALREADY FLOURISHING ONE. COULD BE OPPORTUNITY OF A LIFETIME. INQUIRE AT THE MARSHAL'S OFFICE C/O MATTHEW DILLON, MARSHAL OF DODGE CITY.

Matt studied his words for several moments and then he nodded with satisfaction. Yes, this would do it. All that was necessary was to send the notice out on the telegraph to every reasonable-sized town within four or five hundred miles. That would include Denver, Santa Fe, Kansas City, Oklahoma City, and maybe even Fort Worth, way down in Texas. Matt wasn't sure who would pay for all the telegraphs, but he figured that a collection could be taken up once the word got out that Doc was going to have to cut back on his hours to maintain his fragile health.

Yep, this was the right thing to do, Matt thought. It was right because, if he waited and Doc heard about this plan, the old curmudgeon would raise a fit. Better to send off telegrams and find a young, healthy doctor out there someplace willing to live in a growing and law-abiding Kansas trailhead town. One whose citizens would have little choice but to support a second fine doctor to meet its growing demands.

CHAPTER

2

Festus was downright flustered. Matt had instructed him to follow George Bates out of Dodge City just to make sure that he had been telling the truth and had no further plans to kill Doc. Festus was good at following orders and he took pride in doing exactly what he was told by Marshal Dillon. Some people didn't take orders well, but Festus did, because Matt was his best friend in addition to being a top-notch lawman. The very best, as far as Festus was concerned.

And besides, Matt got paid for making tough decisions. Festus was happy with that arrangement and never comfortable when Matt had to go out of town leaving him in charge. It wasn't that Festus was afraid of making mistakes; nobody was always right. It was just that it was a lot easier to let Matt do the serious thinking and then carry out his orders to the letter.

But this morning there was a problem forcing Festus to make a decision he hoped Matt would approve. Namely, that he stop following George Bates and shoo off all the old women that were now standing outside Doc's office.

There were at least a half dozen, including Bessy Fife, who had a voice that would make the squawk of a crow sound like the music of angels. She was standing right at the head of the line, braying for poor Doc to open up his office and attend to the sick the same as he did every morning.

Just the sight of all those women—none of whom was half as sick as poor Doc—angered Festus. So he marched right up to the head of the line, pulled his hat brim down so hard that the tops of his ears bent outward, and said, "Mornin', ladies."

They paid him no attention despite his good manners. So much for trying to do this the easy way, Festus thought.

"Uh-hem," he began, clearing his throat. "Ladies, I'm sure that all of you must have heard about Doc getting attacked last night in the Long Branch Saloon and then havin' to be brought over here to rest. So why don't you leave him be for a couple of days."

Bessy Fife was tall and nearly as wide as a mule. She had arms twice as big around as Festus's, and when she got riled, she could be tough. Double chins quivering, Bessy raised a ham-sized hand and jabbed a sausage-sized finger between Festus's eyes, saying, "Festus, my gall-stones are a-rollin' around next to my liver and my gizzard is on fire."

"I doubt that," Festus told her.

"Well, you ain't no doctor, so you don't know nothing anyway!" Agnes Alder joined in, her with the face of a prune and the disposition of a teased weasel. "So, Festus, go off somewhere and do something useful so that folks in Dodge won't feel any worse than we already do about payin' your deputy's salary."

Festus knew when he'd been grievously insulted and was ready to go eyeball to eyeball with both old crones. He bristled, stomped his boots up and down, hitched his sagging pants higher, and stuck out his whiskery chin. "I may only be a lowly deputy in this town, but I got orders from Marshal Dillon hisself that the doc is not to be disturbed for a couple of days."

"A couple of days!" Bessy screeched, sending a shiver up Festus's spine. "We'll all be *dead* by then!"

"Well, orders is orders, so you'd better all go home and suffer in silence."

Bessy's meaty fists doubled up and Festus raised his hands to protect himself. What happened next would have been anyone's guess because Doc threw open the door dressed in his regular black striped suit, white starched shirt, and tie. He was pale, but his voice was strong when he said, "Mornin', Festus! Mornin', Ladies. Come on in and take your seats and we'll see what ails you today."

"Now, Doc," Festus objected, "you ain't fit yet to see all these old gals and—"

Festus would have said more, but Bessy bowled him over as she crowded into Doc's office. The other old cows stampeded in behind her, each giving Festus the evil eye.

"Doc, I—"

"It's all right. I'll be fine," Doc promised. "Last night I realized it was only my ulcer acting up again."

"Ulcer!" Festus stared at his longtime friend. "Doc, you was havin' heart troubles. Matthew said you took that there nitroglycerin medicine and—"

"Are you trying to play doctor, too?"

"No, but—"

"I'm fine," Doc repeated. "Now, you just run along and do whatever you do before your usual afternoon nap."

Festus was about to tell Doc that he didn't usually get an afternoon nap, especially after the Texans started arriving with their herds, but the door slammed in his face before he could get that matter straightened out. Back at the office Festus discovered Matt was gone, so he went into the cell and lay down for a spell. Matt had never exactly told him not to sleep in the cell and it sure was a lot more comfortable for a man to catch a short nap there than by laying his head on his desk.

•   •   •

14

"Festus. Festus, wake up."

Festus knuckled his eyes and yawned. "How you doin', Matthew? Is it time for lunch?"

"I already had mine. I'm taking up a telegram collection for Doc."

"Why?"

"Telegrams," Matt said. "I'm sending them out to every town within five hundred miles advertising for a new doctor to help Doc."

"Say now," Festus said, scratching himself good and coming to his feet. "That's a right fine idea!"

"It could save Doc's life. But it'll cost quite a bit to send out so many telegrams."

"Matthew, I'm a little short of funds right now. But payday is next week and—"

"I'll cover your share until then. Is ten dollars okay?"

"Ten dollars!" Festus gulped because that was almost a third of his whole month's pay. "Why . . . why sure, Matthew. If that's the fair share."

"Kitty has put in twenty-five and I'm matching her," Matt told him. "Festus, the thing of it is, we really need to find help for Doc in a hurry. I saw all those women over at his office. I should have guessed that he wouldn't have the heart to send them packing."

"That Bessy Fife and Agnes Alder are both awful," Festus groused. "No wonder Bessy's husband died of drink and Agnes's ran away."

"I know," Matt said. "When they finally left, I made Doc promise to put up his Closed sign and take the rest of the day off."

Festus shook his head. "That won't do no good. As soon as someone has a tooth- or belly-ache, they'll have to see Doc anyway."

"That's why we need a quick response on that telegram I sent out for a new doctor. I made it sound like the opportunity of a lifetime."

"It could be," Festus said, "if Doc wasn't so popular.

Dodge City is growin' bigger and bigger, but poor old Doc is just growin' older.''

"We'll just have to hope for the best." Matt went over and sat down behind his desk. "Did you make sure that Bates left town?"

Festus gulped. "Well, not exactly."

Matt had started to do some paperwork, but now his head snapped up. "Festus, what do you mean, 'not exactly'?"

"I was followin' George Bates just like you said when I came across all them wimmen that were standing outside the doc's door. Now, I know you told me what to do, but I just had to think about which was the most important— seein' Bates ride out of Dodge, or trying to drive off them wimmen."

"But you didn't drive them off, Festus."

"I know that, but—"

"Go check to make sure that someone actually saw George Bates leave town. That shouldn't be too difficult."

"I could ride out to his homestead this afternoon." Festus was feeling guilty now and it appeared he'd made the wrong choice.

"Naw," Matt said. "Just ask around. Someone is bound to have seen him leave town heading for his homestead. That's good enough."

"I'll sure do 'er," Festus said, hitching up his britches and hauling his holster and gun around from where it had gotten pushed up against his tailbone while napping. "Yes, sir, I'll get right on that!"

Festus headed out to find a witness and the first place he went was Delbert's Livery, where, for two bits, a man could turn his horse loose in a corral and have it fed good grass hay. Cheapest livery in town and the one where a man like George Bates would leave his saddle horse when he visited Dodge City.

"Yeah," Delbert Oatman said a few minutes later, "George left his horse here yesterday afternoon. Do you want to look at the animal now?"

16

Festus felt a shiver of dread wiggle the length of his spine. "You sure George's horse is still here?"

"Was the last time I looked. Ain't much of a horse, though. Skinny, jug-headed roan gelding that isn't worth more'n twenty or twenty-five dollars. George uses it to pull a plow when his mule is ailin' and that mule ain't much to look at either."

Festus felt his gut knot like a fist. "I'd better take a look at the roan."

"There it is," Delbert said a few minutes later. "Festus, didn't you know what George's horse looked like?"

"He should have ridden out by now." Festus turned a complete circle, eyes squinting hard as he surveyed the main street. "I guess you probably heard that George got real drunk last night and attacked Doc."

"Yeah, and I figured he must still be in your jail."

"Well, he was," Festus said, not wanting to go into a long explanation. "We let him out this morning after he promised he'd leave town. Said he was selling his place and heading for California."

"California!" Delbert made a face. "Now why would—"

"Look," Festus interrupted, "if George comes for his horse, you tell him to stop by the marshal's office before he heads for home. Can you remember that?"

"Of course I can," Delbert said, looking insulted. "But you just let him out of jail, so why—"

"Just do what I say. And tell George . . . tell him I need to say good-bye."

Delbert appeared confused, but Festus went stomping off to tell Matt what he'd discovered and then to see what they should do next. Halfway down the street, he halted in front of Doc's office and decided he ought to duck in just to make sure that Doc was all right.

He pushed open the unlocked door and poked his head inside. "Doc, it's me, Festus!"

There was no reply and Festus wondered if he should go see if Doc was asleep. But the man was touchy about his back bedroom quarters, so Festus wasn't sure until he heard footsteps.

"Doc, is that you a-walkin' around?"

No answer. Festus drew his six-gun and crouched. Something just wasn't right here and he had a bad feeling he knew what it was—George Bates had lied to him about leaving for California.

"George, this is Deputy Haggen! You come on out here with your hands in the air!"

"Go away, Festus! This is between Doc Adams and me!"

"Not anymore it ain't!" Festus yelled, starting down the hallway toward Doc's living quarters. He was wishing that Matt was with him now but knew there was no time to spare. In fact, he might already be too late.

"Throw your gun out, George!"

In answer, he heard the sound of running footsteps and then the slam of the back door. Festus jumped forward. He'd been in Doc's place enough to know where the back door was, but he meant to catch and arrest George Bates one way or the other.

Festus flew through the open door in time to see George running down the alley. He lifted his gun, took aim, and yelled, "Stop!"

Bates didn't stop. Festus lowered the barrel of his six-gun a fraction of an inch and pulled the trigger. His first shot might have been wide or it might even have passed between the man's legs, but it didn't matter because his second bullet sent Bates tumbling.

Festus sprinted forward, yelling, "Don't move!"

The man couldn't help but move. Bates was squirming and groaning as he tried to stanch the flow of blood from the bullet hole in his thigh.

Festus disarmed Bates, then tore off his own bandanna, shouting, "Hold still or I'll let you bleed to death, dammit!"

"I'd rather die than go to prison! Leave me alone, Festus!"

Festus wasn't sure how to respond, but then Doc came shuffling up the alley with his medical bag. He took one look at the bullet hole and said, "Festus, if he won't lie still while I work on this, pistol-whip him good!"

Doc soon had a bandage wrapped tightly around the homesteader's leg. "Festus, help me get this man into my office. It appears your bullet missed hitting bone or any big arteries, but I'll need to examine him closely to make sure."

"I don't want to live!" Bates shouted, making a feeble effort to break loose.

"Shut up, you fool," Doc muttered. "Festus, hurry and do as I say. He's still losing blood and time is wasting!"

Five minutes later Matt was helping Bates off the examining table and preparing him to return to jail.

"You all right, Doc?" Festus asked, angry at himself for believing the homesteader's lies about going to California.

"Sure am."

"Was he really fixin' to kill you?" Festus asked.

"Well, when I saw him burst into my office, I lit out down the hallway and locked myself in the bathroom. We were discussing my immediate future when you arrived. Thanks for missing your nap and coming by."

"I told you I ain't been takin' naps no more lately!"

Doc winked. "That's what I love most about you, Deputy Haggen, you appreciate a joke."

"Well," Festus groused, "I sure don't think this is very funny."

"It's not," Doc said, his smile fading. "But maybe it's a blessing in disguise."

"How you figure?"

"Bates hasn't been right in the head since his wife and infant son died in childbirth. I was worried about him killing me until I realized that he was probably going to destroy himself first. But now, if he stays in jail a few weeks, I'll have the chance to see him every day. In a while I'm hoping he can come to see things clearly and not only forgive me, but also himself."

"Himself?" Festus asked, not understanding.

"Sure," Doc said. "That poor man feels guilty for not bringing his wife into Dodge City before she went into labor. I warned him that because he is a large man and she was quite young and small, she might have complications."

Festus scratched his whiskered cheek. "So you're sayin' that he *really* hates himself and not you?"

"That's right."

Festus wasn't buying into that horse malarkey. "Well, Doc, you're the one with all the education, but I sure wouldn't count on that one if'n I was you. No sir!"

"Trust me, Festus. George Bates blames himself a lot more than he blames me. If we can keep him in your jail for a month or so, I think I might be able to heal him both in mind and body."

"That'll be up to Judge Brooker."

"I know and he's my friend. Festus, I'm confident that you can count on Bates being in your charge for a good long while."

Festus nodded in agreement. The important thing was that everything had all worked out just fine. Doc was still alive, while Bates was under arrest and no longer a threat. Only trouble was, Festus would not get any more naps on the jail-cell bunk.

CHAPTER

3

D r. Jerome Gentry figured he had worn out his welcome in Wichita and that he was either going to have to kill Samantha Wilcox's jealous husband or hitch up his medicine wagon and make fast tracks for Dodge City.

"If you leave, I'm going with you," the beautiful and buxom blonde said as she finished dressing and then poked her head out of the back of the wagon that served as Jerome's traveling dispensary, examining room, and boudoir. "Doctor, I haven't felt this good in years!"

Jerome could not help smiling. "Perhaps my . . . examination has even more to do with your newfound vitality than the Chickasaw Cure I've been prescribing."

Their smiles faded when they heard the sudden and unexpected pounding of a horse's flying hooves approaching the doctor's medicine wagon.

"Oh, my God! What if it's my husband!"

Dr. Gentry was a cool customer under pressure. "Quick," he ordered, "climb under my bed—no, better if you get into that wooden chest."

"Darling, I'd never fit!"

21

The hoofbeats died and were replaced by an angry voice. "Dr. Gentry, I know you got Samantha Wilcox in your damned wagon! Come out before I come in after you!"

"Who is it?" Jerome whispered, tucking his white silk shirt into his tailored trousers, then reaching for his boots.

"It sounds like Marshal Pinkney." Samantha wasn't giggling anymore. "My God, he'll have you hanged! My husband is his biggest donor at election time."

"All right," Jerome said calmly as he stomped into his boots, shrugged his broad shoulders into his doctor's frock, and then reached for his stethoscope. "Let's just play this out as if you were ill and having a proper medical examination."

Her eyes widened and she stared up at him. "Jerome, are you crazy! The marshal will never believe that!"

Jerome was quite sure that she was correct in that assumption but keeping a brave front was often enough to save the day, so he smoothed her golden hair and then used a towel to wipe the perspiration from her face and neck.

"Samantha, your marshal might *suspect* that we've gone beyond the usual physical examination, but he has no proof. Now compose yourself and let me handle this my way."

"You're a dead man," Samantha breathed, biting her lower lip and appearing as if she were going to weep. "And I'm going to be an outcast! A . . . a jezebel!"

Jerome clasped her pretty face between his hands, and because he was nearly a foot taller and the canvas ceiling of the wagon was pressing down on them, he bent over and kissed her face. "Courage, my love. If we panic, we are both lost. So be brave and remain composed. We haven't been caught in the act, you know."

"Last chance!" the marshal bellowed. "Come on out of there you womanizing scoundrel, or I'm coming in with a gun in my hand and I'll put a finish to your lustful ways!"

Jerome slipped a two-shot derringer in his pocket but knew he'd only use it to save his life or Samantha's, because if he killed this lawman, he would most certainly hang. Even so, he was not willing to be shot because her husband was the marshal's wealthy and influential friend.

Pushing the back door open, Jerome forced a warm smile he did not feel and said, "Ah, Marshal Pinkney! Nice to see you again. But whatever is the matter?"

"You know what the *matter* is, you snake in the grass! Send Mrs. Wilcox out right now!"

Jerome frowned. "You mean Samantha Wilcox?"

"Well, how many other married women have you got in your wagon today? You've dallied with half the—aw, never mind. You're under arrest, Dr. Gentry."

"For practicing medicine?"

Marshal Pinkney snorted with derision. "The kind of medicine you practice don't require a doctor! If you even are a doctor."

Jerome guessed it was time to play the indignant role, one that had often saved his skin in the past. Stepping out of his medicine wagon and drawing himself up to his full six feet four inches, he was an imposing figure as he declared, "Marshal Pinkney, I have impeccable credentials from the Harvard School of Medicine. I'm proud to inform you that I graduated with honors, third in my class out of over a hundred and sixty. If you wish, I will show you my medical diploma!"

"Third, huh?" The lawman shook his head and passed wind to show his contempt. "Only third, huh? Well, I'll just bet that if your professors had worn skirts, you'd have been number one!"

"Marshal Pinkney, I don't know what you mean and I really don't care for the inference that my education had anything to do with the gender of my professors. Furthermore—"

"Shut up and send Samantha out," the lawman growled, drawing his six-gun. "And reach for the sky."

Jerome heard Samantha's muffled exclamation and knew that things were not going well. He also knew that if the woman lost her composure, they were lost.

"Mrs. Wilcox," he said in his calmest manner as he turned toward the open doorway to see her cowering in the front of his wagon, "the marshal wants to see you. My examination is complete."

"Yes, Doctor."

"Mrs. Wilcox, as I was about to say before we were so rudely interrupted, I'm leaving Wichita now, but you will be fine if you take the Cure as I've instructed. Remember, a teaspoon before each meal and—"

Pinkney cocked the hammer of his sixgun. "Doc, I'm running out of patience! Cut the bull and send her out here right now!"

"You are overreacting, Marshal Pinkney," Jerome said, feeling a cold sweat erupt across his forehead but managing to sound calm. "Mrs. Wilcox has been unwell and—ah, there you are!"

To her credit, when Samantha exited the medicine wagon, she appeared composed, although Jerome could well imagine that her pulse was pounding at twice its normal rate, probably around a hundred and fifty beats per minute. Her deep blue eyes were slightly dilated and her cheeks were flushed, but that was probably from their recent . . . ahem, examination.

"Marshal Pinkney, what is the meaning of this intrusion!" Samantha declared, her voice cracking only slightly. "Can't a woman visit her doctor without being embarrassed! Just wait until I tell my husband how you—"

"Aw, stow it," Pinkney ordered. "Right now, if I could figure out a way to get away with it, I'd shoot you both. What am I going to tell your husband?"

Jerome saw Samantha's lower lip begin to tremble and realized she was about to break down and cry. "Marshal," he interrupted, "I suggest that if you must say anything at all, you inform Mr. Wilcox that his lovely wife is now cured of her glandular problems."

Pinkney's jaw sagged and his mouth hung open like a fly trap. The gun in his hand drooped, and before the man could recover, Jerome shook Samantha's hand, saying, "I'm glad to have made your acquaintance, Mrs. Wilcox. But now I must hitch up my wagon and move on in order to help others. There are so many in need and so few frontier doctors that I feel the call of duty."

Tears overflowed, but she managed to squeeze his hand and reply, "Dr. Gentry, you're a *wonderful* physician. Thanks to you, I now feel magnificent."

Jerome offered Marshal Pinkney a brave smile. "There are times," he said, putting a touch of emotion in his voice, "when words are far more compensation than mere money. Good-bye to you and good-bye to Wichita."

Pinkney snapped, "Doc, I should arrest you!"

"Why?" Jerome asked in his most innocent fashion. "Why would someone as intelligent as you want to do something so foolish and ill advised? It would only embarrass Mr. and Mrs. Wilcox and make you the laughing-stock of this fine town. What proof do you have that any wrong was done? Think about it, Marshal Pinkney. Think about it before you do something very, very regrettable for all concerned."

Samantha pressed the point. "Marshal," she warned, "if you don't return to your office and keep still, I'll make sure that my husband *never* contributes another dime to your reelection! And you know that I can do it."

The lawman knew she was telling the truth and that he was on the receiving end of a major disaster. His shoulders slumped with defeat and he started to rein his horse around but hesitated and issued up a final warning. "Dr. Gentry, don't you *ever* return to Wichita! Not while I'm in office."

Jerome expelled a sigh of relief and offered his own parting shot. "And it's nice to see that you have chosen to remain in office, Marshal. Good luck and good day!"

Pinkney rode out from behind the old abandoned barn where Dr. Jerome Gentry had been receiving a growing number of patients, many of whom were urging him to settle permanently in Wichita. "One hour," he shouted hoarsely. "One hour to get beyond the city limits or you're a dead doctor!"

When he was gone, Samantha threw herself into Jerome's arms and squeezed him tightly. "I want to come with you."

"No," he said in a firm but gentle voice.

"Why not! Don't you love me?"

"Of course I do."

"Then—"

"I love *all* strong, passionate, and beautiful woman. Love them far too much to hurt them."

Samantha Wilcox stared up at the handsomest man she had ever seen. "You're finally being honest."

"Completely honest. Samantha, the sad truth of it is that I'm not a one-woman man. Probably never will be. But I do love you. And I'm proud of the way you just handled yourself in front of the marshal and saved us."

"Would you actually have shot the marshal with that derringer I saw you put in your pocket?"

"No," he said. "I've never killed a man before. I really prefer to heal them."

Samantha felt like wailing because she knew that Jerome was going away and she'd probably never see him again. "This kind of farewell happens to you quite a lot, doesn't it?"

What was the point in lying? "Yes."

"Are you even part Chickasaw Indian?"

He brightened. "Of course!"

"And what about the Chickasaw Cure you sell by the caseload?"

"It works!" He grinned. "Keep using it, and when you run out, mix molasses, brandy, and licorice to refill the bottles."

Despite how bad she felt, Samantha had to giggle. "The Cure is just a hoax? No Indian medicine or anything?"

"I didn't give you the *complete* list of ingredients, my dear."

She hugged Jerome one last time. "I don't want to let you go, but I don't want you to break my heart any more than you already have."

"Samantha, you are not only beautiful but intelligent,"

he said. "And that is a wonderful combination."

"Please don't joke right now."

His smile faded. "All right. I am sorry for whatever heartache I might have caused you. But I hope that I've given you some insight into what you really want in life."

"Right now all I want is you."

Jerome shook his head patiently. "Nonsense, my love, you want and deserve much more than me . . . or any man for that matter. You deserve independence from an overbearing and boorish husband that insults and demeans you when he drinks too much whiskey. You want and deserve the children he is unwilling to give; you need a strong and lasting love with someone that respects you. Is there anything I've overlooked or forgotten?"

"No," she breathed. "That covers it. I didn't realize that you had listened so closely these past few days."

"I listened," he said. "But now I have to leave."

"Where will you go?"

Dr. Jerome Gentry extracted a crumpled telegram from the pocket of his white physician's jacket. "They need a doctor in Dodge City. Do you know anything about the town?"

"Only that it is wilder than Wichita and farther west."

"It's probably a wasteland," Jerome sadly concluded. "A raw trailhead town on the edge of the frontier. But . . . but it's a safe destination."

"Will it be any different for you in Dodge City?"

"I expect not."

"Don't you realize that, someday, some husband or boyfriend is going to kill you?"

"I don't like to think about it," he told her.

"Jerome, please *do* think about it, and if you ever decide that you might be happy with just one woman, come back and run away with me."

"I'll do that," he said, suddenly anxious to be out of Wichita before Marshal Pinkney or someone else with murder on their mind came calling.

"Good-bye."

"Leave your husband and find your own happiness," he said, kissing Samantha one last time. "And keep taking the Chickasaw Cure until the last drop is all gone."

"I will. Don't forget me ever, Jerome!"

"I won't," he called as he went to hitch up his mules and make fast tracks westward.

But even as he gave that last lover's promise, Dr. Jerome Gentry knew that he would forget Samantha. Not soon, but eventually. Why? Because there were so many others to meet and treat. And untold new adventures to experience.

"Good-bye, Samantha," he called a few minutes later as he drove his medicine wagon off at a fast, jouncing pace that rattled the cases of newly concocted Chickasaw Cure. "Good-bye Wichita and hello Dodge City!"

CHAPTER

4

Jerome was feeling unexpectedly low as he drove his colorful medicine wagon westward; he was missing Samantha way too much. Why, he wasn't exactly sure. She had not been the only patient he'd "examined" lately, but she was by far the prettiest and most interesting. Women usually told Dr. Gentry their entire life stories, which were often a depressing series of personal disappointments and betrayals. Jerome was a good listener, although he sometimes wearied of hearing about philandering and indifferent husbands. Samantha, however, despite her abusive and domineering husband, had been like a strong and fragrant summer breeze. She'd never once pitied herself or bemoaned her unfortunate condition. She had been fun, passionate, and in the end, when Marshal Pinkney had arrived to confront them, coolheaded and brave.

"I'm going to miss her for a while," he told the matched pair of good Missouri mules he'd named Carrot and Bean, Carrot being taller and coppery-colored and Bean the shorter but stronger. "It's going to be hard to find Samantha's equal in a place as humble as Dodge City."

Jerome had no illusions about the frontier town where he was headed. It would be rough and without much culture. But then, he was accustomed to uncultured places, since his Chickasaw mother had raised him and his brothers in the most abject of conditions back in Tennessee before she'd died of smallpox. After that, Jerome had been shuffled back and forth between a few relatives until he'd been old enough to stand up for himself. Half-starved and lice-ridden, he'd been arrested in Memphis and then hired as a general farmhand and stable boy for the famous Dr. Nathaniel Wellencamp, one of the richest men in that part of the country.

From that lowly point in life, his luck had suddenly turned much for the better. He'd worked hard and distinguished himself, rising quickly among the ranks of Dr. Wellencamp's employees and befriending his son, Walter. Even at that he would never have amounted to much if he hadn't had the great good fortune of saving Walter's life during a swimming accident one hot summer afternoon. Dr. Wellencamp had been so grateful that he'd educated Jerome and sent both the young men to Harvard, where their paths had taken quite different directions. Walter had been spoiled and did not take well to the discipline of medicine and study. Jerome, on the other hand, had—

"Hello the wagon!" a pair of riders called as they approached. "You got any liquor to sell!"

Jerome immediately sized the pair up for a couple of disreputable brothers. They were big men, heavier than he, but not so tall. Both were well armed, slovenly, and unshaven. Jerome patted the derringer in his pocket and wished he had a rifle at his side instead of the medical books that he'd been reading a short time ago.

"Hello," he said without warmth. "Sorry, but I've no liquor to sell."

"Who said anything about buyin'!" the uglier of the two shouted, causing his brother to guffaw.

They both stared at the brightly painted canvas that touted the Chickasaw Cure and Jerome's profession as a doctor. "How about some of that snake medicine you peddle?"

"It's *medicine*," Jerome told them. "And I don't *sell* it, I *prescribe* it for various maladies."

"What?"

"Malarias," the smaller of the two said. "He says that his snake oil is for malaria."

"Well, Hank, we ain't got malaria, but I'll still have a taste."

"Gentlemen," Jerome said, his smile frozen on his lips, "how far is it to Dodge City?"

"Dodge City?" They exchanged glances. "Why," the younger said, "it's over a hundred miles to Dodge! You got still got to cross the Rattlesnake and the Arkansas. Won't be easy with that high-pockets wagon."

"I've floated rivers before," Jerome told them as he picked up his lines and started to give Carrot and Bean a slap across their haunches, signaling it was time to leave.

"Hey, hold up there! We ain't ready to go yet."

"Well," Jerome said, "I intend to reach a settlement tonight. My mules haven't been grained in a couple of days and I could use some cooking besides my own tonight."

"We'll have some of that snake oil you peddle!" the older of the pair said, his voice taking on steel. "You wouldn't want to miss a sale, would you?"

"Gentlemen, I've already told you I don't peddle snake oil but only good medicine, the product of an ageless Chickasaw Indian cure."

"Maybe we got ailments."

"I don't think so."

"Get down and get us some medicine," the one called Hank said, as he drew his six-gun and pointed in Jerome's direction. "We'll start off with a couple bottles of *free* samples, if you don't mind."

"He won't mind at all!" the other chortled. "Not with your hawgleg pointed at his belly."

They both laughed and Jerome decided that he might as well play along with their game and try to get out of this

31

predicament without bloodshed. Besides, his derringer was no match for a Colt .45.

"All right," he said, wrapping his lines around his brake and hopping down to walk around to the rear door of his wagon. "Free samples it is!"

"That's more like it, Doc. I was beginning to think you were kind of uppity. I wouldn't like to have to teach you some good Kansas manners."

"Nor would I enjoy the lesson," Jerome said, deciding to experiment by adding a little emetic and purgative to his Chickasaw Cure just to see how fast and powerfully it would act.

"Gentlemen, I'll have to mix up a fresh batch, but it won't take more than a minute."

"Leave the door wide open so we can see you, Doc. And don't try anything stupid or you'll be wishin' you were a *real* doctor who could dig out bullet holes faster'n we can fill you with 'em."

"Perish the thought," Jerome said, climbing up into his wagon and quickly adding the powerful cathartic calomel, as well as a solution of tartar emetic, to his Chickasaw Cure. He added enough of these two drugs to fill almost a third of the bottle, fearing that any more would cause the potion to taste so vile it would be impossible to swallow.

"There you are," he said a few moments later as he corked two bottles, climbed down from inside his wagon, and walked over to the brothers. "What did you say your names were?"

"We didn't," Hank said, snatching the bottle out of Jerome's fist and uncorking it. "This stuff any good?"

"Sure is. I'll promise it will cure what most ails you gentlemen."

The brothers sniffed like a couple of curs and then swallowed the concoction in big gulps.

"Whew!" Hank choked, tears coming to his eyes. "That stuff is strong! Another bottle!"

"Make that two," his brother wheezed.

Jerome gave them even stronger doses this time and they gulped these down as well.

"I don't feel drunk yet, do you, Lem?"

"Nope. I feel . . ."

Whatever Lem was feeling was left unsaid, although Jerome was pretty sure he could have described it. Powerful and unrelenting cramps deep in their guts.

"Holy Judas!" Lem cried, throwing himself off his horse and racing for the nearest trees.

His big brother wasn't quite so quick. Falling off his horse and hopping back up, Hank ran like a man possessed.

Jerome picked up the man's forgotten pistol and tested its construction by laying its barrel across Hank's cranium just hard enough to put a slight depression on the man's prominent occipital bone. Hank pitched over sideways. Jerome quickly collected their horses, tied them to the rear of his wagon, and climbed back up into the driver's seat.

"Have a good day!" he called out toward the man now so preoccupied with his own problems he didn't even notice Jerome's departure.

Jerome stayed with a homesteader family that night and slept in his wagon hidden inside their barn just in case Hank and Lem were sufficiently recovered to come looking for him. He regretted asking them how far it was to Dodge City and expected that they might even come looking to murder him and recover their horses. With that in mind, Jerome set their animals loose the next morning and continued on his way. At least now no one could accuse him of being a horse thief, which he knew was a hanging offense.

When Jerome first saw Dodge City in the distance, he shaved, expertly cut his wavy black hair and then took a bath in the Arkansas River because he knew that first impressions were very important. Unfortunately, his first impression of Dodge City was not favorable and it appeared to be just another raw cattle railhead town with corrals near the stockyards where the livestock would be and sent back East. Most of these corrals were empty but Jerome knew that would change as soon as the first herds began to arrive up the long trail from Texas. The country was flat to rolling under a rich carpet of spring grass.

The town itself appeared to be the usual collection of saloons, boardinghouses, eateries, and shops that catered primarily to workingmen. To its credit, the founding fathers of Dodge City had planted quite a few trees and Jerome could see a church steeple. Dodge City appeared big enough to have a school and probably a regular doctor. That made him wonder again about the telegram that he'd seen posted in Wichita. He wasn't at all sure why Dodge City had gone to such great lengths to advertise for a new doctor, but supposed that it wouldn't take very long to find out. In a town as wild as Dodge City, it was likely that the former doctor had been shot for failing to save the life of a patient. That kind of thing was not uncommon on the frontier and was why Jerome kept a derringer on his person at all times. Luckily, he was also pretty handy with his fists or a knife.

As soon as Jerome turned his medicine wagon onto the main street, he spotted the marshal's office and guided his team of mules over to a nearby hitching rail, then climbed down and stretched his long legs. His imposing presence and colorfully painted wagon extolling the virtues of the Chickasaw Cure immediately attracted the attention of both young and the old, most of whom were females.

"That snake oil any good for bones?" a woman bent with arthritis demanded, casting Jerome a hard and suspicious look.

"You bet it is! Straighten that back of yours out like a ruler if you drink enough of it according to the directions."

"Hogwash!" the old woman snapped, hobbling on up the street.

Jerome smiled at the other interested parties. "I'm half–Chickasaw Indian, half-Irish, and one hundred percent certified doctor!" he boasted in his commanding voice. "I can cure your boils and heal your sicknesses, but I can't start doing that right at the moment because I first need to find Marshal Matt Dillon.''

"He's been advertising for a new doc ever since our old one had a bad spell a while back in the Long Branch," a young woman with a pretty smile informed Jerome. "I hope that you've come to help Doc Adams."

"We'll see," Jerome said. "May I ask exactly what happened to him?"

The woman looked around, suddenly aware that she was the center of attention. "Well," she said, batting her eyelashes, "I heard that Doc Adams has a problem with his ticker.''

"Ticker?"

"You know," she said coyly, "his heart. Doc Adams has had heart trouble for years. Then, when he was attacked—"

"Attacked?"

"Sure. There was this homesteader whose wife died while having a baby. Doc was there but couldn't save her or her baby. It must have pushed the husband around the bend because he swore to kill Doc and darn near did!"

"That's right," a man said, spitting a stream of tobacco juice in the dust. "If you plan on doctorin' in Dodge, you'd better be good, young fella."

"I'm good, but I'm not God. No doctor is. Anyway," Jerome said, "I'd best see Marshal Dillon."

"Here he comes now."

Matt had spotted the gathering crowd from his office window and then the medicine wagon. He'd turned to Festus and said, "Looks like we got another medicine man selling snake oil."

"You want me to run him off, Matthew?"

"No, I'll go have a talk with him," Matt had decided as he grabbed his hat and headed out the door.

"Hello, Marshal," Jerome said, noting that Matt was even taller than himself. "My name is Dr. Jerome Gentry."

"So it says on your wagon," Matt replied. "And in almost as big letters as your Chickasaw Cure."

"It's a rare and secret medicine made by my mother's ancient ancestors." Jerome could sense the lawman's disapproval and that came as no surprise. "How about a free sample, Marshal?"

"No thanks," Matt said. "Come to my office. I'd like to talk to you a few minutes in private."

"Why sure," Jerome said. He dug two bits out of his pocket and gave it to a large and ornery-looking kid, saying, "You watch over my mules and wagon. If I don't lose anything, there's another two bits coming your way."

The kid nodded and assumed a menacing expression as he glared at his former friends. "Stay back, boys," he ordered.

Satisfied that nothing would be pilfered from his medicine wagon, Jerome followed the towering Marshal Dillon across the street, noticing that the pretty woman he'd been talking to was still watching him. She'd help him forget Samantha unless this marshal proved to be a hard case and ran him off.

"Gentry," Matt said, when they entered his small and cluttered office, "this is Deputy Festus Haggen."

"Well, hello there," Festus said, dropping his feet to the floor. "Welcome to Dodge City."

To Jerome's mind, Deputy Festus Haggen was about the sorriest-looking lawman he'd ever seen. With a high-pitched and whiney voice straight out of the backwoods and a dirty and unshaven appearance, Haggen reminded Jerome more of a town drunk than a deputy. He was of average height with bat ears and a protruding Adam's apple, giving the overall impression of a simpleton.

"Deputy Haggen, it's a pleasure to meet you," Jerome lied, marching over to the deputy and pumping his scaly hand with a surprisingly powerful grip. "A real pleasure."

"Well, thank yew!" Festus looked ready to burst with pleasure and even cast a glance up at Matt to see if he was also pleased by such an effusive greeting.

"Gentry," Matt said, "I know that this is a free country and that some people will say I am acting out of bounds, but I'm going to have to ask you to drive that medicine wagon of yours right on through Dodge City."

Jerome feigned shock and even a hint of indignation. "Why, Marshal," he protested, "surely there's been a misunderstanding. I've never been here before."

"Not you maybe," Matt replied, "but there have been others selling medicines that don't work and only serve to disappoint those in need of a miracle cure. Chickasaw Cure, Miracle Elixir, call them what you will, but they're all just a way to cheat folks out of their hard-earned dollars."

"Marshal Dillon," Jerome said, extracting the crumpled telegram from his coat pocket, "I've come a long way to answer this plea from help. I'm a *certified* medical doctor."

"That I very much doubt," Matt told him.

"Would you like to see my Harvard degree?"

"Not especially," Matt replied. "Fake documents can easily be produced for a few dollars in most big cities."

Jerome took a deep breath. "I *am* a real doctor and I've come to set up practice in Dodge City."

"Driving a medicine wagon and selling snake oil?" Matt asked with unconcealed contempt. "You might fool some folks but not me or Festus."

"That's right," Festus said, "and you shouldn't be takin' folks' money and raisin' their hopes like the last couple of so-called doctors done."

Jerome tossed the telegram down on the marshal's desk. "What can I do or say to convince you that I am a real doctor?"

Festus threw a backward glance at George Bates. "Matthew," he said, "maybe this so-called doctor could have a look at our prisoner? I reckon his bandages could stand being changed."

"Festus, maybe that's a good idea. Okay, Gentry, but if you're a doctor, where is your medical bag?"

"In my wagon."

"Get it and let's see what you can do."

"Is your prisoner dangerous?" Jerome asked, wondering if the man that had attacked Doc Adams was homicidal and if he needed to slip his derringer up his sleeve for protection.

"Not anymore," Matt replied. "And we'll be right at your side, unless you've changed your mind."

"Of course not," Jerome said, heading out the door to get his medical bag.

When the door closed, Festus said, "Matthew, if he's a-bluffin', I'd say that young feller is doin' a pretty good job of it."

"I ain't gonna let no phony doctor look at my bullet wound," George Bates called from his cell.

"He won't," Matt promised. "I'll bet he's going to climb back in that medicine wagon and drive off. That's the last we'll see of Dr. Gentry."

But a few minutes later Jerome was back with his medical bag and a bottle of the Chickasaw Cure. "Open the cell door and I'll have a look at your prisoner," he said, now all business.

"Marshal," Bates protested, "you better keep him out of here!"

"Festus, get the key."

Matt looked closely at Jerome. "Don't try to put anything over on me. I've seen a lot of bullet wounds and keep in mind that our prisoner is not fond of doctors."

"So I've heard," Jerome said. "Did Dr. Adams remove a bullet from his leg?"

"He said it passed through."

Festus went over to the cell and opened it, saying, "You don't look too perky, George."

"I feel like hell, but I got enough left to make that doctor pay if he lays a hand on me."

"Behave yourself," Festus told their prisoner before turning to Jerome and adding, "he's all yours."

Jerome wasn't overly concerned about being harmed. He was bigger and stronger than the prisoner, and besides, the man looked pale and feverish.

"Stretch out on the bunk and relax," he said, taking Bates's wrist and discovering that the man's pulse was quick and shallow. He could also feel the heat of his skin and knew that Bates was feverish.

"I'm going to need to take a look at your leg wound," he said, beginning to unwrap the bandages. "These don't appear to have been changed lately."

"That old sawbones hasn't been around."

"That's because you tried to kill him," Festus said accusingly. "Did you expect Doc to wait hand and foot on the likes of yew!"

The leg wound was badly infected. Jerome bent close and sniffed for the sickly odor of gangrene, but it wasn't yet present.

"Marshal Dillon, this man is going to lose this leg if we can't beat this infection. I need to flush this wound out with a special brand of the Chickasaw Cure that has some of my mother's old medicinal healing powders included. I'd also better consult with Dr. Adams—if he's up to it."

Matt was beginning to think that, just maybe, this young man *was* a real doctor. "Doc is feeling better. I'm the one that has warned him to stay in his bed and rest."

"You'd better send for him at once," Jerome said. "This man is running a high fever and his condition will continue to deteriorate if we don't treat him properly."

"I ain't going to let Doc Adams touch me again!" the prisoner cried. "And I don't much want you to, either."

Jerome shrugged as if he didn't care. "Then gangrene will set in just as sure as the sun rises," he said flatly. "And once that happens, you'll either have to have your leg amputated, or you'll die. So, what's it going to be?"

"Damn you," Bates howled, "the last doctor I had killed my wife and kid!"

"No, he didn't. And anyway, this is different."

"I don't feel so good," the man said, with fear in his voice.

"That's because your leg is infected and suppurating. If you think you feel bad now, wait another day and you'll be out of your mind with pain," Jerome said.

"I'd rather be dead than one-legged."

"I don't think it'll come to that," Jerome told him, although he couldn't be sure. "But I do know that the sooner we clean up that wound, the better. I also suspect that there might be some fragments of lead still in your leg which are causing the infection. I'll need to open it up and make sure."

"Okay," Bates wheezed, eyes now wide open and pleading for help. "I'll let you work on me but not that damned Doc Adams!"

Jerome looked up at the marshal and his deputy. "I'm going to go back to my wagon and mix up a special potion of the Cure that I believe will disinfect that wound."

"Okay," Matt said. "But you'd better—"

Jerome cut him off. "I've already been warned, remember? Marshal, I'm getting a little weary of threats. So why don't you either go get Doc and have him oversee what I do, or else just leave me to practice a brand of medicine that uses the best of two American cultures? In the meantime I'll need hot water—lots of it—plus clean bandaging."

"We can do that," Festus said. "I got hot water in the coffeepot a-steamin'. That be all right, Doc?"

"That will be fine," Jerome answered. "A little coffee in the water won't hurt, either. It might even help."

Festus didn't say anything and neither did the big marshal, so Jerome marched back to his wagon, where he quickly added some special Indian herbs and plant extracts to his usual bottles of Chickasaw Cure.

"You gonna save his leg?" the boy that he'd employed asked.

"I'm going to try." Jerome was aware that there were quite a number of people watching him and said loud enough for most of them to hear, "The Chickasaw Cure rarely fails, and if anything can save that man's leg and life, it's my secret cure."

Armed with several fortified bottles of the Cure, Jerome made his way back to the marshal's office. Without a word, he entered the cell and got down to business.

First, he used Festus's hot water colored by strong coffee to wash out the wound. Bates groaned and quivered.

"Just try to hold still," he told the man when he'd finally gotten the wound cleaned out. "I'm going to use a forceps to see if I can find any pieces of lead that might still be in your leg."

"This is going to hurt plenty, ain't it?" Bates asked, looking scared.

"Not as bad as you might think," Jerome said, hoping this was true. "Try to think about something pleasant."

"Ain't nothing pleasant to think about in my life since Polly and my son died."

"Picture a sunrise or a sunset, the most beautiful you've ever seen," Jerome told the man. "Or a colt running and bucking in a pasture or wildflowers in a meadow. Or the way a fish rises to catch a fly on the water and how ripples form and flow outward like the circle of our lives."

"Why," Festus said, "that's real purty!"

"Picture those things," Jerome ordered his patient as he gently inserted the forceps into the wound and closed his eyes so that every fiber of his being was focused on the instrument in his hand.

Bates groaned and his big, work-roughened hands gripped the edge of his jail-cell bunk. His face turned as white as granite and a pulsating vein in his forehead emerged. Jerome didn't notice any of that as he probed deeper and deeper until he felt what he was sure was either a splinter of bone or a bullet.

"Don't move," he whispered, eyes still shut tightly.

A moment later he extracted a large and twisted piece of lead and grinned. "No doubt that this had something to do with the fact that your leg didn't heal properly."

He laid the bloody forceps down and doused the wound with the medicine he'd concocted.

"Ouch!" Bates cried. "Doc, that stuff burns!"

"It's supposed to," Jerome replied as he rebandaged the wound. "I'll be coming back every four hours to remedicate that wound. We should know in about twenty-four hours if we saved your leg.''

Bates was covered with cold sweat and his voice held a tremor when he said, ''If you saved me, then I'll forever be in your debt, Doc. Don't know how I can repay you, though.''

''Don't worry about that,'' Jerome replied, feeling suddenly drained as he left the cell. ''Well, Marshal?''

''You can stick around,'' Matt said. ''At least until this man either dies or recovers.''

''Thanks a lot,'' Jerome said cryptically. ''And now, if you don't mind, I believe I'll go clean up.''

Festus opened the door, bowing slightly. ''Dr. Gentry, you got me convinced.''

''You'd better reserve your judgment until we see if your prisoner survives,'' Jerome suggested as he emerged onto the boardwalk, where a large and curious crowd had gathered.

''Did you save him?'' someone asked.

''I think Mr. Bates will make a complete recovery,'' Jerome told them, ''but I won't know for sure until my powerful Chickasaw Cure has had time to do its miraculous healing work.''

''If it saves Bates,'' a portly little man in a business suit exclaimed, ''then you can put me down for a couple of bottles!''

''Me, too!'' another said.

Jerome spotted the pretty young woman again. Tipping his hat, he smiled at her and said, ''Good day.''

She blushed and tried to get closer to him. But Jerome pretended not to notice. In truth, he was too excited about what had happened in the jail cell. Yes, he'd gotten lucky and found a large fragment of a bullet that Dr. Adams had missed and that was causing the infection. And because he'd found it, Jerome was pretty sure that he'd passed muster in Dodge City and that he was going to sell barrels of his Chickasaw Cure and see plenty of well-paying patients.

CHAPTER

5

Doc Adams bustled into Matt's office looking angry and upset. Without even stopping to greet the marshal or his deputy, he hurried over to the cell, peered inside at George Bates, and growled, "Did you let that snake-oil peddler change your bandages!"

Bates had been napping, but Doc's furious words brought him awake with a start. "What?"

"Matt!" Doc shouted, spinning around. "Open this door so I can examine my patient."

"Oh no!" Bates cried, now fully awake. "I got a *new* doctor and he's going to save my leg! You stay away from me, Adams!"

The doctor marched over to Matt, tipped his head back, and glared up at him. "Did you really allow that medicine man to attend to my patient!"

"Well," Matt hedged, "I did allow young Gentry to change the dressing. I was just trying to make things a little easier for you."

"Easy?" Doc barked a laugh that held no humor. "For the last thirty minutes all I've heard is how this charlatan saved my patient's leg and life! Have you any idea how that makes me feel?''

Matt was beginning to think that he did. ''Simmer down, Doc. How about a cup of coffee?''

''I don't need coffee, I need a drink!''

''I got some whiskey in my desk drawer,'' Festus offered. ''But it's awful early in the day to get a toot on, Doc. And anyway, it might be bad for your weak heart.''

''My heart isn't weak, you fly-bitten idiot!''

''Easy,'' Matt said, taking Doc by the arm and almost forcing him to sit. ''What's got you so riled? All Gentry did was change George's bandages.''

''And dig out lead in my leg that you missed!'' Bates shouted. ''Are you goin' blind, Doc!''

''Shut up,'' Matt ordered his prisoner.

Doc had been about to shout something, but instead he asked, ''Did Gentry really find a piece of bullet in George's leg?''

''He did,'' Matt admitted, feeling almost guilty.

''Let me see it.''

''Festus?''

''Why sure, Matthew. I done saved it to give to George as a souvenir.''

Festus had cleaned the misshapen piece of lead and carefully placed it next to a chaw of chewing tobacco. ''Here it is, Doc,'' he said, presenting it in the palm of his open hand. ''No wonder that leg wound wasn't healin'.''

Doc didn't touch the piece of dark, twisted metal. Instead, he shook his head and muttered, ''I don't know how I could have missed anything that big.''

''Doc,'' Matt said in a gentle voice, ''you were in great pain. It's easy to see how you could have missed it, given the circumstances.''

Doc didn't seem to be listening. He got up and shuffled over to the cell, saying, ''Matt, I need to see what kind of bandaging job that young man did on your prisoner.''

Matt unlocked the cell with a stern warning. ''Bates,

you'd better behave yourself or I'll see that you have two bad legs.''

"I don't want Adams near me!" Bates cried, recoiling against the back wall of his cell. "Go get Dr. Gentry!"

Doc hesitated, then turned and retreated. "If George insists on the Indian medicine man, then let him have him."

Matt intercepted his old friend. "Doc, you haven't had your coffee. Sit down and let's talk."

"Nothing to talk about," Doc said, eyes distant and face lined with age and fatigue. "It looks to me like I got some competition."

"Some *help*, Doc."

"Is it true that you sent a telegram all over the country saying that I wasn't capable of taking care of the medical needs in Dodge City?"

"Doc, you're completely turning this thing around. All I did was send out a telegram asking for a little medical assistance. Nothing more."

"Well, it worked. Now you've got a handsome, smooth-talking snake-oil peddler who must have, somewhere along the line in his sordid past, extracted a few bullets. He's got everyone to thinking that he is a real doctor . . . one better'n old broken-down Doc Galen Adams. Isn't that right?"

"Of course not! Doc, you don't have to defend your record in Dodge City. You've saved dozens of lives. You're a fine doctor."

"But I'm old and tired, Matt."

"You're just recuperating from some heart trouble. And besides, no one in this town is about to forget all you have done. You've earned their trust and they won't forget you, not ever."

"Oh really?" Doc smiled sadly. "Well, an hour ago I had a line of patients waiting outside my office, but they've suddenly disappeared. And do you know why? They disappeared because everyone is talking about this Dr. Gentry and his Chickasaw Cure."

"Doc, listen—"

"No, Matt, *you* listen. You should have at least asked

me before sending that telegram. I deserved to know."

"You're right. I'm sorry."

"Well, so am I. Just please don't do me any more favors. Just . . . just keep your big nose out of my profession."

"Doc, has it occurred to you that Gentry might be the real thing?"

"Of course it has! And to tell you the truth, I hope he is qualified, because I could use some professional help."

"Then—"

"Let me finish," Doc said, cutting Matt off. "I want another doctor in town, but anyone who drives a medicine wagon and peddles a miracle water called the Chickasaw Cure can't possibly be on the level. Matt, I'd stake my life on the fact that Gentry is nothing but a fraud."

"No, he ain't!" Bates shouted from his cell. "He's a better doctor than you ever was!"

Doc made a sound deep in his throat that was half rattle and half growl. Then, before either Matt or Festus could say or do anything, he was out the door.

"Matthew, he's pretty upset," Festus said, looking worried. "Do you want me to bring him back?"

"No, that would only make things worse. Let Doc cool down awhile."

"All right, but what'll we do about Dr. Gentry?"

"Festus, I don't know yet," Matt said a bit testily. "What would you suggest?"

"I got nothing in mind."

"Well," Matt said, "neither do I. But if Dr. Gentry is for real, then we ought to consider ourselves fortunate. And if he's not, someone could die."

Festus scratched his scraggly beard and frowned. "You mean he could kill someone by treatin' 'em wrong?"

"That's it exactly."

"Holy cow!" Festus exclaimed. "I'd feel awful if we let him treat folks and he killed one."

"So would I, but for now, there isn't much else that we can do. I'll take a look at his medical-school diploma and then write his college to see if Gentry really attended and graduated. But it will take quite some time to get a reply.''

"Matthew, I think Jerome Gentry is a real doctor," Festus said. "And the Chickasaw Cure might be powerful medicine. Why, I remember one time up in the mountains when my uncle Jethro got drunk and shot hisself in the foot—blew off his big toe—or maybe it was the middle one, and—

"Festus?"

"Yeah, Matthew?"

"I've already heard that story about a hundred times. Why don't you go find and keep an eye on Gentry. I want to know what he's up to and if he's selling snake oil."

"Might not be snake oil atall."

"It's snake oil," Matt said. "Just go find him and report back to me like I asked."

"Why sure. But I expect that Doc Gentry is probably going to put his mules up at the livery and then go to eat, maybe have a steak at Delmonicos, and then look Doc up for a palaver. Or he might look up Doc first and then—"

"Festus!"

"Yeah?"

"Get busy."

"Sure thing, Matthew," Festus said as he headed out the door and then down the street. Rounding a corner, he practically ran over the town drunk, poor, besotted Louie Pheeters. Louie was stretched out on the boardwalk, dead to the world.

Festus grabbed Louie and hauled him over to the nearest horse trough. "Come on, it's time to wake up and get yourself something to eat."

Louie smelled bad, so Festus dumped him into the trough and let him either sink or swim.

"D-damn, Festus!" Louie spluttered, scrambling out of the water and shaking like a dog when it wants to rid itself of water. "Why'd you do that!"

" 'Cause you stink!"

"Well, so do you, but I never did anything mean about it."

"Aw, the only mean part about tossin' you in that water trough is how it'll foul it for the horses," Festus snorted. "Now, Louie, you know that Marshal Dillon said he'd lock you up the next time he found you passed out drunk on the boardwalk."

"I ain't drunk, Festus, I'm just tired and now I'm cold and wet," Louie whined. "Never knew you was so ornery."

"Go back to your own place and sleep it off and don't let me catch you out drinkin' tonight," Festus told the man as he continued along.

"Morning, Deputy Haggen!"

"Mornin', Mr. Halligan," Festus said, not even breaking stride and wondering where that medicine wagon and Dr. Gentry had gotten to so fast.

"Say," Halligan called, grabbing Festus by the sleeve, "what do you think about that new young doctor that just arrived in Dodge? Ain't he something, though! Guess he saved your prisoner's life. Funny that Doc Adams missed that piece of your bullet. I guess old Doc is slippin' pretty bad, huh?"

Festus didn't like Halligan. Small in stature and well into his fifties, the man was a professional busybody who loved nothing better than to spread malicious gossip. No matter what facts he heard, they were sure to be twisted around to Halligan's own belittling point of view. As far as Festus was concerned, people like Halligan were an affliction and caused far more trouble than they were worth.

"Doc isn't slippin'," Festus snapped. "He just missed a little piece of bullet lead, that's all. Weren't for Doc, George Bates would have bled to death."

"Maybe," Halligan said, "but if it wasn't for Doc Adams, Mrs. Bates and her baby might still be alive."

Festus slapped Halligan's hand away from his sleeve. "Now, you don't know that for sure and it ain't right that you or nobody else should blame poor old Doc."

"Maybe not," Halligan said, looking injured by Festus's reprimand, "but from what I hear, this new doctor is selling some real good medicine and he knows what he's about. You ask me, I think Doc Adams ought to take down his shingle. Maybe he could even sell out to Dr. Gentry and retire.''

''Well, dagnabit!'' Festus swore. ''You got it all figured out against poor Doc! And him that saved your hide that time that you accidentally broke through the floor of the that upstairs balcony and broke your arm and nearly hanged your sorry self. Have you already forgotten how it was Doc who set that arm and got your neck twisted around so you didn't look back when you was supposed to look forward!''

''I ain't forgot,'' Halligan said, looking indignant, ''but my neck still hurts and my arm ain't never got back its natural strength.''

''That ain't Doc's fault.''

''Maybe it is and maybe it isn't, but I'm going to buy some of that Chickasaw Cure. The writing on Dr. Gentry's wagon said it will ease the pain of old injuries.''

''So will a bottle of tarantula juice,'' Festus snapped, looking all around. ''Now, where did Dr. Gentry go?''

''He drove that wagon around to the livery. I heard that he's going to park there and use his medicine wagon as his office in the day and his sleeping room at night. Smart young fella, if you ask me. Maybe Doc Gentry won't charge so much as Doc Adams, either.''

''Go on with you!'' Festus ranted. ''I ain't got time for listenin' to your prattle.''

Halligan's face colored. ''Deputy, you've no right to talk to me that way and I know when an old doctor ought to step aside for a young one!''

Festus's mood was grim when he reached the stable and saw the medicine wagon but no Dr. Gentry. He went into the barn and found Delbert Oatman was pitching hay to the stalls. ''Where's Doc?'' he asked.

''I don't know. He probably went to get something to eat.''

''I seen his wagon out yonder. Delbert, are you gonna let him stay here and sleep and work outta it?''

"Why not? He's going to doctor a sick horse of mine and give me a bottle of his Chickasaw Cure every now and then for my rheumatism. Besides, hay prices are down and his mules won't eat much. Maybe havin' the doctor here will bring me some additional business."

"Ain't right that a doctor should work out of his wagon parked in a stable."

"Well, Jesus Himself was born in a stable and he did a lot of healin'," Delbert said, looking smug, "or have you forgotten your Bible teachings?"

"I ain't forgot," Festus replied. "Did Gentry tell you anything else?"

"Like what, for instance?" the liveryman asked as he leaned on his pitchfork.

"Well, you know!"

"No, I don't."

Festus was getting exasperated. "For example, did that young feller say anything at all about how long he was fixin' to stay in Dodge City?"

"Nope."

Festus scowled. "You sure ain't any help."

"Why are you askin' about Dr. Gentry like he was fixin' to start trouble? I had heard from Barney down at the telegraph office that Marshal Dillon sent out the word that Dodge City needed another doctor. I think that was a fine idea and our prayers have been answered. Bates would have lost his leg without this new doctor."

"Seems that you're awful trusting," Festus said. "Bates ain't cured yet by a longshot."

"Well, even if he dies," Oatman snapped, "he'll do it without a big piece of lead buried in his leg."

Festus decided that this was another fine fool not worth talking to anymore. He marched out of the livery and went back around to the medicine wagon, thinking that maybe Gentry was inside.

"Hello in there!"

There was no answer, so Festus tried the door, but it was locked.

"I guess there's nothin' to do now but to track him down and see what his plans are so I can tell Matthew," he muttered.

He hitched his pants and hurried up the street, thinking that most people sure had a short memory when it came to good deeds. For too many years Doc Adams had worked himself toward an early grave caring for people and most of the time never even getting paid for his time or his medicines. Doc was expected to get up at all hours of the night, often to patch up some drunken fool who'd gotten hisself shot or stabbed. He'd gladly drive his buggy out in a blizzard to help someone and come back to Dodge half-frozen and himself sick.

And after all he'd done, he made one bitsy little old mistake and suddenly everyone was turning against him and running to Doc Gentry as if he were the second coming of Jesus Christ. It just wasn't right.

"No wonder Doc is so grouchy all the time," Festus said aloud. "He probably knew people would treat him this way the minute they thought someone better come along."

"You seen that new doctor?" he asked Percy Crump, the undertaker, who was standing outside his business smoking a cigar.

"Nope," Percy said. "I hear that he saved your prisoner's life. That'll cost me, Festus."

"Well, I'm right sorry to hear that, Percy! Fact of the matter is, George wouldn't have died either way."

"That's not what I hear," Percy said. "I've been told that he had gangrene and pustulation of the leg and would have died if it hadn't been for Dr. Gentry and his Chickasaw Cure. You buy any yet, Festus?"

"Why a-course not! I'm just fine."

"Well, I been havin' some back pains. Working over a body and trying to make 'em look better than they ever did in this world takes its toll on your back. I . . ."

Festus didn't want to hear any more. For crying in the beer, now the town's undertaker was complaining about how he'd lost business. Was everyone in Dodge City crazy?

When Festus returned to the office, Matthew was gone, probably to get something to eat or take care of some business. Festus poured himself a cup of coffee and collapsed in his desk chair. He removed his hat and hiked his boots up on his desk, then sipped his coffee.

"Hey," Bates called, "how about some of that coffee?"

"Sorry, you had your share already this morning with breakfast."

"Come on," Bates pleaded. "What's a cup of coffee gonna hurt?"

Festus pretended not to hear, but his conscience got the better of him, so he couldn't even enjoy his own coffee. Finally, he got up and poured Bates a cup.

"Don't spill it, 'cause I mopped up your floor last week."

Bates sipped at his coffee for a few minutes, then asked, "You think I'll go to prison?"

"I don't know. That's up to Judge Brooker."

"I wouldn't do anything more to Doc," Bates said. "I swear that I wouldn't."

"I don't know about that," Festus said, shaking his head. "You tricked me and Matthew once into believing that you were heading for California and then you went after Doc again. You can't be trusted, George."

"Oh yes I can. You just don't know what it's like to lose someone you love."

"I lost my mother and I sure loved her. Lost a lot of my kinfolk that I loved."

"But none of 'em was your wife and your firstborn son. That's a lot different."

"Maybe so," Festus allowed. "But dyin' is dyin' and livin' is livin' and you don't seem to be doin' very good at the latter. You need to put the past behind and get on with your life."

"I will, if the judge don't send me away to prison. Festus?"

"Yeah?"

"You got a good heart and I wanted you to know that I

don't hold it against you the way you shot me in the leg.''

"Glad to hear that," Festus said, casting the man a side-ways look. " 'Cause I was wonderin' about that, seein' as how you're so big on holdin' a grudge.''

"If Judge Brooker lets me go, you can escort me all the way to California. Maybe you'd like it so much you'd want to stay.''

"Nope. Dodge City is where I belong.''

"You ain't cut out to be a deputy," Bates opined with a rueful shake of his head. "You're way too nice a fella.''

"I can be as hard as a horseshoe.''

"No, you can't. You're too good-hearted. Now, Matt Dillon isn't. He'd as soon shoot a man as arrest him.''

Festus jumped up, spilling his coffee. "That's a lie, George! I don't know why you want to say something like that when it ain't true. I've known Matthew a long time. Worked for him for eight or nine years. I've never once seen him kill or pistol-whip or even punch a fella that didn't need it.''

"That's not what I've heard.''

"Then you've heard a bunch of lies!''

Bates drained his coffee cup and placed it on the floor. "Well," he said, "it don't matter none to me, but I can tell you one thing—there's some changes needed right here in Dodge City, starting with Doc Adams and then Marshal Dillon. You ask me, I'd say Dr. Gentry is going to run Doc out of business and that *you* ought to run for marshal next election.''

"What!''

"You heard me," Bates said. "Why be second fiddle when you can be first?''

Festus went over and retrieved the coffee cup. "You listen here, George Bates, you're dead wrong about every-thing and I'm plumb sick of hearing you run off at the mouth. So shut and leave me in peace.''

Bates spat on the floor. "You can mop that up the next time, Deputy. And maybe I was wrong about you being nice, 'cause you sure lack ambition.''

"And you lack makin' sense!"

Festus tromped back to his desk to finish his coffee. Sure, it was mean of him to think it, but he almost hoped Judge Brooker was in a bad mood and would sentence George to prison for a year or two. That might be the only thing that would shut the fool up and keep him out of trouble.

CHAPTER

6

That evening, Jerome decided to celebrate his auspicious arrival in Dodge City with a big steak dinner and chanced upon a small and newly opened café called Clancy's Place. The attractive, auburn-haired woman who cooked and waited on the customers was Rita Clancy. Outgoing and in her mid-thirties, Rita was a hard worker and an excellent cook. Her husband, Mike, however, was lazy, profane, and slovenly with a protruding beer belly that refused to be confined by his shirts. That evening, Mike was recuperating from a bad case of the scoots because he had consumed nearly two pounds of tainted pork and a half-dozen bottles of beer for breakfast.

Shorthanded and forced to work the kitchen as well as wait on their customers, Rita had been angry through most of the early evening and it had been all she could do to smile. She was thinking that her café would go broke if the cowboys didn't arrive soon with their herds of cattle. She was also thinking that she ought to get rid of her no-account husband and the sooner the better. But those dark thoughts all evaporated the instant that Jerome appeared.

"Hi!" he'd called out in greeting, just like a big, over-grown kid without a care in the world. "Is this place any good for steaks?"

"You bet!" Rita shouted from her kitchen as she brushed back her hair and smoothed her grease-stained apron so that her hourglass figure was sure to be noted and admired.

As she took his order, prepared and served his steak, Rita could hardly keep her eyes off Jerome and decided he was the handsomest hunk of manhood she had ever laid eyes upon.

"More coffee or pie, Dr. Gentry?" she asked for the third or fourth time after he had finished.

"No, ma'am! I'm full. How much do I owe you?"

"Just eighty-five cents." Rita decided this was no time to be bashful, so she added, "But, Dr. Gentry, I'd rather have a bottle of your Chickasaw Cure than money."

"That's easy enough," Jerome replied, thinking that he might mosey on over to the Long Branch Saloon and see what the town had to offer in the way of entertainment. "Just come by my wagon tomorrow and I'll give you a bottle."

"Well," Rita said, her mind in a tizzy, "I need the medicine tonight. You see, my . . . my friend has a very upset stomach. He . . . I mean *she* is sicker'n anything, actually, and I was hoping—"

"Of course!"

Jerome realized that all the other customers had finished their meals and departed while he'd been eating and perusing the latest issue of an eastern medical journal discussing the dangers of bloodletting and the advantages of using African leeches rather than ones from Asia.

"I suppose that I could go to my wagon and bring you back a bottle," he offered. "I'm parked at the stable, which is not very far."

Rita removed her apron. "I need some fresh air."

"Fine," he said. "Then let's go."

Rita locked the door and glanced up and down the street,

hoping that no one important was watching her leave with the doctor. Her heart was pounding and she felt nearly giddy as she walked side by side with Jerome toward the stable. If it had been a hundred miles instead of just two blocks, she would not have minded at all.

"Have you lived in Dodge City very long?" he asked.

"Less than a year."

"Do you like it?"

"It's all right," Rita said, not wanting to talk about herself and certainly not wanting him to know that she was married. "I mean, it's pretty nice. Everything changes when the Texans start arriving with their big herds of cattle. Then it's a lot more exciting and fun."

"Probably better for your business, too," Jerome said, glancing over toward the Long Branch and hearing a piano playing a lively tune that he could not identify. "Has your friend been sick very long?"

"Uh . . . no."

"Well, that's good." Jerome looked up at the stars and tasted the warm, sweet wind coming off the grasslands. "Just give your friend a tablespoon of the Cure four times a day. It will straighten out her gastronomical problems or you can have your money back."

"Where did you come from?" she blurted.

"Tennessee, and just about every other place back East that you can imagine. I'm a half-breed, you know." Jerome found the North Star off the Big Dipper. "I'm very proud of my Indian mother. She was Chickasaw and they're fine people."

"I'm sure they are," Rita said as they left the glow of the city lamplights and plunged into semidarkness. Instinctively, she reached out and took his hand. "Sure is dark."

"I should have retrieved a bottle of the Cure alone," he said. "But we're almost there."

"Do you like living in a wagon?"

"It's fine for now."

"Everyone is hoping you stay in Dodge City. Old Dr. Adams is worn-out and crotchety all the time."

"Maybe he just needs a vacation," Jerome suggested. "I meant to go by and introduce myself, but I just didn't quite get around to it. Ah, here we are!"

He fumbled for the key and got the door open. The interior of the wagon smelled of licorice and herbs. "I'll just grab a bottle and be right with you," he said, climbing up inside.

Rita couldn't help herself. She jumped into the wagon, and when he turned around with a look of surprise, she wrapped her arms around his neck and kissed him full on the mouth.

"My, my," Jerome breathed. "There's nothing wrong with the way that you're feeling."

"No, there isn't."

Jerome kissed her again and felt her shiver. "Has it been a long time since you been kissed?"

"A long time since I wanted to be kissed is closer to the truth. Can we close the door?"

"You think we ought to?"

"I do," Rita said in a voice she hardly recognized. "Oh yes, I do!"

Jerome thought that was an excellent idea and it was quite a while before either of them had another word to say.

"You were wonderful, Doctor," Rita finally told him when he sat up and lit a candle.

"So were you."

"I've got to go now, but I'll be back tomorrow night."

"Why?"

"Well . . . you know. So we can be together again."

"Rita," he said, "I had a wonderful time, but you are married."

"How'd you know?"

"While you were in the kitchen, I remarked to one of the other diners that you worked too hard. That's when I learned about your husband, Mike Clancy."

"Oh." Rita wanted to die of shame.

He brushed back a damp tendril of her hair and touched

her cheek. "I'm glad we had a little time together, but this isn't going to work very well. Is Mike . . . violent?"

"Whenever he drinks too much he hits me. He's hurt men in bar fights, too."

"Leave him and go find someone else. The way you cook, you'd be successful anywhere."

"Do you really think so?"

"I'm sure of it."

"We could leave Dodge together. Maybe go to Wichita and—"

"No," he said, remembering Samantha and the Wichita marshal who'd run him out of town, "that would not be a good idea."

"Then we could go to Denver or Santa Fe."

"I'm going to stay in Dodge City awhile."

"What about us?" Rita could feel her eyes stinging with tears.

"Come by once in a while and we can talk about you and Mike."

"I don't want to *talk*!"

"Then go away," Jerome told her, "before Mike really hurts you."

"To where? With what!"

"I don't know. Maybe you can sell the business. Beg, steal, or borrow enough funds to start up again. Rita, you're young, strong, and smart. You don't need a man who gets drunk and beats you. You don't need someone who won't pull their own weight."

"But couldn't we—"

"No," Jerome said as gently as possible.

"Okay." Rita wrapped her arms around his neck. "I don't regret this and I'll probably come back for more."

"Just make sure that there isn't a bandanna tied to the doorknob," he told her.

"A what?"

"A bandanna." Jerome grabbed a red one and waved it. "I tie them on the doorknob when entertaining."

"Oh." Rita wanted to laugh and she wanted to cry. "I imagine that you often have company."

"I like company," he said simply. "And yours was especially wonderful."

She took a deep breath and kissed him one last time. "I could get addicted to you, Doctor. In fact, I already am."

"No you're not," he said. "You're just tired of being hitched to a loser. Get rid of him and you'll do far better."

"We could be a team."

"Good night, my dear Rita."

"Good night."

Rita left in a hurry, and because she could not bear going home to face her husband, who was probably still awake, she returned to the café and spent the next few hours cleaning the kitchen and polishing the silverware.

"Dr. Gentry is right," she decided aloud as she finally closed up and started for home. "I need to leave Mike and move on."

On her way home, Rita remembered that she had completely forgotten to get a bottle of Jerome's Chickasaw Cure. No matter, it would give her a good reason to stop by some night when there was no bandanna tied to his doorknob and have one last, bittersweet farewell.

After Rita had left, Jerome cleaned up and strolled over to the Long Branch, but not before passing Clancy's Place and seeing Rita inside. The woman was special and deserving of happiness. Would she leave her worthless husband and Dodge City to strike out on her own? Jerome hoped so.

"Welcome to the Long Branch," a pretty girl in a lacy pink dress said when Jerome walked in the door. "It's the friendliest saloon in town!"

Rita was instantly forgotten as Jerome allowed himself to be escorted across the floor to the long polished walnut bar with the fine back mirror.

"So," another woman with wavy red hair and a generous smile said, "you must be the famous Dr. Jerome Gentry everyone has been talking about."

Jerome thought her magnificent. "Ma'am," he said, "I'm afraid that you have the advantage on me because I don't know your name."

"Kitty," she told him. "I own this place and this is my bartender, Sam. Just tell him what you are drinking."

"Rye whiskey is fine," Jerome said, eyes flicking to the square-jawed bartender with the genial smile and big hands before he looked back at Kitty. "This is a very nice saloon."

"I take a lot of pride in the Long Branch. It's the friendliest saloon in Dodge City and serves the best liquor. You might pay a penny or two more than at some of the slop joints, but we believe you'll think the Long Branch is worth a little extra."

"I'm already a believer," Jerome said, glancing around at the huge and ornate interior, complete with hanging chandeliers and poker and roulette tables. "This establishment mirrors the beauty of your smile."

"Why, thank you," she said. "And now, there's someone I want you to meet. Grab your drink and come on over so I can make the introduction."

"It was a pleasure to serve you," Sam said, pushing a full glass of rye across the bar top and then wiping up a few spilled drops.

"Dr. Gentry," Kitty said, leading him to a table where a rumpled old man sat nursing a drink, "this is Doc Adams. I think it's time you two finally met."

"Dr. Adams!" Jerome said, extending his hand. "I've heard so much about you!"

"Yeah," Adams replied sourly as he ignored Jerome's hand, "you've heard that I'm old and washed-up."

"No, sir!"

"Don't lie to me!"

Before Jerome could reply, Kitty hurried around behind Doc and placed her hands on his drooping shoulders. "Now, Doc, where are your usual good manners?"

"They're gone," he snapped. "And why wouldn't they

be! One day I'm Dodge City's medical salvation, the next I'm relegated to the dustbin.''

"Dr. Adams," Jerome said, "I'm sure that we can work together and—"

"No we can't!" Adams glared at him fiercely. "I'll be damned if I'll work with a snake-oil peddler. Now get out of here and leave me alone!"

Jerome could feel the heat in his cheeks as he stormed outside, but Kitty overtook him and grabbed his arm.

"I'm sorry! I didn't think Doc was that bitter and upset."

Jerome took a deep breath. "It's all right, Kitty. The man has probably spent some of the best years of his life in practice here for very little gain other than his sense of doing good to others, and now he feels betrayed."

"That's about the size of it," Kitty agreed. "It'll all work out. Just give Doc a little time."

"Sure."

"Come back in and I'll buy you a drink on the house," Kitty offered.

"Naw, I think I'll pass." Jerome gazed up and down the nearly deserted street and his eyes came to rest on the nearest saloon. Reading the sign, he asked, "What's the Bull's Head Saloon like?"

"Rough, Doctor. You wouldn't fit in."

"Maybe I would."

Kitty shook her head. "I've spent most of my life learning how to read all kinds of men. The good and the bad and all in between. Believe me, you don't belong in the Bull's Head."

"That bad, huh?"

"It's operated by a man called Bull. He was a bare-knuckle prizefighter for a lot of years and it shows. Bull keeps the peace . . . most of the time when he's sober."

"He sounds like an interesting character. I think I'll go make his acquaintance. Unless, that is, you want to join me back at my wagon for a little of the Cure."

Kitty cocked an eyebrow. "A woman could get in big trouble with your kind of cure, Doctor. I'll pass."

"Too bad. Maybe another time?"

"No, thank you."

Jerome shrugged and tipped his hat before he headed on down the street toward the Bull's Head. He was still a little upset about the way he'd been publicly humiliated by Doc Adams just a few minutes earlier and he wasn't ready to go to sleep.

I wonder if I'll wind up like Doc Adams, old and feeling threatened by someone younger, Jerome asked himself as he plowed through the swinging doors of the Bull's Head to find a very different scene from the one he'd left at the Long Branch. Most obvious was that the patrons were scruffy and boisterous. Instead of chandeliers, there were just lamps and smoky candles. The bar was as rough as the customers and was tended by a big, fierce-looking man with a bald head covered with scars.

"Rye whiskey," Jerome ordered, easing up to the bar and wishing he'd brought his hideout derringer.

"Comin' up, Doc," Bull growled as he splashed amber liquid into a dirty glass and shoved it across the crude bar top. "Be two bits."

The rye was so raw that it burned Jerome's eyes and made them weep. "How do you know me?" he asked.

"Everybody knows everything about everyone in Dodge," Bull told him. "Or at least they think they do. Anyway, you're the talk of the town."

"Why?"

"Well, not only did you save George's life, but you've just bedded one of the most beautiful married women in town tonight!"

Jerome might have fallen over if he hadn't reached out and supported himself on the bar. "What are you talking about?" he managed to sputter.

"Ah, come on, Doc! Nothin' happens here without me or some of my boys knowing about it. And to tell you the truth, you are in bad trouble."

Jerome tossed down the drink and hammered it down

hard enough to let Bull know he needed a refill. "People talk too much."

"Yeah, sure," Bull agreed, "but you shouldn't have taken Mrs. Clancy to your wagon. That was a big mistake."

Denial tried to form in Jerome's throat, but it died still-born and he choked, "How did you know?"

"Doc, people ain't blind! And I'm afraid that there's gonna be hell to pay in the mornin'!"

"Why?"

"It's simple," Bull said, leaning closer. "Mike Clancy is crazy jealous and he'll come looking for you with a gun or a knife. Probably both. So either he'll kill you, or you'll kill him. My money is on Mike."

Jerome steeled himself. "Bet however you want, but if Mike comes to kill me, I'll set Rita free once and for all."

"Brave talk," Bull said. "I thought doctors were supposed to save lives."

"We are, but nothing in the Hippocratic Oath says we need to be martyrs."

Jerome ordered another whiskey and regarded it for a moment, aware that all conversation in the Bull's Head had died. "And besides," he added, raising his glass, "nobody lives forever."

"That's the spirit!" Bull roared. "Boys, we're gonna have a good fight tomorrow!"

"We will if Dillon and Festus don't interfere," someone down the bar yelled.

That was when Jerome decided that the most prudent thing to do was to pay a hasty visit to the marshal's office early in the morning.

"Good evening," he said, starting for the door and thinking that one way or the other, Rita would probably be liberated from her violent and worthless husband tomorrow morning. He just hoped that her freedom didn't cost him his life.

CHAPTER

7

It was barely daylight when Jerome was suddenly awakened by an angry shout outside of his wagon. He also heard someone trying to tear open his locked door. Jerome groaned and sat bolt upright, more asleep than awake.

"Come out and fight!" Mike Clancy roared.

"Mike, leave him alone!" Rita cried. "It wasn't his fault! I'm the one to blame!"

Jerome heard the sound of hard flesh striking soft, yielding flesh, followed by a cry of pain. He jumped up, throwing off his blankets, and shouted, "Don't hit her, I'm coming!"

"You'd better or I'll kill you both!"

Jerome took a series of swift, deep breaths, closing his eyes so that he might quickly collect his senses. There was no need to panic. He had been in dozens of fights and believed there were few men who could whip him. The trouble was, a man like Rita's husband would likely have a gun or a knife.

With that in mind, Jerome shoved his derringer into his pants pocket, then pulled on his boots and finally his shirt.

"Are you coming out or am I gonna have to drag you out!"

"I'm coming!"

Jerome stood just inside the door and took a few more deep breaths. He was scared, but then he'd always been scared before a fight and that had never stopped him from doing his best. He clenched and unclenched his fists and reached for the doorknob.

"Don't come out!" Rita cried. "Mike has a club!"

Jerome grabbed a yard-long iron pry bar he used to move sticks and logs around in his campfires and threw open the door. Mike was standing at the foot of his doorway with a short piece of lumber clenched in both fists. Even in the semidarkness, Jerome could see that he was crazed with fury.

"Get back and give me room," Jerome ordered, holding the pry bar before him at chest level.

"Sure," Mike growled, backing a half step.

Jerome could see that Rita's husband was a big, big man. Not just in the belly but all over. Mike wasn't especially tall, but he had a thick chest and massive shoulders.

"Look," Jerome offered, "maybe we can talk this out."

"Get down here and take your medicine, Doc!"

"Don't do it!" Rita sobbed. "He'll beat you to death!"

The sight of Rita filled Jerome him with cold rage because she had been savagely beaten. The left side of her face was so battered that her eye was swollen shut and her lips were pulpy with torn flesh and blood.

"All my life I've hated bullies," Jerome breathed, coming down the steps with the pry bar balanced in his hands.

With a strangled curse, Mike swung his club and it whistled downward in a tight, wicked arc that would have crushed Jerome's skull like an eggshell. Throwing both hands up before him to block the strike, Jerome caught the board squarely against the pry bar and snapping it like a matchstick. Before Mike could recover, Jerome changed his grip and used the pry bar as a spear, punching him in the mouth and cracking his teeth like hard rock candy.

"Owww!" Mike cried, retreating as he spat blood and fragments of bone. He shook all over, then lowered his head and charged with his massive arms outstretched. Jerome took a step back and braced the pry bar against his wagon an instant before the big man impaled himself.

Had the bar been sharp instead of blunt, Jerome knew that it would have killed his attacker. Instead, it brought Mike to howling. Jerome stepped back and raised the iron bar overhead. He might have crushed Mike's skull if Rita hadn't intervened.

"No!" she begged. "If you kill him you could hang!"

With the bar still poised overhead and trembling in his fist, it took several moments for Jerome to regain his composure. "You're right," he said, tossing the bar aside with a warning: "Mike, if you ever touch Rita again, I'll make you wish you'd never been born."

He took her hand, saying, "Come inside. I'll see what I can do for those bruises."

Jerome lit a candle, found some water and began to gently wash Rita's face. "Oh, Jerome," she whispered in desperation. "What am I going to do!"

"I'll take you to the marshal's office and you can swear out a warrant to have your husband arrested. He'll be locked up and that will give you time to close your business and leave Dodge City. It will be all right. Do you have any money so that—"

Mike suddenly loomed in the wagon's open doorway with a six-gun pointed at Jerome's chest. "Doc, you're a dead man!" he choked through his broken teeth.

"No!" Rita cried, throwing herself at her husband and taking the bullet that was meant for Jerome as they both tumbled down the stairs.

Jerome yanked out his derringer and jumped to his doorway. Mike was shoving Rita away and trying to raise his six-gun when Jerome fired. His first bullet went wide, but the second struck Mike in the arm and knocked his six-gun spinning. Jerome vaulted out of the wagon and they fought over the dropped Colt revolver like wild animals. Mike managed to grab the pistol first, but Jerome twisted it back, breaking his opponent's trigger finger and causing it to discharge tight between them. The blast ignited their shirtfronts with burning powder.

Jerome felt the heavy man's body shudder and then go limp. He smothered the embers on his shirtfront and rolled away with Mike's six-gun grasped firmly in his hand. He would have fired again, but it was clear that Mike was dying, so he crabbed on his hands and knees over to Rita who lay gasping. When he gathered her into his arms, her eyes fluttered open for an instant and she asked, "Darling, did you kill him?"

"Yes."

"Thank God!" she whispered.

"Hang on, Rita!" he pleaded, starting to lift and carry her back up in his wagon so he could see how badly she was wounded.

"No," she told him, "don't . . ."

Jerome heard the death rattle in her throat as she slowly expelled her last breath. Crushing her against his chest, he buried his head against her bosom and wept.

"All right, Dr. Gentry," Matt Dillon said, several hours later. "One more time. What caused Mike to attack you just after daybreak?"

Jerome knuckled his eyes. "I imagine that he heard that his wife and I were talking last night and became jealous."

"That doesn't seem like enough to send a man into a killing rage. Why don't you tell me *all* of it?"

"I've told you all that you need to know."

"I'll be the judge of what I 'need to know'! The rumor is that you entertained Rita Clancy in your wagon last night. Is that true?"

"I'd rather not say, Marshal."

"If necessary, I can ask around and find out."

"Marshal, what good would that do except to cause tongues to wag even faster? Rita is dead! Can't we at least put her to rest without slandering her name?''

"Maybe you should have thought about Rita's reputation before you went for a walk in the moonlight," Matt said with anger edging into his voice. "If you had, maybe none of this would have happened."

"Did you see her face!" Jerome exclaimed, coming out of his chair. "Did you see the way Mike had beaten her? And I'll bet it wasn't the first time, either. What about you, Marshal? Did you pretend not to notice when it happened in the past?''

"Now, hold on there!"

Festus pushed between them. "Simmer down! Hasn't there been enough trouble already for one day?''

Matt relaxed. "Festus, you're right. But I'm not sure whether to lock this man up for murder, or let him go on his own promise that he'll stand before Judge Brooker.''

"Well, Matthew, we know the murder weapon belonged to Mike Clancy. And it's pretty clear that Doc Gentry was probably sleepin' when Mike showed up. So I think the judge is going to rule that the doctor acted in self-defense.''

"That's what you think?" Matt asked.

"Why sure! Everybody in town know'd that Mike was a wild man, and if anybody so much as looked at his wife, he'd beat 'em up. Dr. Gentry is the only one who didn't know about crazy Mike.''

Matt sat down for a moment to think the matter over. "All right," he decided. "Dr. Gentry, I won't jail you because what Festus says makes sense. But if you try to leave Dodge City before you see Judge Brooker, I'll lock you up and throw away the key. Is that understood?''

"Sure," Jerome said, feeling washed out and depressed.

"I'll tell you something else," Matt solemnly added. "When I advertised for a doctor, I never expected someone like you to answer my telegram. You've been in Dodge City less than two full days and already two people are dead."

"The only regret I have is that I didn't brain Mike Clancy when I had the chance," Jerome said tightly.

"Hey, Marshal!" George Bates shouted from his cell. "Are you forgettin' how Dr. Gentry saved my life? And, Doc, ain't it time you changed my bandages again and cleaned out that hole in my leg? Don't want to let it get bad again."

"All right," Jerome said, feeling a sudden and overwhelming urge to get away from people. "I'll be back later to change that dressing. Right now, though, I need some fresh air."

There were people outside and most of them had heard about the killings and wanted to talk, but Jerome put his head down and brushed everyone aside. He marched up Front Street past the Dodge House Hotel and then cut across the street past the railroad depot and followed the tracks out of town. He didn't stop until he was miles away from Dodge and then he angled away from the tracks and walked out into the open prairie, where a man felt humble and where a sea of white and yellow wildflowers were blooming.

Taking a deep breath, he sat down and then stretched out full length to watch towering windblown clouds configure castles, bays, and bridges. He thought about Rita and then about Samantha, and finally all the other women he'd known. In his own way, he'd loved every one of them deeply.

"I always tried to give as much as I got," he told the sky. "But this time . . . this time, well, I ruined everything. Because of me, Rita Clancy is dead."

Yet even as he judged himself guilty, Jerome knew that he wasn't really responsible for Rita's death. She'd chosen to come to his wagon so he'd loved her and then tried to protect her, but everything had gone wrong. My mistake was in not finishing the man when I had the chance. And because I didn't, Rita took the bullet that was meant for me. And that's something I'm just going to have to live with the rest of my life.

The brassy Kansas sun slid across the afternoon sky and settled low in the west before Jerome felt up to facing anyone again. As he had in the past, he vowed that he would never again become involved with a married woman.

"Dr. Gentry," a young man in a rumpled coat said, rushing up to him. "I'm a reporter. Would you tell me what happened this morning?"

"I'm sorry," Jerome said, barging into the marshal's office and closing the door behind him.

Festus jumped up. "Are you all right?"

"No."

"Everybody in town has been a-pesterin' Matt and me, wantin' to know what happened this morning. I been a-tellin' 'em to mind their own business and that Mrs. Clancy was shot by her husband. But they sure are nosy."

"Death always draws flies," Jerome said, recalling words his mother had once spoken in reference to the morbid curiosity of certain people.

"You don't look so good."

"I feel pretty bad about Rita. She took *my* bullet, Festus."

"She did?"

"Yes."

"Well, don't be too hard on yourself, Doc. Matt and I are partly to blame, too."

"Why?"

"We've arrested Clancy more'n once because he beat up on his wife. Matt and I were talkin' after you left and we both agreed that we should have had the judge send the man off to prison. But Mrs. Clancy wouldn't press charges."

"Why?"

"I don't know," Festus said, shaking his head sadly. "But she wouldn't. And Mike was pure poison."

"I can't imagine why she ever married him."

"They say Mike Clancy was once an important young man. I heard he has a ranchin' family down in Texas. Big ranch, too. But someone said he killed a man in cold blood.

Matt and I could never get the truth of that and I doubt that his wife believed it, but I do.''

"So do I," Jerome said. "He would have killed me in a heartbeat. I'm just sorry I didn't finish him off when I had the chance.''

"And we're sorry we didn't get him into a prison," Festus said sadly. "Say, I see that you have your medical bag. Gonna take a look at Bates?''

"Yeah," Jerome answered. "Why don't you open the cell?''

"About time you come back," Bates said looking petulant. "My leg wound has been botherin' me some this afternoon. I sure wouldn't be happy if it was getting worse.''

"Lay down and be quiet," Jerome ordered as he quickly unwrapped the bandages and then examined the bullet wound carefully.

"Well, Doc?''

"It looks much better.''

Bates lifted his head and managed to grin. "It does?''

"Yes. You don't have to worry about losing your leg anymore.''

"Hallelujah!" Bates cried. "I knew you and that Chickasaw Cure would save me! And say, don't you worry too much about killin' Mike Clancy. Someone was bound to do it sooner or later. And, as for his pretty young wife—''

"George, do me a favor and just shut up. All right?''

"Sure," George said. "But I just wanted you to know that I think you're the best doctor I ever had. Doc Adams is washed up and—''

"George?''

"Oh, yeah. Sure.''

Jerome rebandaged the wound and Festus let him out and relocked the cell, saying, "Doc, how about some coffee?''

Jerome slumped down in Matt's empty chair. "Where is the marshal?''

72

"Havin' dinner with Doc and Miss Kitty over at Delmonico's."

"Do you have anything except coffee?"

"You mean like the hair of the dog?"

"That's right."

"Sure," Festus said, fetching a bottle out of his desk drawer. "I can't drink 'cause I'm on duty. I don't drink much anyways. My family drinks enough moonshine every month to float a barge."

Jerome studied Deputy Haggen thoughtfully. His first impression had been of a backwoods bumpkin. But he'd since come to regard Festus in a far better light. Sure, the man was unshaven and unkempt, but he was obviously intelligent and dedicated both to his job and to Marshal Dillon.

"Where did your family come from?" Jerome asked.

"Way back in the mountains. The Haggens is a clannish bunch and not much given to socializin' with outsiders."

"How'd you wind up in Dodge City?"

"There was some trouble," Festus said vaguely, "and anyways, I like Matthew and this here job pays real steady."

"Would you like to be promoted to marshal someday?"

Festus made a face like he'd bit into a lemon . . . or worse. "Now why'd I want to put up with all the whinin' and complainin' that Matthew has to listen to from everyone from the mayor on down to the town drunk? No, sir! You couldn't pay me enough to take Matthew's badge and neither could Chester Goode, Matthew's deputy before I was hired. Matthew is the best marshal I ever seen and I'm happy jest to be his deputy."

"Then you're the rare man satisfied with his lot."

"Sure am! Why, my lot is good compared to them crazy Haggens up in the mountains. They is always feudin' and fightin'. I tell you, I wouldn't change places with them, nor Matthew nor nobody."

Festus offered Jerome his bottle, but there was something lumpy floating around in it, so Jerome declined. "On sec-

73

ond thought, I better get something to eat. One last question.''

''Shoot.''

''Did Rita Clancy have any relatives that ought to be notified of her death?''

''Not that anybody knowed about,'' Festus said. ''But I expect a name or two might come up. Why do you ask?''

''I'd like to write and tell them that she was good, and brave. That she saved my life by jumping between me and her husband when he opened fire.''

''I'll keep that in mind in case we do come up with a relative or two.''

''Thanks,'' Jerome said.

''Doc, are you going over to Delmonico's to see Matthew, Kitty, and Doc?''

''No,'' Jerome decided, ''I don't think I could stand putting up with Doc's insults tonight. I'll find someplace else to eat.''

''You might try them pickled pigs' feet over at the Skullery,'' Festus suggested. ''You can get 'em served up hot with fried onions and chicken necks.''

''I'll keep that in mind,'' Jerome managed to reply, realizing that he wasn't very hungry after all.

Jerome was almost back to the livery and his wagon when a horse and rider came galloping into town. Jerome's hand was reaching for the door key when the horse suddenly veered toward a pen of horses and its rider tumbled into the dark street.

''Help!'' the man cried, trying to rise but failing. ''Help!''

Jerome ran over to the rider and saw that he was a young cowboy. ''Are you shot? What's wrong!''

''North of the Cimarron River, some rustlers ambushed us for our herd of cattle,'' the kid whispered. ''Pa sent me a-racin' north to try and get help. But I got winged tryin' to get past 'em. You got to help us, mister!''

''You're in bad shape,'' Jerome told him. ''I need to see

if I can get you to Doc Adams's place and we can fix you up."

"Never mind me! My pa and brothers are gettin' killed! They're outgunned bad!"

"We'll help them," Jerome said, not at all sure what could be done as he lifted the cowboy and started back into town for help. "You can tell Marshal Dillon all about it."

"But you got to hurry!"

Stopping outside the Delmonico restaurant, Jerome shouted, "Marshal Dillon, a man has been shot! Doc Adams!"

Matt was the out the door first, followed by Kitty and then Doc. The marshal took one look at the wounded cowboy and said, "Who did this!"

"Cattle rustlers down south jumped his family's herd," Jerome answered.

"Bring him to my office," Adams said, starting off up the boardwalk.

"Marshal," the cowboy managed to choke as he stared at the tin badge on Matt's broad chest, "we were ambushed by rustlers. Our cattle were all stampeded and—"

A sudden spasm caused the cowboy to stiffen in Jerome's arms and then groan in pain.

"Don't try to talk anymore," Jerome ordered, hurrying after Doc Adams.

"But the marshal has got to help or . . ."

The body in Jerome's arms suddenly went limp. Jerome stopped and laid the kid down on the sidewalk under a lamp, then reached for his pulse.

"Is he dead?" Matt asked, hovering close.

The pulse was weak, but steady. "No," Jerome said, scooping the cowboy back up again. "He just passed out."

"Did he say how far south it was when he was ambushed by those cattle rustlers?"

"No," Jerome said.

"Well, then, did he at least give you his name or that of the ambushers?"

"No!"

"In here," Doc Adams called, unlocking his office door and making room for Jerome to sweep inside with the wounded cowboy as he blocked Matt's forward progress.

"Doc," the marshal said, "I can't do a damn thing to help him unless I know more about—"

"Later," Doc said, looking up at the marshal, who towered over him. "Right now, we're trying to save a life."

"Sure," Matt said, taking a back step. "But as soon as you find out something. Anything that—"

Doc Adams slammed the door shut. "All right, Dr. Gentry," he ordered, "bring him into my examining room and let's hope we don't have *three* people going to Boot Hill today."

They tore open the cowboy's jacket, then his shirt, to expose the gaping bullet hole in his shoulder. Jerome said, "I think the bullet missed the right lung, what do you think?"

"I agree," Adams said, reaching for cotton and chloroform.

Jerome was concerned about how much blood had soaked into the cowboy's shirt and pants. "It's a miracle that he's even alive, given so much loss of blood."

"Cowboys are as tough as the Longhorn cattle they drive," Doc Adams replied. "My surgical instruments are over in that metal tray on the counter."

Jerome removed a scalpel, forceps, and several other instruments he thought they might need. When he turned back, he saw that Doc Adams had soaked chloroform in a wad of cotton and was placing it over the cowboy's face.

"Doc," he asked, "do you really think we need that?"

"I do," Adams replied. "Otherwise, he's likely to come awake in the middle of our surgery and then we'll have hell to pay."

Jerome wasn't so sure about that, but he didn't say anything. He did, however, monitor the cowboy's pulse, and when it slowed, then stopped, he shouted, "Doc, his heart quit!"

Doc Adams paled and jerked the chloroformed cotton away. Quick as the strike of a snake, he slammed his clenched fist down on the cowboy's bare chest. Once, then a second time, and hard.

"What are you doing!" Jerome exclaimed in astonishment.

"It's worked before," Doc said, looking pale and shaken.

And sure enough, the cowboy's heart started. Jerome could hardly believe it as he scrubbed away the blood so they could get a better look at the wound.

"The shoulder is pretty torn up," he said, rolling the kid over slightly. "And the bullet is still inside."

"Hand me my forceps!"

Jerome gave the instrument to Adams, who sleeved sweat from his brow and immediately bent forward. But the old doctor was shaking so badly he could hardly get the forceps into the bullet wound. Adams looked ready to faint.

"Doc," Jerome said, "sit down and let me give it a try."

Doc shot him an angry look. "I can do this. I've removed hundreds of bullets!"

But Doc couldn't do it. Cold sweat was pouring into his eyes and he began to shake as if he had the ague. Twice, he pushed the forceps into the bullet hole, but his hands were so slippery with blood and his own cold sweat that he couldn't grip them properly.

"Here," he finally choked, giving up. "You try it!"

Jerome's nerves were steady and so was his hand. In less than a minute he found and then extracted the bullet. "Let's patch him up," he said, looking to Doc for bandaging.

But Doc was sitting slumped in his office chair. He'd removed his spectacles and his head was cradled in his hands.

"Are you all right!" Gentry called.

"Yeah," Doc Adams whispered. "I . . . I think so."

"We're going to do just fine," Jerome told him. "This kid is going to pull through. He's *got* to."

He expected a response, but Doc Adams said nothing.

Maybe he's having a heart attack again, Jerome thought. Maybe he's the one that I should be working on right now.

CHAPTER

8

Matt was waiting outside in the predawn darkness when Doc Adams wobbled outside. "Is the kid going to make it, Doc?"

"It's hard to say," Adams replied, leaning against a porch post and then sitting down heavily on the boardwalk. "He's lost a lot of blood and that's a nasty bullet hole in his shoulder."

"Did you get the slug out?"

"Dr. Gentry did. But it was deep and . . . well, Matt, only time will tell. On the positive side, the kid is young, strong, and tough. On the downside, he's lost so much blood that he might not pull through."

Matt looked at Festus, then back to Doc. "Was he able to tell you any more about the trouble he and his family had down south with those cattle rustlers? Anything that would help Festus and me figure out what we can do to help?"

"No," Doc said. "And, to be honest, I nearly killed him during surgery. The kid's heart even stopped once."

"What?"

"You heard me, Matt. His heart stopped! I might have caused him brain damage," Doc said, looking sickly in the lamplight. "I don't hold much hope for the kid."

Matt shook his head. "Sometimes trouble comes in streaks. First your heart troubles, then the killing of Rita Clancy and her husband, now this."

Doc peered at him over his spectacles. "Matt, I have a confession to make. Just listen, all right?"

"Sure."

"If this cowboy survives, it will be because of Dr. Gentry, not me. I got dizzy in there and I made some mistakes that could prove fatal."

"Hold on, Doc," Festus protested, "you're not yourself. You've had health troubles and you've been under a strain."

"I'm past my time and I've lost the touch. I could see that watching Dr. Gentry. That's not to say that he doesn't need a bit of seasoning. But I was wrong about him—he's a fine doctor and will become an excellent surgeon."

"So are you," Matt told his old friend. "Don't forget that I've seen you save a lot of men that other doctors would have given up on."

"I can't go on living on my reputation."

"No one expects you to," Festus argued. "Doc, the problem is that you need a good rest."

"That's not in the cards right now. If the kid survives, it's going to be touch and go for several days. He's slipped into a coma and might never awaken."

"I still need to know about the shooting he was involved in," Matt said. "If it's just a few miles south of Dodge, then I'll head out that way. But it might be as far south as the Cimarron River. The thing of it is, I can't leave things here for too long."

"I can't help you, Matt."

"Well, can't you at least give me some idea of how long ago that kid was shot?"

"My best guess would be that he was in the saddle at least two days."

"Two days!" Matt stared. "With that torn-up shoulder?"

"That's right," Doc answered. "After the surgery, we found bloody rags in his shirt where the cowboy had plugged up the bullet hole. I expect that is why he's still alive."

"But he was bleeding when we brought him here," Matt said. "I saw it."

"Sure," Doc replied. "When that cowboy fell off his horse, he reopened his wound. The kid is real tough. Be a shame if he died after fighting that hard to get help."

"But I can't help him, Doc! Not without knowing where he and his herd were ambushed. My job is—"

"Matt," Doc said wearily, "you don't have to tell me what your job is. I know it almost as well as I know my own. And as for going down there to find out what happened, you'd better just wait and see if the kid survives. Otherwise, there is no telling what you might be riding into and you wouldn't know who was guilty or not guilty."

"Did Dr. Gentry hear anything from the kid before he lost consciousness?"

"Only that his was a family outfit and they were ambushed north of the Cimarron."

"That's no help," Matt said. "Each spring there are dozens of family outfits driving Longhorns north out of Texas. Who knows how many of them might have already been ambushed and their cattle stolen? Why, if the bodies were buried and then the cattle run over the graves, there would be no way to ever find them or discover the murderers. The trail down to Texas could be a burial ground for all we know."

"I see what you mean," Doc said, looking grim.

"Doc, I need to put a stop to this now, and that kid in your office might be my only chance to save others."

"If the kid lives," Doc said, "he ought to be able to tell you what you need to know."

"What are his chances?" Festus asked.

"I'd say about one in five."

"I sure hate to just sit around and wait," Matt complained. "We don't even know if the rustlers are heading for Dodge City. Could be they are going to Witchita or even Abilene. They might even trail 'em all the way up to Kansas City, ambushing other small outfits and swallowing up their cattle along the way."

"I hadn't had time to think of that," Doc said, "but you could be right. Still, you don't have any choice but to sit tight and wait. In a day or two at the most we'll know a lot more. Besides, you work for the people of Dodge City."

"Yeah, but if there is trouble coming, I'd like to know about it in advance. Festus and I could have a posse waiting for them if we knew who they were. The last thing I want is a shoot-out on Front Street."

"Hold tight," Doc advised. "If the kid comes around, I'll try to find out who shot him."

"Thanks, Doc."

"Don't thank me, thank Dr. Gentry. I don't know why I gave the cowboy so much chloroform."

"Don't be so hard on yourself," Festus said. "You're just plumb worn-out. Where is Dr. Gentry?"

"Inside. We'll be spelling each other until we see what happens."

Matt sat down beside his old friend. "You need to go to bed and get some rest."

"I can't. Not now."

"Doc . . ."

"Stop worrying about me!"

"That's impossible," Matt said. "We've all been through too much together."

"And it's taken its toll," Adams said, reaching into his vest pocket and dragging out a pill.

"Heart medicine?" Festus asked.

Doc didn't answer. Instead, he drew himself up slowly and shuffled back inside.

"Matthew, he looks awful!"

"I know, but he's too proud to rest."

"It's gonna kill him if he don't."

Matt shrugged. "He knows that, Festus. But he's the doctor, remember."

"You want me to ride south and scout around for trouble? If this one was shot trying to escape, probably his whole family is dead."

"Tell you what," Matt said. "Ride south but not for any more than two, maybe three days. Most likely you'll start meeting the first herds coming up. Since we don't even know who shot the kid and ambushed his family, you're going to have to be real careful."

"Some of 'em will likely recollect I'm your deputy, Matthew. They're gonna wonder what I'm doin' pokin' around down there."

"You're right. Tell them I fired you."

"Huh?"

"You heard me," Matt said. "Tell them we had a falling-out and you were fired. Act like you're real angry. If you come upon the kind of men who would ambush the kid's family, they'll appreciate the fact that you're not in good with the law anymore. Maybe you can even join up with them."

"You make it sound real easy."

"It won't be," Matt admitted. "But you've been here long enough to know which trail bosses are honest and which aren't to be trusted. What you'll be looking for is a bigger outfit. One with some hard cases on the payroll. Men who look like they know how to use guns and aren't worried about prison or a hangman's noose."

"Well," Festus said, scratching his whiskers, "there's a lot of them Texas outfits that are a little on the shady side. And they's some pretty rough customers among 'em, as you well know."

"Festus, I'd go myself except that I'd scare off our ambushers and we'd never catch them. Just act like you're broke and looking for some cowboying work."

"But, Matthew, I *ain't* no cowboy! Why, I couldn't rope my own foot!"

"Then hire on as cook or horse wrangler, if you think

you've found the right bunch." Matt stood up. "Did you check to see if the kid's horse had a brand?"

"No, sir."

"Well, that might be all he has to give us," Matt said. "I'll ask Dr. Gentry if he said anything else that might help before he lost consciousness. And also check to see if he had any saddlebags. There might be something we can use there."

"I'll do 'er, Matthew."

"Festus?"

"Yeah?"

Matt looked at him closely in the strengthening light. "Whatever you do, don't take any chances. If whoever jumped this kid's family even suspects that you are still my deputy, they'll kill you without hesitation. What I want you to do is to find them, then come back here and we'll set a trap."

"Yes, sir."

"Here comes Dr. Gentry," Matt said. "Maybe he can give us some more information to work on."

Jerome was wrung out but optimistic, and greeted the pair of lawmen by saying, "The cowboy has got a better than even chance."

"Doc Adams gave him only a one-in-five chance," Matt said.

"Well, Doc Adams is tired. If the cowboy makes it through today, I think his chances are excellent."

"But no word of who ambushed him?"

"No," Jerome replied. "That makes it real tough, doesn't it?"

"It sure does," Matt agreed. "Doctor, I'd like you to go through his clothes for any personal information he might be carrying."

"You mean like a letter or something to identify him?"

"That's right. Festus is going over to the livery to see if his horse has been branded. But even if it has been, that doesn't mean much of anything. Branded horses are bought and sold all the time."

"I see what you mean," Jerome said. "Well, I'm going to get a few minutes' rest while the kid is asleep and then return to watch him closely. If your prisoner starts complaining from his jail cell about his bandages needing to be changed, tell him I'll get around to it by this evening."

"I'll do that," Matt agreed.

Jerome looked to Festus. "If you're heading over to the livery, I'll walk along with you."

"Sure," Festus said, yawning as they started off.

"Deputy Haggen, lately it seems as if I'm a magnet for trouble," Jerome commented as they walked down the street.

"That kid getting shot ain't your fault. In fact, Doc Adams says that you're the one that just saved his life."

"I don't know about that. He could still die, given how much blood he's lost."

"Be a damn shame," Festus said. "I wonder how many was in his family that got ambushed."

"I don't have any idea," Jerome replied. "But I sure hope there were no women."

"Never even thought about that."

"I did," Jerome said, thinking of Rita. "In this country, it seems that good women die young."

When they returned to Delbert's Livery, the cowboy's horse was tied and Delbert was waiting. "I heard about the trouble," the liveryman said. "I caught up that loose cow pony and already gave him some hay and water. He has been grazed across the rump with a rifle slug and I put some salve on it. Doc, you might want to apply some of your Chickasaw Cure."

"Yeah," Jerome said as he and Festus went over to examine the cowboy's black gelding with three white stockings.

"Nice horse," Festus said, noting all the dried blood on the saddle. "But he's sure been run long and hard."

"No saddlebags," Jerome said, noting the old single-shot percussion rifle resting in the saddle scabbard.

"He's branded, though," Festus said, running his hand over the animal's hip. "Must've done it when he was just a colt, 'cause you can hardly see to read it."

"You got that right," Delbert agreed. "I couldn't make it out."

"Looks like a Rocking R to me," Festus commented, running his thick fingers lightly over the animal's sweat-caked coat. "Yep, it's the Rocking R fer sure."

"I never heard of that one," Delbert said with a frown. "But then, if this is a Texas horse, there's no reason why I should have."

"Oh, it's a Texas cow pony, all right," Festus told them. "The saddle, bit, and bridle make that much plain. *South* Texas, way down near the Rio Grande, would be my guess. Big Bend County, maybe."

"How'd you know that?" Jerome asked.

"I been down into Mexico and all through that country a time or two and the cowboys favor a little bit of Mexican silver. I noticed it in the kid's spurs and you can see it in this here spade bit."

"Why, you're right!" the liveryman said. "Festus, you're pretty good!"

"I just been around a little," the deputy said, lifting up the gelding's right forefoot and examining its shoe, then the others one by one until he was back around to the left forefoot. "Pretty good job of horseshoeing."

"And I suppose that you can tell where *that* was done, too," Delbert said folding his arms across his chest. "Any silver in those shoes, Deputy Haggen?"

Festus either missed or more likely ignored the livery man's sarcasm. "Nope. Just the usual old iron. But you can see that whoever done this know'd what they was a-doin', 'cause they did some fancy work on the back pair of shoes to correct this animal's stride. I'm no blacksmith, but I'd say this horse might have a tendency to overreach hisself when he gallops real hard."

Delbert Oatman looked as impressed as Jerome felt.

"Are you thinking that those back shoes might help you—"

"Doc," Festus said, cutting him off because he didn't want anyone to know that he was riding south in search of the cowboy's family and stolen herd, "I think some of your Chickasaw Cure might be good for that rump wound."

Gentry understood at once and nodded to Festus.

"Well, I'll tell you this," Delbert said, "when you go back around the barn for some, you're likely to meet a crowd."

"What do you mean?" Jerome asked.

"I mean people been comin' around askin' when they can buy some of your Chickasaw Cure medicine. They heard what it did for Bates's leg and they want some for themselves."

"Then I'll have to oblige them," Jerome said, not much wanting to be bothered but knowing he needed a fresh infusion of cash; he was nearly broke and had yet to collect a fee for his medical services.

There were six people waiting to buy the Chickasaw Cure and each of them wanted two or three bottles. At two dollars a bottle, it amounted to a pretty fair chunk of cash.

"Just remember that taking it orally works better than rubbing it in a wound, insect bite, or on a stiffness or old injury," he told them all. "And don't be shy about coming back and buying more, because it sometimes takes a while to act."

When they were gone, Jerome went inside and cleaned up. He felt like lying down and taking a nap, but he was so tired that he knew sleep might prove elusive. So he changed his clothes and decided to go get some breakfast. Also, he knew that he would not rest until he checked up on the cowboy again, just in case.

Festus was sitting outside Doc Adams's office, and when he saw Jerome coming, he said, "I didn't want to go in there and wake up Doc or maybe the kid. But could you go through his clothes, just in case there's some identification or something?"

"Of course," Jerome said.

He came back outside a few minutes later. "Festus, I'm sorry, but there was nothing that would help. No letters or anything. The only thing that the kid had on him that could possibly be helpful was this old Barlow knife with the initials F.R. carved into the handle."

Festus took the pocketknife. It was a good one and he studied the initials for several minutes, then gave the knife back to Jerome. "Keep it in case the kid lives. Every cowboy takes pride in havin' a good pocketknife and I'll sure remember them initials."

"But it isn't much to go on."

"No, it's not," Festus agreed. "But you never know. I might even find them initials on something else and there'd be a valuable tie-in to who ambushed this boy and his family."

"When are you leaving?"

"Right about now, I reckon," Festus replied. "I packed my saddlebags and had somethin' to eat."

"I almost wish that I was going along with you," Jerome said.

"I'd enjoy your company, but I think your time is better spent right here in Dodge City. Old Doc Adams, he don't look good at all and he's a-talkin' like he's ready to quit practicin' medicine."

"He's got a lot of years left," Jerome said. "Doc is very tired and discouraged. He could use a long vacation."

"Well, that's what Matthew and I keep a-tellin' him!" Festus shook his head. "But old Doc, he's as stubborn as a Missouri mule knee-deep in a field of ripe oats!"

"I'll keep an eye on him," Jerome promised. "I'll try to help out so that he gets some rest."

"You'd be doin' everyone a favor if you helped Doc to get better," Festus said. "Well, so long, there."

"When will you come back?"

"That all depends." Festus squinted one eye and toed the ground with his boot. "If'n I get lucky and find them ambushers, then I'll stick with 'em like sap on a tree and get word to Matthew. But if'n I don't, then I expect to be back in a week.''

''Be careful.''

''Oh, I will, Doc! I'm not ready to poison good ground yet!''

Jerome watched Deputy Haggen go down the street in his peculiar, rocking way. The man ducked into the marshal's office for a moment, then reappeared with Matt Dillon. After a few moments of conversation, Festus climbed onto a bay horse that was just as sorry and disreputable looking as himself and rode south.

CHAPTER

9

Festus was happy enough to do what Matthew needed done. In fact, he was pleased that the marshal had entrusted him with such an important job. It was, Festus thought, far easier to see if he could ferret out a bunch of murderin' Texas cattle rustlers than it would have been to stay in Dodge City and be responsible for handling all the trouble that came from the so-called upright citizens. People like Mr. Brodkin, the banker, who was always spouting off about how he and Matthew should be doin' this or doin' that. Or Nathan Burke, the freight agent and town gossip, who created more hard feelings and hot air than those old biddies Agnes Alder and Bessy Fife all put together.

The trail south was well traveled and Festus expected that he'd soon be meeting up with a few of the earliest herds. Sometimes they even sent a man up ahead to stake out a piece of the prairie south of town for grazing their herds. Festus was no cowboy, but he knew that most of the time the Longhorns arriving were in pretty poor condition. They would fatten quickly on this good Kansas grass. And all the while the cattle buyers would be making the rounds and trying to buy whatever they could as cheap as possible. If a rancher or trail boss were in a hurry, he'd sell out quick and head on back to Texas. But if he could afford to keep his wild cowboys on the payroll an extra few weeks or even longer, he might end up getting top dollar.

All these things Festus knew well from previous years. Dodge City had started out as Fort Dodge, a place to protect overland travelers from Indians who raided all along the Santa Fe Trail. In time, Fort Dodge had become a mecca for buffalo hunters. "Hiders," they were called and a smellier, rougher bunch never lived. The buffalo hunters with their big rifles had shot out all the herds in the 1870s and then the "bone bandits," as Festus called them, had picked the prairie clean. And so, what the United States Cavalry had never been able to do, the buffalo hunters had accomplished, and that was to force hungry Indians onto the nearby government reservations. It hadn't been pretty and it hadn't been nice, but that was the way Dodge City had started and danged if it hadn't turned into a pretty decent town.

Festus didn't see anyone that entire first day of travel. Just a few head of antelope, a pair of coyotes, and a stray horse that he tried to catch, but that kept running off. If he'd been a cowboy and had a little time, he might have tried to run the animal down and rope it, because the animal was a handsome pinto with plenty of speed. But Festus wasn't a cowboy and so that was out of the question. He did, however, practice trying to rope little bunches of scrub brush and then pulling them out with his horse, but he usually missed and the horse wasn't too pleased about pulling anything more than was necessary. After an hour or so of that, Festus coiled his lariat and gave the effort up entirely.

That night he made camp in the lee of a hill where he found an old cowboy camp. There was some charred timber with a little burning time left in them and Festus got a fire to blazing. He had packed some chicken and cold biscuits and danged if he didn't also have a bottle of beer to wash it all down. It was not, he decided as he lay warm in his bedroll watching the stars roam around the heavens, a bad way to spend the night.

But the next morning, Festus awoke to discover that his horse, despite being hobbled, had managed to travel about a half mile in search of the choicest grass.

"Well dagnabit anyway!" Festus fumed, pulling on his boots and grabbing his hat before he set out after the animal.

The hammer-headed gelding with the big jug head waited until Festus was almost up to him before he shied away, and then took off with surprising speed. Festus had never seen an animal move so fast with its front legs tied together, but this one had mastered the art of hopping like a crow.

"Come on back here, you jug head!" Festus yelled, running after the animal, which seemed intent on returning to Dodge City and causing him great mortification. "Come back here or, by gawd, I'll plug you!"

Festus was so mad that he actually did yank out his six-shooter and fire it into the air. And the gelding stopped cold stone still.

Festus took a bead on the gelding, declaring, "If you're teasin' me and take off runnin' again, I'll put a hole in your ugly hide!"

The bay gelding twisted its pencil-thin neck around and regarded Festus's approach warily. It snorted, but it didn't run away again.

"Damn your hide!" Festus complained, grabbing it by the halter and starting back toward his camp. "I sure don't have time for this nonsense!"

The bay was compliant as Festus broke camp without taking the time to brew some coffee. It grunted as he pulled the cinch tighter than usual and then resisted the bit by clamping its front teeth together so that Festus had to jam his fingers up behind the teeth and pinch its tongue.

"Next time I get a raise, I'm gonna trade you in for a decent horse that appreciates the fact that it hardly ever gets rode. If I had your life, I'd be lickin' my master's hand like a dagnabbed dog!''

After that first scare and trial, the morning passed pleasantly enough. Festus enjoyed being alone and he liked to think his curious thoughts about life and the universe and how everything that God made just seemed perfect and necessary. Well, *almost* everything. For instance, he'd never been able to figure out why God made flies, fleas, and mosquitoes. Maybe it had something to do with Adam and Eve eatin' that apple when they shouldn't have, but Festus wasn't sure about that.

The sun was almost directly overhead when he finally saw a herd of cattle, the first of the season coming over a hill. It was a big herd of bawling Longhorns, with their horns a-clickin' and a-clackin' like a Mexican girl's castanets when she danced.

A big old brindle-colored steer with a cowbell around his neck was in the lead and the rest were following like a litter of kittens. When the cowboys saw Festus, one came galloping on ahead to meet him. Festus recognized the man but couldn't recall his name.

''Howdy!'' the Texan called.

''Howdy!''

''You a Dodge City cattle buyer?''

''Nope,'' Festus said.

''Well,'' the cowboy answered, ''you sure look familiar.''

''I was a Dodge City deputy,'' Festus told the man, figuring he or one of his friends would remember anyway. ''But I quit and I'm looking for work.''

The cowboy blinked, then removed his hat and scratched the plastered-down part of his hair. ''Well, Mister, why'd you come down here, then? We're almost to Dodge.''

''I know that,'' Festus said, suddenly realizing how ridiculous he must have sounded. ''But, well, I was just hopin', is all.''

''Mister, we don't need nobody and, no offense, but you don't look like a hand to me.''

"I'm . . . I'm a wrangler. I can cook, too."

"Oh," the cowboy said, "well, I sure wish we'd have met up with you a couple months ago! We've gone through three cooks and fired them all. Boys nearly hanged one down the Pecos River because he made us all sick. But we picked up a Mexican who can make a mean pot of chili and we've done just fine ever since."

"Some Mexicans are pretty good cooks," Festus agreed. "You come a long way, did you?"

"Long way. How is it in Dodge City? Marshal Dillon still there?"

"Yeah, he's the one that fired me."

"He's a hard man," the cowboy said. "I behave myself in Dodge, but some of the boys have had their skulls tapped and wound up in your jail."

"Matthew don't stand for no trouble," Festus said, a little too proudly. "Mind if I pass on by your herd?"

"Heck no! Sorry we can't give you work. Don't expect you'll find much with any of the other outfits behind us, either. Wrong end of the trail, you know."

"Yeah, I know."

They galloped back to the herd, and when they reached it, the cowboy said, "Mister, if I were you, I'd get a better horse. That plug you're ridin' ain't never gonna get you to Texas and it sure ain't going to help you get work."

Festus swallowed the insult and rode on around the herd. He studied the animals closely, looking to see if any had newly altered brands. But he didn't see a one. They were the Bar B outfit and, to his recollection, a pretty good bunch of boys.

The next herd was no more than ten miles back and it was huge. Must have been a thousand or more cattle. None of the cowboys paid Festus any mind and he rode up to the chuck wagon hoping that the cook might feed him and want to talk. But the cook hardly even looked up when Festus shouted, and kept his wagon rolling north.

Festus studied the passing herd and saw nothing that would indicate any brand changes. He also tried to look at the brand on each horse just to see if, by chance, he spotted a Rocking R. But this was the Spear S Ranch, one of the bigger outfits, with a reputation for being cheap and not very neighborly.

He came across two more herds before sundown and even managed an invitation to eat and spend the night with the second one. The trail boss, a rugged-looking man named Ace Benton, said over their evening coffee, "Haggen, I think you should have stayed in Dodge City. You'll find no work on this trail. Not until next spring."

"Well, that is probably true," Festus said, looking suitably depressed.

"Can you rope, tie, and brand cattle?"

"Calves, I can. Where I growed up we had pigs."

Benton made a face. "Pigs?"

"Yes, sir! We'd raise 'em up to about two hundred pounds, then butcher and boil 'em."

"Well," Benton said, shooting a hard glance at his cowboys, who were trying to keep from laughing outright, "you won't find no work with pigs on this cattle trail."

"Well, I know that, Mr. Benton, but I was wonderin' if there might be some *small* family outfits that could use an extra hand. You know, maybe one of 'em got hurt, or somethin'."

"There's small outfits, all right. Plenty of them. But they don't pay anything."

"You ever heard one called the Rocking R?"

"No."

"I have, Boss," a lean cowboy with a droopy mustache said. "I heard of that brand."

"Where are they at?" Festus asked, trying not to sound excited.

"They are from down around Del Rio, beside the Rio Grande. Small family outfit. Only reason I ever heard of 'em is that one of my friends worked for 'em a spell. They was a real poor outfit, or so he said. Not much water or grass down in that dry, hot country."

"How far is Del Rio, do you suppose?"

"Far as hell," the cowboy said.

"Do you recall the name of the man that owned the spread?"

"No, sir, I do not," the cowboy answered. "But I do recall that they was a family outfit and paid poor wages and served bad food. That's all that I remember my friend sayin'."

"Why are you askin' about 'em?" Benton inquired. "Being as how they're so far south, and all."

"Oh, I had just heard about 'em from a friend and wondered if they were drivin' a herd north."

"Not too likely," Benton said. "Say, you ought to get a good horse, Festus. No self-respecting cowboy would ride yours."

"He's not so bad," Festus said, not sure why he felt any need to defend the jug head. "He's steady."

"Steady?" Now even Benton was having difficulty not laughing. "Jaysus, man, the only thing steady about that hog-headed son of a gun is the beat of his lazy heart. He's got feet like kettles, and when you took the saddle off, I saw that he was swaybacked in addition to his knock knees."

"He can run a little," Festus said, starting to feel testy.

"He should run to the boneyard!" one of the cowboys said under his breath, causing everyone to burst out laughing.

Festus finished his meal and jumped to his feet. "Well," he said, "I reckon I know when I been insulted."

"It ain't you we're a-funnin', Festus! It's that ugly critter you're riding!"

More laughter. Festus grabbed up his bedroll and walked outside the circle of the campfire. He threw the bedroll down and yelled, "Good night and I'm sure glad that horse of mine gave you such pleasure."

Benton came over after the guffaws of laughter died and squatted down on his boot heels. "I apologize if we rubbed you a little hard, Festus. But that's the way of it with cowboys. There's nothing sacred to 'em except their wimmen."

"No harm done," Festus said, still smarting from their laughter.

"If you're broke, you can trail on up with us to Dodge City," Benton offered. "I could pay you a couple of dollars and, of course, feed you until then."

"Much obliged, but no thanks."

"You headin' down to Del Rio to see those people?"

Festus sat upright. "What give you that idea?"

"You seemed pretty interested in them, is all. I figured there was more to it than you were sayin'."

"Maybe I heard that there's a pretty daughter in the family."

"Maybe, but I doubt it." Benton rolled a cigarette and struck a match. When he spoke again, his voice was soft and low. "I also doubt that you quit Marshal Dillon. I figure that you're down here because of some trouble."

"You got a real fine imagination."

"I'm no fool, Haggen. You ride into my camp on a horse that ought to have been shot because it's so sorry, then you eat my grub and tell me you got fired by Matt Dillon. So I offer you a few days' work and you turn it down, and all you're really interested in is the Rocking R; some little bitty half-starved outfit down around Del Rio. What's really going on, Deputy?"

Festus pushed himself up on one elbow. "How long have you been coming up the trail with a herd?"

"Four years. I was one of the first."

"Yeah, I know."

"I always kept my cowboys in line when we got to Dodge City. I never caused you no grief, did I?"

"Not that I can remember."

"Well," Benton said, "once Johnny Singletary nearly bit the finger off a saloon gal, but that was because she had her hand where it didn't belong."

"I remember. Doc Adams sewed it on but it turned black and he had to cut it off again. They call her Four-fingered Flora now. She's still a pickpocket, and worse."

"The point is," Benton said, "maybe I can really help you if you tell me what to look for."

"All right, but you got to promise not to say anything to anybody. My life could depend on it."

"You got my word," Benton gravely told him.

In a few hushed words, Festus recounted the story of the young cowboy and how his outfit had been ambushed and he'd been able to get away. He ended by saying, "The kid was unconscious and may not pull through. All I know is that his horse carried the Rocking R brand and he had a Barlow knife with the initials F.R. carved into the wood handle."

"That sure ain't much to go on," Benton said.

"Matthew thinks that there could be a lot of other little outfits that are being ambushed for their herd and horses. He says that they could be buried right under the Chisholm Trail and their bodies would never be found."

"That's sure true enough," Benton allowed. "But I never heard or seen anything to make me think that killin' is goin' on."

"That's because you have a big herd and crew," Festus told him. "But a little outfit with maybe only four or five men, they would be the ones that would be attacked."

"What about brands?"

"You know they can be altered pretty easy. There are also cattle buyers that don't worry about 'em."

"Then Marshal Dillon needs to start keeping track of the brands and Bills of Sale."

"He doesn't have time and neither do I. Heck, when the cowboys hit Dodge City, it's all that we can do to keep a lid on the pot so trouble don't boil over!"

"Yeah," Benton said, "I see what you mean. Can I help?"

"You can keep your eyes open for outfits that have fresh-branded cattle, and if you spot 'em, go in and report 'em to Matthew."

"What about you?" Benton asked.

"I'm just going to keep ridin' south. I'd consider it a big

favor if, when you reach Dodge, you stop by and tell Matthew that you seen me and heard about this little outfit down by Del Rio.''

''You're not planning on riding that far, are you?''

''I will if I have to,'' Festus decided.

In the morning, he said good-bye and headed on down the trail, sure hoping that he wasn't going to have to ride all the way to Del Rio.

CHAPTER

10

When the office door opened Matt looked up expectantly, hoping to see Festus come shuffling in the door, but instead, it was Dr. Gentry.

"Come to change your prisoner's bandages," Jerome informed him.

Matt retrieved the cell key. "How's our mystery cowboy?"

"He's still unconscious, but his pulse is a bit stronger. I sure wish we could get some food down him. I've been able to get him to swallow water, but not much. The kid needs to eat or he'll waste away and we'll lose him."

"What does Doc suggest?"

"Absolutely nothing."

"What do you mean?"

"Doc Adams has given me complete responsibility."

"Why, is he that busy seeing other patients?"

"No," Jerome answered, "he's stopped seeing them, too."

"Good! Then he's finally resting."

Jerome was about to answer when the prisoner interrupted them, "Hey, Doc! I've been waiting all morning. You're kind of late today."

"I've been real busy," Jerome replied, unable to mask his annoyance because Bates was far too demanding. He turned back to Matt Dillon saying, "Marshal, could I have a word with you in private?"

"Why . . . why sure."

"Hey," Bates called, "what about me!"

"I'll be back soon," Jerome told the prisoner.

When they stepped outside, Jerome sat down in one of the wooden chairs lined up in front of the office and motioned Matt to do the same. "Marshal," he said without preamble, "I'm worried."

"Don't you think the cowboy will live?"

"I can't say," Jerome replied. "But that's not what I was referring to. I'm worried about Dr. Adams."

"We all are," Matt said. "His heart hasn't been good for years and—"

"It's not his heart that I'm most worried about," Jerome said, cutting off the marshal's words, "it's Doc's spirit. He's just given up since I removed that bullet from the cowboy's shoulder and hasn't shown any interest in the kid's recovery. I thought he would help me try to think of some way to bring the kid around, but he doesn't even want to discuss medicine."

"Hmm," Matt mused. "Maybe Doc feels that there isn't much that can be done."

"I've considered that possibility," Jerome replied. "And that may well be the case. But you'd think Doc would at least be helping me change those shoulder dressings. And there's the matter of his other patients."

"What's wrong with them?"

"He's refusing to see them! And, to be honest, a lot of them have decided to start coming to me for their ills. Marshal, I think Doc has decided to quit practicing medicine altogether."

"What!"

Jerome expelled a deep sigh. "Doc Adams has slipped into a deep funk."

"Oh now, hold on there. You don't know Doc the way I do," Matt said. "Doc has never been what I'd call a happy man. He doesn't smile a lot or even laugh much, but he enjoys life in his own cynical and sarcastic way."

"Not now he doesn't," Jerome stated.

"Why not?"

"I have the feeling that as long as he was the only doctor in this town, he felt very important and—"

"He was very important," Matt interrupted. "He *is* very important."

"I know that's true and you know that's true, but I'm afraid that Dr. Adams doesn't."

"Do you think that I need to talk to him?"

"Someone he trusts and knows has to," Jerome said. "I'm a newcomer in town. And I can't remind him of all the things that he's done for Dodge City. However, you sure can."

"I will," Matt promised. "It's just that I haven't seen Doc since Festus left last week."

"That's my point," Jerome said. "Nobody has seen him. Before I arrived, everyone was seeing him for their ills, but that's all changed. Couple that with Doc's recent heart problem, and you can easily understand why he suddenly feels useless."

"Well, yes," Matt agreed, "and it probably didn't help that he failed to detect that metal in Bates's leg wound. I know that it hurt his professional pride. Add to that the chloroform overdose. Did he really cause that cowboy's heart to stop?"

"I can't say one way or the other, Marshal. I wouldn't have given the kid any, but Doc was worried about him awakening all of a sudden in the middle of our surgery."

Matt scowled. "I'm going to ask you a hard question and I hope that you'll give me an honest answer."

"I'll try."

"Has Doc lost his medical skills?"

"Of course not!" Jerome snapped. "But you can't expect a man of his age and physical condition to have as steady a hand or as clear an eye as someone my age . . . or even yours. Doc is worn-out and his nerves are frayed. He's probably scared about dying of a heart attack and he's been worked far too long and hard. What he needs is rest, but I don't think he ought to stop working altogether."

"I agree," Matt said. "But if his patients have lost faith in him . . ."

"Look," Jerome explained, "I'm the new guy in town and I've been lucky enough to have corrected a few of Doc Adams's mistakes. Suddenly, I'm the savior of Dodge City . . . a healer who can do no wrong. Unfortunately, that makes Doc seem less of a physician than he is. But that will change."

"How?"

"I'll make mistakes," Jerome told him. "I already have with Rita Clancy."

"That was different. We're talking about your medical judgment, not your moral judgment."

"Either way," Jerome said, "I will make mistakes and some of them might cost lives. Doctors aren't gods, and we do occasionally lose patients despite our best intentions. Once I do that, the citizens of this town will turn back to Dr. Adams and I'll suddenly be out of favor."

"That's a pretty harsh assessment," Matt said. "Nobody with any sense seriously believes you're infallible."

"Yes, they do," Jerome argued. "And, if you saw the way I'm selling the Chickasaw Cure and the lines of Doc's patients that I've been treating, you'd believe me."

"I'll talk to Doc," Matt repeated. "But, with Festus gone, I'm stuck here most of the time and—"

"I'll watch your patient while you're gone," Jerome offered. "Go see Doc now. You'll find that he's in his nightshirt lying in bed probably staring up at the ceiling. His mental condition worries me far more right now than anything physical."

"Okay, thanks," Matt said, giving Jerome the cell key.

"Bates isn't dangerous or I wouldn't just go off and leave you alone with him in an open cell."

"I'm not worried. With only one good leg, how far would he get even if he did knock me in the head?"

"Not far. I'll see Doc right now."

"Marshal?"

"Yes?"

"Don't tell him what I've said about being despondent. Just remind Dr. Adams that he's still needed."

"That's easy because it's true."

"Of course. I need his experience and advice with respect to that cowboy. If we can't manage to bring him back to consciousness, I'm afraid that he will slowly waste away and die."

"We can't let that happen," Matt said. "Not only for the kid's sake, but also for any other small outfits on the trail that might also be in danger of being wiped out for their cattle. And Doc, thanks. When you arrived in Dodge driving that medicine wagon, I judged you a charlatan."

"Sure. Just another snake-oil peddler out to make a few fast dollars before he disappeared in the night."

"That's right," Matt said. "And when Rita Clancy was killed . . . well, I was about to run you out of town."

'You would have been justified."

"No," Matt said, "it would have been a big mistake."

"I hope you're still thinking that after I make a mistake that proves fatal."

"You won't," Matt said, then remembered Rita Clancy and added, "as long as you stay away from married women."

"Right," Jerome agreed.

"Look, I'm sorry. That last remark wasn't necessary."

"Oh yes, it was," Jerome replied. "Good luck with Doc. Right now what he needs most is a trusted friend."

Matt headed over to Doc's office and found him lying in bed just as described, except that his eyes were closed. Assuming that he was sleeping, Matt started to turn and leave, but stopped when Doc opened his eyes and said, "Matt. I'm just resting."

Matt was shocked by the depth of sadness and despair in his old friend's voice. He pulled up a chair to the bedside. "Doc," he lied, "you're looking better and better."

"Liar. I look as old as dirt and ready for the grave."

"Cut it out! You're only what? Sixty?"

"I wish," Doc Adams said. "But never mind my age. You're no longer a spring chicken, either."

"We've both been worn hard," Matt agreed. "But I'm far from washed up as a lawman and you're nowhere near the end of your medical career."

"Now, *that's* where you're wrong. I'm finished, Matt. Lately, I've been thinking more and more of my younger sister back East."

"You've made fun of Agnes for years. She's a religious fanatic and keeps threatening to come to Dodge City and make her life's work saving your soul."

"Agnes means well," Doc said defensively. "She has always loved me and she means well."

"Fine," Matt said, "but why are we talking about her now?"

"I'm going to ask her to come live here and take care of me," Doc announced, avoiding Matt's eyes. "Either that, or go back and live with her."

"What!"

"You heard me. I'm in no condition to waste my breath repeating myself."

"Doc, you told me a hundred times that you would never live back East again because the climate doesn't agree with you."

"Nonsense! They don't have tornadoes like we do in Kansas! And it doesn't get any colder than here. Why, Kansas burns you up in the summer and it freezes you in the winter."

"Forget the climate," Matt clipped. "The point of it is that you wouldn't like it back there and you sure don't want to live with your sister. Two days of her trying to reform you to her idea of religion and you'd be on the first train back to Dodge City.''

''I . . . well, I don't know. I guess it might be better to have her come here and live with me.''

''No one could live with you, Doc! You're way too ornery and set in your ways.''

Doc wasn't listening. ''On the other hand, if I went back East,'' he mused, ''I could sit on Agnes's porch in a rocking chair. She's supposed to be a good cook.''

''You like to eat out every evening. Doc, you're talking crazy.''

''No, I'm not. You see, Agnes is lonely since her husband died. We could be of comfort to each other.''

Matt shook his head. ''Doc, you'd either be bored to death, or you'd just give up and die.''

''No one lives forever. Matt, I've already had a good life.''

''It's not over. You've a lot of good years left to practice medicine in Dodge.''

''My time is past,'' Doc said, chin jutting out the way it always did when he was going to be especially stubborn. He poked a finger at Matt and said, ''And I just hope that when your time to quit arrives, you'll be man enough to admit the fact and retire with some dignity.''

Matt came to his feet. ''Doc, you're deliberately trying to get me angry enough to stomp out of here so that you can lie in bed and feel sorry for yourself.''

''That's not true, but you *are* angry, so I guess I can still tweak your nose out of joint. You and Festus are easy. Now, Miss Kitty . . . well, she almost never takes my bait and so is a far greater challenge.''

Matt sat down again. ''Listen,'' he said earnestly, ''I know that you feel bad about missing those pieces of lead in George Bates's leg and about the chloroform overdose.''

''Bad? That is a huge understatement. If we were back East at a big hospital, I'd have my license pulled for—''

''This isn't 'back East' and you've been on your own

and doing well for a lot of years. This town needs you, Doc!''

"Not anymore. Not with Dr. Gentry walking on water and selling cases full of his Chickasaw Cure.''

Matt came back to his feet. "Look," he said, "I came over here to see how the cowboy was doing.''

"No, you didn't," Adams argued. "You came over to try and change my mind about retiring.''

"I didn't even know that you were considering something that ridiculous.''

" 'Ridiculous'!'' Doc's eyes blazed. "Well, Marshal Dillon, if you don't marry Miss Kitty one of these days and start thinking about your own retirement and future, you'll wind up as alone and useless as I am!''

"I'm leaving," Matt announced. "Maybe you'll be fit company to talk to tomorrow.''

"If I'm strong enough, I might start packing.''

"What about your practice?''

"I could trade it to the town's new medicine man for a case or two of his Chickasaw Cure! Who knows? If Agnes doesn't want to come to Dodge City and care for me, then I guess the thing to do would be for me to go join her so that I'd at least be buried among my family.''

"You've always hated your family!'' Matt stormed. "You want to be buried with family? All right, die right here in Dodge City because *we* are your real family.''

"I need to get drunk," Doc said, tossing his covers aside.

"No you don't. You need to get to work.''

"Matt, get out of here before I find a tourniquet and try to strangle you good.''

Matt left the man to wallow in self-pity. Maybe Doc would quit and go back East where he'd quickly die because he'd have nothing more to live for than Agnes's company and a rocking chair. But Matt wasn't ready to give up on his old friend. Not nearly. He'd ask Kitty to visit right away and he'd send Festus over the minute his deputy returned from his cattle investigation. Festus was always a wonderful antidote for Doc's poor disposition. The two of them would argue and give each other hell, but before they parted, they'd both be feeling a whole lot better.

Yes, Matt thought, *Festus is exactly what Doc needs to snap him out of his blue funk. But where is he? Festus should have returned to Dodge by now. What if something went wrong down the trail to Texas? Matt hadn't even asked Festus if he was going to follow the Chisholm or the Western Trail down into Texas.*

Matt shook his head with worry and thought, *Hurry back, Festus, or Doc might be gone before you can needle him back into good-humored sanity.*

CHAPTER

11

When Matt had left, Doc lay back down in bed for a few minutes thinking about their disagreement. Doc liked to argue and he was frequently at odds with folks, especially his best friends. But this time, the argument had been uncomfortably personal. What Matt did not understand was how it felt when a man got old and past his prime. When a physician began to lose his touch, the results were often fatal. Overlooking bullet fragments in George Bates's leg would have proved fatal or, at minimum, necessitated an amputation. Using too much chloroform on the still-unconscious cowboy was another example of what could happen when a physician had lost his nerve, judgment, and skill.

No, Matt did not understand. He was still in his prime and would be for several more years. But God help him if he didn't quit before he lost his ability to uphold the law. That could also be fatal—to himself.

For almost an hour, Doc went over his own rationale for retirement, and at the end of that time he was even more convinced that he had made the right decision. However,

Matt might have been correct about him needing to stay in Dodge City rather than go back East and live with Agnes. In the first place, Doc did love Dodge City and had invested his best years here helping to build something that would outlast the cattle trade. From buffalo to bones to these huge Texas cattle deliveries, Dodge had always been a lively and interesting town, one undergoing continual economic changes. Doc knew that the days of the cattle drives could not last. This country was too fertile and, sooner rather than later, it would all be farmed and fenced. When that happened, real permanence and stability would finally take place. There would be fewer saloons, dance halls, and brothels, and more churches, fraternal halls, and schools. Doc knew that he wanted to live long enough to see those positive and lasting changes.

Well, then, I'll send for Agnes. She can come here to live and I'll pay her something to cook and take care of me in my dotage. I don't think she has much money and maybe, after all these years, we can become friends, he thought.

With that decision made, Doc got up and dressed, then sat down at his writing table and composed a telegram. He would send it to Agnes, explaining that poor health had forced him to retire, and inquire if she would come live in Dodge City as his helpmate and companion.

But what if she comes and all we do is fight? Doc fretted. Then what am I going to do? Oh well, I'll worry about that then.

Feeling as if he'd made the best decision, Doc pulled on his coat and went down the hallway to check up on the cowboy. The kid was still breathing, and when Doc felt his pulse, it was fast but steady. Doc thumbed up one of the cowboy's eyelids and studied his pupil. He decided that the kid might make it after all, no thanks to himself.

"Keep fighting," Doc told the pale and unconscious figure, then cynically added, "you're too young to die, but then, that doesn't count for anything out West."

Doc grabbed his hat and headed for the front door, intending to go directly to the telegraph office. He hadn't seen Agnes in more than twenty years. But she'd kept in touch, and when her husband had died, she'd written almost every month. Not that Agnes had anything to say of interest, but the fact that she was his sister and cared enough to keep in contact meant something. In fact, it meant quite a lot now that he was feeling so poorly and near the end of his days.

"Hi, Doc," Percy Crump the undertaker called, hurrying up to him on his long, spindly legs. "Has that young Texas cowboy died yet?"

"No," Doc snapped, offended by the hopefulness in Crump's beady eyes.

"Well, I hear that he's the same as dead," Crump said, not one to be easily discouraged. "I guess that Marshal Dillon sent Festus down to find his kinfolks in Texas. Probably to see if they want to send someone up to make funeral arrangements."

"That's ridiculous!" Doc snorted. "Nobody even knows what the cowboy's name is, much less if he has any kinfolk that care enough to handle his burying."

"I went over to the stable and took a look at his horse and outfit. Nice horse. The saddle ain't bad either. Ought to bring fifty dollars. Maybe a little less."

"Percy, what are you babbling about?"

"His horse and saddle! Fifty dollars would give him a pretty good send-off. I'd handle everything and maybe I could even find him a clean shirt and—"

"Darn it, Percy, the poor kid isn't dead yet and you're already hovering around like a starving vulture!"

The undertaker recoiled. "Now, Doc, that's no way to talk to an old friend."

"If you keep talking like that, we're not going to be friends anymore," Doc retorted. "What's the matter, is business slow right now?"

"It isn't the best," Percy admitted. "Burying the Clancy couple helped, but before them, it'd been more'n a week since old widow woman Hastings died of consumption."

"It wasn't consumption and damned if I can work up much sympathy for you!"

Percy Crump assumed a haughty air. His long, hooked nose went up as if he were sniffing the wind and he declared, "I can see that the rumors about your failing health and disposition are entirely true. Doc, you shouldn't offend your undertaker."

Doc could scarcely believe what he was hearing. "Percy, are you *threatening* my last remains?"

"Enough said," Crump replied, turning and marching away stiff-backed.

"You *are* a vulture!" Doc shouted before continuing on toward the telegraph office.

"Mrs. Winslow," Doc said. "How are you feeling today?"

The matronly wife of one of the town's most successful mercantile stores replied, "Very well, Dr. Adams."

"Gout not bothering you for a change?"

"Not at all."

"You haven't been in for your medicine," Doc said, feeling guilty. "I've got some—"

"Not necessary," the woman interrupted. "I'm on some *new* medicine and I'm feeling quite good."

" 'New medicine'?"

"The Chickasaw Cure," she replied. "I never expected to feel so good after all these years! You really ought to try some yourself, Dr. Adams. It might do wonders for your own poor health."

Doc was too stunned to reply before the matronly woman bustled on down the boardwalk. But when he recovered from his surprise, he snorted, "Chickasaw Cure! Hogwash!"

Thanks to Mrs. Winslow, the undertaker, and no fewer than three more of his patients who either avoided his greeting or confessed to being converts to Dr. Gentry, Doc was in an especially foul mood by the time he reached the telegraph office.

"Hey, Doc," Barney said, thumbing up his green eyeshade to expose his receding hairline. "I thought you were on your deathbed from the way folks were talking. You don't look so good."

"Well, you don't look so good, either," Doc told the crusty old telegraph operator. "Do you suppose we could skip the insults today and just conduct business?"

"Sure," Barney said. "You want to send a message?"

"That's the idea," Doc replied, reaching into his front pocket and retrieving the note he'd written to Agnes. "It's all there. Just send it along and I'd appreciate it if you kept the message confidential this one time."

Barney's mouth turned down at the corners. "Doc, I never tell people what ain't none of their business."

"Sure," Doc said, reaching for his wallet, "and most cowboys want to be preachers and prohibitionists."

"Huh?"

"Never mind. How much to send that message?"

"Let me count the words. Doc, you could save some money by eliminating about half of what you said."

"Yeah, but then I wouldn't be saying but half of what I want to say, you idiot!"

Barney jumped out of his chair, fists clenched. "Idiot! Is that what you called me?"

"What's the matter? Is your hearing gone, too?"

Barney shook his knobby fist. "Doc, if you wasn't such a sick man, I'd come around this counter and beat you to within an inch of your miserable life!"

"Come on!" Doc shouted, balling up his own fists. "I could whip you on my deathbed!"

For a moment Doc thought that Barney actually was going to come around and fight. And that would have been just fine. He hadn't been in a good scrap in years and he could feel his tired old blood began to course with excitement. But then he suddenly felt a shortness of breath and a tingling in his nose and maybe . . . maybe some pain and numbness on his left side.

"Doc, are you all right? What's wrong! You're turnin' white!"

"I'm . . . I'm all right," Doc gasped, leaning on the counter for support and forcing himself to settle down and breathe deeply.

"Geez, Doc! You ought to go to bed. I could hunt down Dr. Gentry. He's got this stuff called the Chickasaw Cure and it's a wonder tonic, I tell you. You ought to—"

But Doc shook his head. "How much do I owe you for the telegram, Barney?" he breathed.

"Sit down while I count. Geez, I'm sure glad that you're sending for Agnes. I just hope that she isn't too late."

"How much!"

"One dollar and fifteen cents," Barney said. "What if she can't come? You look terrible! Do you want me to go find Dr. Gentry?"

"Barney, just do me a favor and send the telegram. And I really would appreciate it if at least one person in this town didn't know about Agnes by this time tomorrow."

"Doc, I told you that I respect the confidence of . . ."

But Doc didn't wait any longer. He was fed up with Barney just like he was fed up with all the other fickle people in Dodge City that he'd treated and who now considered him little more than a walking corpse. An object to be pitied . . . or avoided.

A drink at the Long Branch, Doc thought. And maybe a little intelligent conversation with Kitty. Or at least something pretty to look at for these poor, failing old eyes.

"Doc!" Kitty cried loud enough to be heard by half the patrons in the Long Branch. "Doc, you look awful!"

"Well, thank you very much and good night!" he shouted, wheeling around and heading back outside.

But Kitty caught him before he could make a respectable exit. "Oh, Doc, I'm sorry!" she exclaimed, grabbing his sleeve and pulling him around. "It's just that I've heard that you aren't feeling well and—"

"Maybe I have had better days," he spluttered with righteous indignation, "but I sure don't need to be constantly reminded of it!"

"Doc, I apologize. Come on in and we'll have a drink and talk."

"I'd better warn you that I'm in a foul funk. I've fought and snapped at every idiot I've seen in the last hour."

"Well," Kitty said, kissing him on the cheek, "you're not going to treat me that way, are you?"

"Not unless you humiliate me again before all your other customers."

"I swear I won't do that. And, if you're really nice, I'll even have Cherry come over and sit on your lap."

It was a joke and it brought a smile to Doc's face because Cherry weighed at least three hundred pounds. Round as a cherry pit and sweet as the cherry candy, Cherry was immensely popular with the regular customers and probably made more in tips than any of Kitty's other girls despite her dimensions. She also had the finest voice in Dodge City, although bellowing Bessy Fife loudly proclaimed that distinction among her church acquaintances.

"All right," Doc promised, "you win. Get us a bottle of your best rye whiskey and my disposition will improve."

"Sam," Kitty called to her bartender, "the usual for Doc and me."

Sam came over to their table with two clean crystal glasses. He uncorked the bottle and hesitated, looking closely at Doc.

"What are you staring at, Sam?" Doc demanded.

"You don't look so good. Are you sure you ought to be drinking with your bad heart and all?"

"Sam, *I'm* the doctor! *You're* the bartender, or have you forgotten!"

"Gosh, Doc," Sam said, looking hurt, "I was only thinking of your poor health. I didn't mean—"

"It's all right, Sam," Kitty said, giving Doc a disapproving look. "Our friend is just a little oversensitive right now."

"You got that right," Doc groused, tossing his whiskey down neat. "I'm sick and tired of everyone telling me how bad I look and how I ought to be taking some of that voodoo firewater that Dr. Gentry is peddling out of the back of his wagon.''

"Say, Doc, now, that stuff works real good!'' Sam told him earnestly. "You remember that rash that I had on my— well, you know. Anyway, that ointment you gave me didn't do much, but I been washing it with some of that Chickasaw Cure stuff and it's almost gone!''

Sam grinned hugely and Doc would have tossed his drink in the bartender's face except that his glass was empty and Sam was normally a good fellow.

"Sam,'' Kitty said, glancing over at the bar, "you've got customers to serve.''

"Oh, yeah. Sure! But you ought to try some of that new stuff before Dr. Gentry sells out.''

Doc refilled his glass and emptied it. Kitty studied him in silence until he grew uncomfortable and asked, "What are you staring at me for?''

"Like everyone else,'' Kitty answered, "I'm very worried about you, Doc. You've never been a real cheerful soul, but your mood sure has gone downhill since your heart trouble. Are you afraid of dying?''

"What?'' Doc could not believe what he'd just heard.

"I asked if you were afraid of death,'' Kitty said, tossing her own drink down and refilling her glass. "Because, if you are, you ought to read the Bible.''

Doc gaped. "I don't believe what I'm hearing here! We're in your saloon and you're *preaching* to me?''

"I'm not preaching,'' Kitty said with annoyance. "But sometimes it helps to read the Bible and to pray. I'm not ashamed to tell you that. Doc, we've talked about God and religion before, so don't act so shocked.''

"I think I'll get drunk alone,'' Doc told her. "Would you mind leaving me in peace?''

"As a matter of fact, I would. Now, what is the problem?''

"The problem is that I'm in poor health and have been replaced and that I feel . . . useless.''

"Doc, you aren't useless. You're beloved in Dodge City.

If there were a poll of who saved the most lives or did the most good, you'd probably be at the very top of the list.''

"Bosh! Everyone has written me off, and even the undertaker is eyeballing me like his next potential client—which I very well may be.''

"Stop it!'' Kitty ordered. "Stop this kind of talk right now or I will let you drink alone.''

Doc could see that she was serious. Kitty was no bluffer and she rarely got mad, but mad she was right now. He took a deep breath. "All right,'' he agreed. "But I think you should know that I have just sent a telegram to my sister asking her to come to Dodge and take care of me in my retirement.''

"'Retirement'?''

"That's right.''

"Can you afford to retire?''

"I can. Enough of my former patients still owe me barter of all kinds and descriptions in lieu of cash money. So much barter, in fact, that I can hire Agnes to run a junk shop, where we shall undoubtedly make far more money than I ever did in the practice of medicine.''

Kitty laughed outright, causing Doc's mood to brighten just as it always did in her unfailingly cheerful and lovely company.

"Well,'' she told him, "I'm glad that you haven't lost your wit and wry humor.''

"I guess I haven't,'' he confessed, "but I did send for Agnes. I'm surprised that Barney hasn't already rushed over here to tell everyone in your saloon, or at least run out in the street to proclaim it in a loud voice.''

"Doc, don't be so hard on Barney. And anyway, let's get back to your sister, Agnes. You told me that you never got along with her.''

"I didn't.''

"Well, then?''

"She's all the family I have . . . or at least that has cared enough to keep in touch,'' Doc explained. "She's widowed and lonely. I just think that maybe I can help Agnes and she can help me. That's all. Nothing more.''

"Doc, that's a sweet sentiment. Family is very important.''

"You think so?''

"Sure!''

"I never seen any of your family. Or Matt's. And when Festus's family comes into Dodge from the hills, there's always trouble.''

"Festus's family is . . . unique,'' Kitty said with a half smile. "But we're not talking about his family, we're talking about you sending for a sister that you have often derided and ridiculed as being stingy, ugly, and bossy.''

"She's all of that and religious, too. She doesn't approve of drinking, gambling, smoking, or cussing, all of which I do to excess.''

"Then what makes you think you can get along with her?''

"Kitty,'' Doc said, refilling both their glasses, "I can't answer your question. But what if I have another heart attack? What if I become paralyzed and can't take care of myself?''

"Then we'll find someone to help you,'' Kitty said. "You know that.''

Doc raised his glass and studied it thoughtfully. "Yes,'' he said after a few moments, "I know that you, Matt, Festus, and a few other of my real friends would do everything in your power to see that I was comfortable. But that's a lot to ask of friends and I'd rather ask it of my sister and then leave her my worldly possessions. She doesn't have much, from what I gather from her letters. Agnes needs help and . . . it's clear, so do I. In fact, I'd thought to go back and live with her, but Matt made me realize that I wouldn't be happy back East. So I'm inviting Agnes out to Kansas.''

"Will she come?''

"I don't know. Maybe.'' Doc sipped as his drink. "It's one of those things where you decide to put it up to fate, or God or whatever, and see what happens and hope it is

118

for the best. If Agnes comes, I'll try my darnedest to see that she is rewarded and appreciated.''

"Doc," Kitty said, "I don't want to sound . . . harsh, but you are not an easy man to get along with, under even the best of circumstances.''

"Neither is Agnes, so we'll be even. And besides—''

"Doc!''

He looked around to see Matt and Dr. Gentry coming over to join them. Matt looked troubled and said, "Are you sure drinking is good for you?''

"Of course I'm sure!'' Doc looked at Gentry. "Everyone I've been meeting can't say enough about your Chickasaw Cure. I'm almost tempted to try some myself, except that I don't drink bad liquor.''

Gentry colored with either embarrassment or anger, Doc didn't know or care which and then the young doctor said, "It's good to see you up and about.''

"Yeah," Doc said sarcastically, "I'm sure you're delighted.''

"Doc, stop it!'' Kitty scolded him in an angry voice. "You don't have to be insulting.''

"That's probably true," Doc said, forcing a smile. "Gentlemen, why don't you join us? The drinks are on me tonight.''

Matt and Gentry exchanged worried glances, but they sat down, and before they could say anything more about his health, Doc said, "Matt, what's this I hear about Festus heading off for Texas?''

"He's not supposed to go that far," Matt replied. "I told him to ride south for a couple of days and see if he could learn anything about that young cowboy. Festus should have been back by now.''

"Any idea what might have happened to him?'' Doc asked.

"None at all.''

"Well," Kitty said, trying to sound a note of encouragement, "Festus is more than capable of taking care of himself under any and all circumstances. I'm sure that he's just fine. In fact, he's probably enjoying the chance to get off by himself.''

"Yeah," Matt said, "you're probably right. But I sure wish that he'd let me know what he's up to and what he's found out."

"I'll bet you hear from him soon," Kitty said.

"I hope so."

Doc knew Matt well enough to read the worry in his eyes. And he supposed Kitty and the others must have guessed it as well, because the mood went flat and little more was said, either about his poor appearance or about the whereabouts of Deputy Festus Haggen.

CHAPTER

12

Festus forded the Cimarron River, hardly getting the bottom of his pant legs wet but knowing the Canadian would be far deeper. He had two days of foul weather with heavy thunder and lightning, but discovered an old buffalo hunter's dugout and holed up during the worst of the storms, then continued south, meeting new Texas herds most every day. He visited each outfit, offering the same story about getting fired as a Dodge City deputy while he studied brands looking for the Rocking R or evidence of brands that had recently been altered.

"We're takin' our herd all the way to Wyoming this year," one grizzled old Texan from down near San Antonio announced. "Figure to fatten 'em up on that northern grass and sell 'em to the army for top dollar."

Festus wished the rancher well and kept riding south. He was surprised at how many of the herds weren't going to sell their cattle in Dodge City but were instead continuing on, where they hoped to sell them at northern mining camps, Indian reservations, and to various railroad companies building lines ever farther westward. One outfit called the Slash Knife was driving three thousand head of Longhorns all the way to Canada!

On the day that Festus saw the wide Canadian River, he also met an outfit quite different from any he'd met thus far. The first thing he noticed was that their herd lacked conformity; it was composed of mostly Longhorns but also some Mexican cattle and even a few milk cows. His suspicions were also raised because the outfit's remuda was much larger than necessary, given the number of cowboys and cattle.

With very few exceptions, Festus had been treated hospitably by the drovers, but this bunch was standoffish. Instead of the usual greeting, these men were silent and taciturn. Instead of the usual chuck wagon, this bunch of hard cases operated out of a couple of big Conestoga wagons packed with goods concealed by heavy canvas tarps.

The more that Festus studied this outfit who had just swum the Canadian River and were drying out in preparation for moving north, the more he felt something about them was peculiar.

"Howdy, there!" he called, riding into their camp without an invitation.

A pair of big galoots sauntered out to meet him. "That's far enough, stranger," the larger of the pair said, holding up his hand in a gesture that discouraged any farther advance.

Festus felt their suspicion and disfavor, but that made him even more determined to play the congenial fool. He dismounted and walked forward with an outstretched hand. "Glad to make your acquaintances!"

They ignored his hand and one bluntly asked, "Stranger, what do you want?"

"Why, I was hopin' for a little chow," Festus said, rubbing his belly. "I been out of grub since yesterday morning and my stomach is sure complainin'."

"We don't give drifters handouts."

"I don't want no charity! I got cash money to pay for victuals!" Festus patted his pocket with his left hand, keeping his right hand near his gun. "I got plenty of money. I was fired up in Dodge City and am looking for a job."

"Then keep looking," the larger one growled. "We don't want your money and we don't need any more hands. Besides, you ain't no cowboy and you ain't a Texan, either."

"Well, that's true enough," Festus admitted, "but I am good with horses. I see you have a lot of extras. Maybe we could strike a deal."

"What kind of a 'deal'?"

"As you can see," Festus said, jerking a thumb back over at his own horse, "my animal is not the best. Now, I was thinking that since you got so many horses, we might work out a trade. Of course, I'd give you money to boot."

The man looked past Festus at his horse, then spat a stream of brown tobacco on the grass. "That sorry creature you are ridin' wouldn't bring twenty dollars at killer prices. No thanks."

"My horse hates water and I probably won't be able to get him to swim that Canadian."

"Well, you're just in all kinds of trouble, ain't you? No grub and a horse afraid of water. But your troubles don't concern us so take 'em and git!"

"Look," Festus said, growing desperate to get among this outfit's horses and cattle so that he could have a close look at their brands, "I have over a hundred dollars cash money. I'll pay you *twice* what one of your best horses is worth . . . if you throw in a couple pounds of beans, flour, coffee and just enough to see me on down the trail."

"*You* got over a hundred dollars?"

"That's right."

"Stranger, you don't look like you got two nickels to rub together."

"Well," Festus said, managing to look injured, "I most surely do and I am hungry and in need of a better horse, and you have some fine ones. I'll make it well worth your time, so what do you say?"

"Waco?" the big one said with a scowl. "I ain't opposed to making a profit off this fella's misfortune. Are you?''

"I guess not," Waco allowed, eyes boring into Festus. "Stranger, we buy good saddle horses from farmers and small outfits as we travel north. Then we trail 'em along with our herd and sell 'em for a hefty profit."

"That makes good sense."

"It makes us extra money."

"Well," Festus told them, "I'll pay you better'n you'll get up north for the right horse. Are your sure they're all sound?''

"You bet, which is more than you can say about that plug you're riding."

"You got me over a barrel," Festus admitted, looking downcast. "I know I'm gonna get skinned by you fellas, but I am in a bad fix. What do you say?"

"All right," Waco decided, "ride in among our remuda an' pick a horse. Rope him and switch saddles and bridles. By then, I'll have one of the boys sack up a few eats and you can show us the color of your cash. But you'd best have the money to pay for our trouble."

"Yes, sir!" Festus slapped the bugle in his pocket, which was nothing more than a dirty bandanna. "I wouldn't put you fellas to no trouble without payment. That wouldn't be smart of me, would it?"

"It sure wouldn't," Waco said ominously.

Festus smiled nervously and then took a deep breath and rode around the pair toward the remuda, not entirely sure that he wasn't about to get a bullet in the back. There was no help for it, though. He had to demonstrate that he was stupid and trusting so that they didn't get suspicious.

The bullet did not come but Festus was sweating profusely by the time he rode in among the large remuda looking for a horse with a Rocking R brand. He found it right away. In fact, he counted seven saddle horses with that brand. One of them was a handsome dapple gelding that was a real eyeful, long-legged and deep-chested. Festus judged the horse to be a swift and powerful runner.

"I choose the gray!" he called to the watching crew.

"Rope him," Waco ordered.

Festus knew his chances of roping the dapple gray were slim to none, but he figured that his ineptitude might be amusing enough to distract Waco and his cowboys while he inspected a few cattle brands. So he untied his lariat and made a big show of fashioning a noose, feeling them watching his every move.

When he began to swing the lariat around and around overhead, the horses started to move away and Festus spurred his sorry bay after the dapple. It bolted and he made a pathetic show of flinging his noose, which missed badly.

"Whooee," one of the cowboys exclaimed, "what a sorry roper he is!"

Festus ignored the comment and began to coil his rope. He heard Waco order one of his cowboys to go catch the dapple, and an instant later a lean and hard-faced Texan vaulted into the saddle and went flying after the horse. He had it roped in nothing flat, giving Festus only a few minutes to really study the herd. But it was time enough. There were plenty of cattle with freshly altered brands, and although there was not enough time for a close inspection, some of the altered ones looked to be Rocking R.

"If you can't ride any better than you rope, this horse is gonna be too damned much for you to handle," the Texas cowboy said with unconcealed contempt as he led the dapple over to Festus.

"It's my money that buys him and I'll worry about that," Festus said, dismounting to unloosen his cinch. As fast as he could, he bitted and saddled the dapple, then turned his bay gelding in among the remuda. He mounted and immediately felt the animal's spirit and power.

"Hey!" Waco called. "Let's see your money!"

Festus didn't have anywhere near a hundred dollars and he wasn't exactly sure what to do next. One thing for sure, he wasn't going to ride back to Waco and confess that he was fifty or sixty dollars short.

Trying to buy a little time and distance between himself

and what he was now sure were a bunch of ambushers and cattle thieves, Festus called, "I just want to ride him a minute to make sure he's sound!"

"Of course he's sound!" the cowboy who'd caught the dapple yelled. "You saw him bolt and run!"

Yeah, Festus thought, reining the tall gelding around and driving his spurs into its ribs, but not like he's gonna have to run now in order to save my lyin' hide!

His move caught the men completely off guard. One minute he was a sorry, trusting fool, the next minute he riding like a wild Comanche.

Festus heard their shouts of anger and surprise followed by a furious volley of gunfire. But the dapple was extending the distance between himself and the gang with every powerful stride.

Another couple of hundred yards and I'm out of their pistol range, Festus reckoned. Just another couple of seconds.

Festus heard the boom of the massive buffalo rifle an instant before he felt the blow graze his ribs, nearly tearing him out of the saddle. He dropped his reins and grabbed his saddlehorn as the dapple ran as if its tail were on fire. He felt light-headed and bent forward as a second boom clipped the crown of his hat and sent it spinning into the sky.

"Ya! Ya!" he shouted, forcing the horse to run even harder. Its ears were laid back flat and it seemed almost to sail across the grassland, but Festus knew the horse could not outrun a .50-caliber bullet.

The third shot was clearly one of desperation and meant to drop the horse, but it was a shade high and smashed into the cantle of Festus's saddle, passing through rawhide and leather to tear a hunk out of his buttock. Festus howled and his fingers laced themselves in the gray's streaming mane and he held on for dear life.

He didn't dare look back for another mile, and when he did, Festus saw three cowboys hot on his trail. He tried to assess how badly he'd been wounded, but it was impossible. His ribs felt broken, his butt was numb, and there was a lot of blood leaking down his pants and filling his boots, but he was sure the wound was not mortal. Festus worried that the blood loss might cause him to lose consciousness and slip from the saddle. If that happened, he was a dead man.

Festus reined the gray down, knowing that he had to conserve the animal's strength. He tried to recall how far north it would be before he came upon one of the herds he'd already visited. Five miles? No, more than ten. But it had been a large outfit with at least thirty cowboys. They wouldn't let him be murdered by his pursuers, would they?

"Hang on!" he told himself as he struggled to stay in the saddle.

The cowboys must have been riding horses they'd been on all morning, while Festus's gray was fresh. That was the only possible explanation as to why they didn't outride and overtake him. That, and the fact that he had chosen to steal an exceptionally strong and fast mount.

There was more scattered gunfire and even a few rifle shots, but none of them were close, and when Festus looked back several miles later, the cowboys had fallen far behind and were grouped in a bunch. It looked as if they had given up the chase.

Now that he was no longer in any immediate danger, Festus's bullet wounds pained him mightily. His broken or cracked ribs and his poor butt were on fire. Furthermore, he felt dizzy and weak as he slowed the dapple to a jog that would conserve its strength, but only added to his misery.

The afternoon grew long, and when Festus topped a hill and looked south, he didn't see his pursuers anymore. He thirsted for water; his mouth felt parched and his throat too dry to swallow. He watched the sun sink into the western horizon and then the first stars twinkle in the darkening sky before he finally saw a trail-herd campfire up near the Cimarron.

"Hello the camp!" he called a while later as he rode

through the already bedded-down herd of Longhorns.

"Who goes there!" a man called as he stepped out of the firelight.

"Festus Haggen! I'm the fella that you met this mornin'. The one from Dodge City riding the ugly bay horse!"

"Well, you ain't ridin' him now," the trail boss observed, coming closer. Festus remembered the man's name was J. B. Logan and he had several cowboys at his side. "What's the matter with you, anyway?"

"I been shot," Festus replied. "I need some help."

Logan hurried forward and helped him out of his saddle, "What happened! How'd you get this gray horse?"

"It's a long story," Festus gritted, feeling as if his legs were dead. "Do you have medicine and bandages?"

"Did you steal this horse?"

"Yeah, but he was stolen from someone else." Festus clenched his teeth to keep from crying out with pain, then managed to gasp, "I could use a swallow of whiskey."

"Cookie," the trail boss shouted, half carrying Festus to their campfire, "bring whiskey and some towels over here. This fella is all shot up!"

Once he was laid out beside the fire, Festus took three or four swallows of whiskey and tried to keep from yelping as they removed his clothes and bandaged his gunshot wounds. When they'd finished, Logan said, "Haggen, you'd better start explaining what happened and how you got that fine horse."

So Festus told them about the Texas cowboy who was still most likely unconscious up in Dodge City and how he'd been ambushed and about his Rocking R brand and lost herd of rustled cattle.

"I said this morning that I was fired up in Dodge City, but I wasn't," Festus added. "I'm still Marshal Matthew Dillon's deputy and he sent me down here to learn who shot that boy and rustled his herd. I found the thieves just south and they shot me as I was trying to get away."

"How do we know you didn't just steal that gray and are telling us a lie?" Logan asked.

128

"You'll find my deputy's badge in my saddlebag."

"Take a look!" Logan shouted.

"I found it!" a cowboy said a few minutes later, bringing the badge over to show his boss.

Logan nodded. "All right, Deputy. What's going to happen now?"

"Most likely they know I've been shot and they'll come hunting for me and that dapple gray. So you got to hide me in your chuck wagon and help me reach Dodge City."

"That's where we're headin' anyway, but what about the gray horse you took? We can't hide him!"

"Then have someone turn him loose out yonder."

Logan nodded with understanding. "Johnny, unsaddle the gray and set him free out in those hills off a mile or two."

"Leave the saddle on," Festus advised. "That way, they'll figure I fell off someplace in the dark and died. Maybe they won't look so hard for me anymore."

"All right." Logan glanced up at Johnny. "Just take the horse off a couple miles and turn him loose."

"Damn shame to just give him up," Johnny complained. "He's a real fine animal. Ought to be worth fifty dollars easy."

"Do it!"

"Yes, sir!"

Festus heard the drumming of hoofbeats a few minutes later and said, "I'm feeling pretty low. If they come—"

"Let's get him in the wagon and under the tarp!" Logan shouted. "No telling when we could have unwelcome company."

Festus didn't remember much after that. Logan had doctored his wounds and promised that he was in no danger of dying, although he was going to be out of commission for a good long while. Mostly, though, Festus just felt the need to sleep.

Waco and three of his outlaws arrived early the next morning while Festus was still asleep. They were greeted by

Logan and his men with courtesy but not friendliness.

"Ain't seen anyone on a gray horse," Logan told the big man and his hard-faced companions. "Sorry."

"He's a stinkin' horse thief," Waco hissed. "We're offering a hundred-dollar reward so we can hang him."

"A hundred dollars would be a nice bonus," Logan said, "but we still ain't seen him."

"Maybe he's gone back to Dodge City," Waco said, looking north. "If he has, we'll find him and settle up there."

The ambushers rode off, continuing to search. Later, one of Logan's cowboys saw them with the dapple gray they'd found, heading back south to their herd with the animal in tow.

"Deputy, what's going to happen when we get you to Dodge City?" Logan asked as they started the herd north again.

"I'd say all hell is going to break loose when Marshal Dillon learns what I found out down here," Festus replied.

"We're all Texans and we don't much like the idea of our own kind killin' and rustlin' . . . especially from our own kind," Logan grimly told him. "We'd help you."

"Much obliged," Festus said weakly, "but you'd better know that Waco and his bunch aren't going to hand over their guns without a fight. They mean business."

"I could tell that last night when I dug lead and leather out of your bee-hind," Logan answered before he galloped up to the head of his herd and started pushing them toward the nearby Cimarron River.

CHAPTER

13

Festus stayed hidden in the chuck wagon all the way up to Dodge City. He was in considerable pain and anxious to tell Matthew what he'd discovered. During the long hours while he lay in the wagon, Festus spent quite a bit of time wondering how they'd arrest Waco and his Texas outlaws. He'd counted eight in that outfit and all of them looked to be tough and seasoned gunmen. The thing was, Festus decided, he and Matthew would have to try to get the drop on them real sudden like. But how could he help Matthew do that without Waco recognizing him?

Festus chewed and worried about that dilemma and he still didn't have an answer when Logan and his cowboys finally reached their grazing ground south of Dodge and the railroad tracks.

"I haven't seen any sign of that bunch of killers and cattle thieves closing on us from behind," Logan announced. "But we've been pushing harder than normal, so they might not be along for a couple of days yet."

"That makes sense," Festus replied. "Do you reckon

you could help me get into town so I could tell Matthew what happened?''

"Of course, but I'm not sure that you're up to riding.''

Festus frowned. "Why don't you jest fetch Matthew for me? Tell him what happened and that I'd be obliged if he'd bring a buckboard for me to ride.''

"I'll do that,'' Logan agreed. "And I'll offer him the same help that I offered you.''

"You're a good man, Mr. Logan, and I sure am grateful.''

"Texans ought to look out for Texans. That young cowboy that rode into Dodge shot up, do you think he survived?''

"I don't rightly know,'' Festus replied. "Doc Gentry and Doc Adams both worked on him, but he hadn't regained consciousness by the time Matthew sent me south. I sure hope he pulled through. Not only for his sake, but also because we'll need his testimony to convict Waco and his bunch of rustlers and murderers.''

"And there's no doubt in your mind they are the guilty ones?'' Logan asked.

"There sure ain't,'' Festus said, squinting through one eye. "And danged if I don't want to see them face Judge Brooker and go off to prison or hang for their crimes.''

Logan nodded with agreement and set off for town with about half his crew after giving orders to the ones that would stay to guard the herd. Festus watched them ride off at a gallop. The cowboys hadn't been paid yet and wouldn't be until this herd was sold, but they had a few dollars and a powerful thirst for whiskey after their long ordeal. They'd whoop it up pretty good, but Logan would keep them under control just in case Matthew would need them to help arrest Waco and his outlaws.

Festus hated just lying in the chuck wagon and feeling so useless to Matthew. He'd do all he could to help out, but to be honest, he was not nearly up to snuff. He'd do his job, and with Logan's help and maybe a few others that Matthew could usually depend upon to be sworn in as deputies during emergencies, they'd be able to handle those outlaw Texans.

Festus must have dozed off, because when he awakened, it was to feel Matthew's big hand on his shoulder. Beside him was Doc Adams looking none too pleased.

"Well, Festus," Doc complained, "I hear you finally took a bullet in your brains."

"Not my brains, Doc, my . . . oh, dagnabit, you shouldn't ought to talk like that, Doc."

"Roll over so I can get a good look at the damage," Doc ordered.

"I sure don't much enjoy doin' this!"

"Shut up and do as I tell you. Modesty doesn't become you, Festus."

After a quick examination of both wounds, Doc said, "Looks to me like you'll pull through."

"Well, of course I will!"

"But we need to get you to bed where you'll have to stay until a lot of healing takes place."

"Doc, I can't do that just yet," Festus said, looking up at Matthew. "We got big trouble."

"That's what Mr. Logan said when he barged into my office," Matt replied, looking anything but pleased. "He told me about your escape from that gang. Why'd you take such a big risk?"

"They wouldn't let me near their livestock, so I had to come up with a story and then steal one of their horses to get away alive."

"Festus, all I wanted you to do was to just size up the herds and come back to Dodge so we could figure out what to do."

"I'm sorry, Matthew, but I did the best that I could."

The marshal's rugged face softened. "Of course you did. It's just that I feel bad about you getting shot."

"Don't feel sorry for him," Doc interrupted. "Festus is never happier than when he's forced to stay in bed."

"Now, Doc, that ain't a bit true!"

"Let's help him into the buckboard," Matthew said. "We've got blankets for you to lay on, but it will still be a rough ride."

"Well, this here rickety old chuck wagon ain't no carriage, I'll tell you!"

They helped Festus into the buckboard and then drove him into Dodge City, going up the backstreets and then the alley.

"Matthew, I'd rather stay at the office than at my little room," Festus said. "That way I could at least watch Bates and help out some."

"Fair enough," Matthew said. "Is that all right with you, Doc?"

"Sure is," Doc said. "We can play cards and drink Festus's coffee while you figure out what to do next."

Festus was relieved that he could still be of some help. And maybe, if Waco and his boys didn't show up for a few more days, he'd even be able to help Matthew arrest that bunch.

"Hey, Festus," Bates called with a big grin as they helped him inside, "someone shot you in the butt, huh!"

"That's enough of that," Matthew warned. "Festus, since the cell bunk is occupied, we need to fix you up another out here."

"No need for that," Festus assured him. "Jest lay some blankets out on the floor between our desks and that's where I'll sleep."

"Are you sure?"

"Yep."

Just then, Jerome entered the office. He looked at Matthew, then Doc Adams, and then at Festus, who was stretching out on the floor and said, "What's going on here?"

"Festus was wounded," Matt explained. "Doc Adams says he's been shot in the brains but that he'll recover."

Jerome came over and knelt beside Festus. "You all right?"

"I could maybe use a few bottles of your Chickasaw Cure."

"I'll bring them next time," Jerome promised, ignoring Doc Adams's snort of derision. "Don't worry about that."

Jerome went and checked on Bates's leg and said, "You're healing fast. I won't need to be changing your bandages but every other day now."

"You hear that, Marshal? Doc Gentry says that I'm healed. What do you say about me leaving Dodge City?"

"Like you promised last time before you attacked Doc again?" Matt asked.

"Aw, let him go," Doc Adams argued. "He isn't a threat to me anymore and he's just costing the taxpayers money."

"Judge Brooker isn't due back for another week or so. All right, Bates, I'll turn you loose. But if I see you in town after sundown, you'll be back in that cell."

"You won't find me in Dodge City even an hour from now," Bates promised as Matt unlocked the cell and turned him loose. "California, here I come!"

Doc Adams and Doc Gentry both left at the same time as George Bates, and now that he was alone with the marshal, Festus said, "Matthew, Mr. Logan and his cowboys have offered to help us arrest Waco and his bunch."

"I'm not sure that we need them."

"Waco and his boys are real hardcases," Festus warned, "and I can tell you that they're not going to give up without a gunfight."

"Tell me everything you can about them and what you saw," Matt said. "Don't leave out a thing."

Festus recounted every detail that he could remember about the outlaws and, when he was through, said, "What about that young cowboy?"

"He's still in a coma," Matt said gravely. "There's some question of whether or not he'll ever regain consciousness."

"I'm sorry to hear that. Won't we need his testimony in order to convict that bunch of murderers and thieves?"

"Maybe not," Matt answered. "If we can prove those brands were altered, we can send Waco and his bunch to prison for a long time. Then, if the kid does come around, we can have them tried for murder."

"So how are we gonna arrest 'em?" Festus asked.

"After what you've told me, I think the best way would be to wait until they come into town. They'll have to leave part of their gang to guard and watch the herd, so they'll be split. With luck, we can get the drop on Waco and whoever he's with, and then the others wherever we find them."

"Say, Matthew, why didn't I think of that! Makes a lot more sense than riding down south and facin' all of them together."

"Well," Matt said, "it sounds good but we won't know until we've tried it out. It's important that you stay under cover so that the outlaws don't know you're alive and in Dodge City, which would make arresting them much more difficult. As far as they know, there are no witnesses that can put them behind bars."

"But won't they hear about that wounded cowboy?"

"I won't give them time," Matt vowed. "You've given me a good description, and as soon as they ride into town and go their separate ways, I'll be out there making arrests, starting with this Waco fella."

"He's a real bad one, Matthew. We can't take any chances 'cause he's the sort that would as soon kill a man as not."

"I'll keep that in mind," Matt promised. "In the meantime, there's nothing either of us can do about that bunch until they arrive. Right now, I'm going to go make sure that Bates really does leave Dodge City this time."

"I'll be able to help you by tomorrow," Festus called to his boss. "Next day at the latest."

"Fine," Matt said, not believing a word of it; he'd seen the bullet wounds and knew that his deputy was hurting far worse than he'd ever admit.

Matt started on his rounds, and when he'd completed them, he made a point of passing by Delbert's Livery, where he saw Mrs. Nelson exiting Doc Gentry's medicine wagon. Her husband, Harvey, had made a small fortune in mining up near Cripple Creek in the Colorado Rockies and then had retired to Dodge City. Harvey's health was not the best and Matt wondered if Linda had bought some Chickasaw Cure.

"Afternoon," he said to the woman as she started back into town. "How is Harvey feeling today?"

Startled, the attractive woman dropped her handbag, pretty brown eyes flashing with anger. "Marshal," she said breathlessly, "you shouldn't sneak up on a person!"

"I'm sorry," Matt replied, picking up her handbag and realizing that it was empty except for a few items of clothing. "You look upset. Is Harvey okay?"

"He is very strong."

"I'm sure that he is," Matt said, noticing her flushed cheeks and that her eyes were red, as if she'd just been crying. "I thought you were probably buying him some of Dr. Gentry's medicine. It seems like everyone in town is buying that stuff. Maybe you're not feeling all that well yourself, huh?"

"Whatever do you mean?"

"You look a little upset and feverish, that's all."

"I do . . . yes, I know I do!" She brushed her forehead with the back of her hand. "I am not feeling all that well, which is why I was visiting Dr. Gentry."

"I see."

"He really is a *fine* doctor."

"I'm sure that he is," Matt said, studying the woman closely and realizing that her hair was disheveled and her powder smeared, which was odd, because she was always fastidious about her appearance, even, some women said, to the point of being vain.

"Well, Marshal Dillon, I better be getting home. Dr. Gentry has prescribed a treatment that I should begin administering right away."

"Say hello to Harvey for me," Matt told the woman as she hurried away.

Matt frowned and then he walked up to the medicine wagon and knocked on the door. "Dr. Gentry?"

Jerome did not open the door but called, "Yeah?"

"Matt Dillon here. Can we talk?"

"Be right with you, Marshal!"

When the door opened, Matt's worst suspicions were confirmed. Jerome's handsome face was also flushed.

"Can I do something for you, Marshal?"

"I just saw Mrs. Nelson leaving."

"Yes, I'm afraid her husband isn't feeling well."

"That's not what she just told me."

He swallowed. "It's not?"

"Why don't we have a private word inside your wagon?"

"Have I done something to upset you?"

"You sure have," Matt said, pushing his way inside and closing the door. "You've been at it again."

"What do you mean?"

"Mrs. Nelson," Matt growled. "She's all tousled and her cheeks are flushed."

"What are you trying to say?"

"Holy cow, man, didn't the death of Rita Clancy teach you anything?"

"Marshal, you're out of line!"

"No, you are," Matt said angrily. "Harvey Nelson is a good man and you're taking advantage of his wife. Now, it either stops right now, or I'm ordering you to leave Dodge City."

"You don't understand," Jerome said, "Mrs. Nelson is—"

"Married! Doc, you've already been instrumental in the death of one married woman and I'll be damned if I'm going to let you be the cause of another. Harvey may be unwell and he may be too old for his wife, but he is not too old to use a gun, and he is an expert marksman."

"So I've heard," Gentry said. "He is also dying of a cancer, and if that isn't bad enough, he won't live long enough to see his newborn son or daughter."

Matt's jaw dropped. "What!"

"I saw Mr. Nelson last night and again this morning to help relieve him of some pain. The gentleman is dying and still has no idea that his wife is pregnant. She just asked me to confirm her suspicions and I complied. As you might expect, the woman is extremely upset. I gave her some laudanum for her husband's pain."

Matt sat down heavily. "Harvey Nelson is dying?"

"Yes."

"And Mrs. Nelson is with child?"

"That's right. She will bury her husband, sell out their holdings in Dodge City, and then return to live with her parents in Kentucky. For many reasons, some of which are financial, you can understand why she would prefer not to have this news become common knowledge."

"Of course," Matt said, feeling like an idiot. "Does Doc Adams know?"

"I suspect not. Dr. Adams seems to have given up medicine except for treating Festus. When we left your office a short while ago, he asked if I was interested in buying his office and medical practice."

"What did you say?"

"I said I had very little money. He told me that didn't matter, that we could work something out on terms."

"I wish . . . ah, never mind."

"No, finish what you were going to say, Marshal."

"I wish he wouldn't quit," Matt said. "And that hasn't a thing to do with you. It's just that I'm afraid that he'll sit down in a rocking chair and die an unhappy man."

"You have to allow him to do as he wishes," Jerome said. "But if it's any consolation, I think that he is going through a spell that will soon pass."

"You do?"

"Yes."

"There's going to be some trouble coming our way," Matt said. "I'm going to try and keep it under control, but I might not be able to prevent someone from getting shot. What I'm saying is that I expect that we might need both you and Doc Adams in the next day or two."

"I'll be ready to help any way that I can and I'm sure we can also count on Doc Adams."

"I sure am sorry about Harvey Nelson. He's a pretty good man."

"So his wife tells me," Jerome said. "She also said that they'd been trying to have children for many years without any success. Maybe this child they've created is a gift from God for Mr. Nelson's present suffering."

"I owe you an apology, Dr. Gentry."

"Yes," he said with a smile, "you do. And I accept it. As for this other trouble that you've spoken of, well, I am not without some talent with a gun or a rifle."

"No, Doc. You just keep selling the Chickasaw Cure and helping folks in Dodge. Festus and me will take care of that other stuff."

"Whatever you think best," Jerome said. "And I know that you will tell no one about the Nelsons. The news will be out soon enough, but they should have the right to set the time and the place."

"I couldn't agree more." Matt ducked his head and went back outside.

"Marshal?"

Matt turned around. "Yeah?"

"I understand how it must have looked and seemed when Mrs. Nelson left this wagon only a few minutes ago. Given that, I think that you were right to come up with your conclusion."

"I have backaches," Matt told him. "Most often when I sit in my office chair too long. Do you think that your Chickasaw Cure could help that?"

"Of course, but so would sitting up straight and keeping your shoulders from slumping forward. You're a big man, Marshal, and you have a tendency to stoop a little. You should work to improve your posture both when you walk and also when you sit. Marshal, I suspect that is the real cause of your backaches."

Despite all the bad news and the impending trouble, Matt

had to chuckle at that as he headed off to see an old gambler friend who liked to play penny ante poker at the Alamo Saloon when he wasn't sitting around the cracker barrel at one of the general stores playing a mean game of checkers.

Alvin Nash was tall and dignified, and to look at him, you'd swear that he was a successful banker, editor, attorney or . . . cattle buyer.

Yes, Matt thought, if anyone could con Waco and his bunch of murderers and thieves into thinking he was a legitimate cattle buyer, it was Alvin Nash.

CHAPTER

14

"Alvin!" Matt called out in greeting when he entered the Alamo Saloon and saw his friend dealing cards at the back table with a couple of locals who were also well into their sixties.

"Say, if it isn't Marshal Dillon! Have you finally come to arrest me for cheating these fellas out of their cookie money?"

"No," Matt said, nodding to the other grinning players. "But I would like to have a private word with you." Nash tossed his hand in and collected a stack of chips that Matt knew didn't amount to more than a couple of dollars. "I'll be back, so keep the cards hot for me."

There was some good-natured grumbling and even a couple of crude remarks, but nothing more. Matt knew that Alvin Nash always bought the beers and often dinners for the less talented players at his table. A natty dresser and somewhat of a dandy, Nash was a former Mississippi riverboat gambler who had won and lost several fortunes but managed to come out on top of that dangerous game. For Nash, small-stakes poker with his friends was just an enjoyable way to pass the time when he wasn't playing horseshoes or checkers, two other games of skill at which he was almost unbeatable.

When they were outside, Matt led Nash around behind the building and said, "Alvin, I've no right to ask, but I need a big favor."

"Name it, Marshal."

In as few words as it took, Matt explained about Waco and his outlaws coming up the trail. "They're a bad bunch. They killed that young cowboy's family and they also shot up Festus."

"Yeah, I heard about that. So what exactly do you want me to do?"

"I'd like you to ride south and meet them, posing as an eastern cattle buyer. Gain their confidence and report back to me when they reach the grass south of Dodge. If possible, make a deal and get Waco into the bank, saying you'll pay in cash. Then I'll slip in and disarm him."

"What about the others?"

"Festus and I hope to catch them by surprise. If it goes as I hope, not a shot will be fired. But I wouldn't try to kid you for a minute . . . there's a risk to what I'm asking."

"I enjoy risks," the former riverboat gambler said, actually looking excited. "Risks and the dangers they bring are what keeps a man sharp. Hell yes, Matt, I'll enjoy playing this game!"

"Listen, Alvin. I know you're a cool customer, but Festus barely got away from that bunch with his life."

"I mean no offense when I say this, but Festus is as transparent as a shot glass. I'm surprised that you even sent him to try and fool those Texans."

"I didn't have much choice."

"Sure you did! You could have sent me instead."

"I'm asking you to go now. They're close enough to Dodge City that it would not be unusual for a cattle buyer to arrive in their camp looking to gain a price advantage."

"What are cattle selling for right now?"

"Between thirty-six and forty-one dollars a head, depending on their condition and uniformity."

"Good enough," Nash said. "Do you want me to leave right now?"

"The sooner the better. It's important that you intercept that bunch before they hit town."

"Then I'll be on my way. Describe them."

Matt told Nash about the altered brands and the Conestoga wagon he needed to look for rather than the usual chuck wagon.

"I'll serve them to you on a platter," Nash promised. "I know a few of the cattle buyers and I'll even borrow their business cards to make me look more authentic."

"Don't take any unnecessary chances," Matt warned. "If these people so much as suspect that you are a phony, they'll kill you without hesitation. As it is, I'm worried that one of them who has been to Dodge before will recognize you."

"I'll wear a partial disguise," Nash decided aloud. "Marshal, after this is over, you'll owe me a good dinner at the Delmonico Restaurant, complete with wine and some expensive French brandy."

"I knew you'd cost me plenty," Matt complained with a smile before he headed back to his office to check on Festus.

Alvin Nash rented a fine horse and buggy, then drove the rig around behind his neat and well-kept house on Spruce Street. Whistling a Texas song about a love-lorn cowboy, he went inside and changed his appearance. His hair, beard, and mustache were silver, so he brushed them liberally with bootblack and found a pair of weak spectacles that gave him a peculiar bookish appearance that was, he decided, suitably disarming. He pushed a derringer up one sleeve and another derringer in his boot top after deciding not to wear a Colt revolver, which would be at odds with his otherwise benign appearance. He did, however, have a pepperbox revolver which he slipped into a leather briefcase that the Texans would assume contained documents. Nash realized that the pepperbox was as likely to misfire and blow off his own hand as do mortal damage to the Texans, but it was such a mean and intimidating weapon that its presence was reassuring. A man would have to be crazy to risk the wrath of such a devastating weapon at close range.

It was well into the afternoon and Nash had greeted and passed two herds before he saw the towering white canvas of the Conestoga wagon and knew that he'd finally encountered the enemy. He flicked trail dust from his jacket and drove confidently on to hail the cowboys riding point.

"Good afternoon!" he shouted. "Are those fine Texas Longhorns for sale?"

"Hell, yes, they are!" the nearest cowboy replied. "You got a pile of cash, Mister?"

"Not on me, of course, but at the bank. Who is in charge?"

"Go get Waco and tell him the first buyer is so eager he rode out to meet us," the cowboy told his companion.

Nash started to flick his reins, for he preferred to ride in among the cattle, but the Texan blocked his path. "Reckon this is near enough for you right now."

"But I would like to see the condition of your herd," Nash protested.

"That'll be up to Waco to decide. He'll be along directly."

The cowboy was right. The trail boss soon arrived, and after giving Nash a long and critical inspection, he said, "Are you cattle buyers so eager that you're coming out meet us this year?"

"Early bird gets the worm," Nash said, hating himself for stooping to use that hackneyed phrase but thinking it suited these circumstances. "How many head do you have, Mr. Waco?"

"We got exactly 2,357 head. How much you payin'?"

"Top dollar is thirty-eight, but your cattle appear to be . . . well, not at all uniform, the way they like them back east."

Waco spat a stream of tobacco juice at the churned-up cattle trail, then began to rein his horse around. "We can do a lot better than thirty-eight a head when we reach Dodge."

"Wait a minute! I . . . I might be able to go forty dollars. That is, if these cattle are in good flesh."

"They're light, same as all the cattle when they arrive after being pushed a thousand miles or more," Waco said bluntly. "We both know that, but we also know they'll fatten up fast on this rich Kansas grass. Me and the boys don't mind waiting an extra couple of weeks while they graze and put on weight. Dodge City is a good town to let off steam."

"That it is," Nash agreed making sure he looked worried. "But it does take money to have fun in Dodge. I'm prepared to pay you cash on the barrelhead."

"No thanks. We'll see what your competitors have to offer."

"You might be sorry! There are a lot of outfits driving up not only the Chisholm, but also the Western Trail this year. Why, some estimate as many as a quarter of a million. That will make shipping cattle go real slow. Besides, Waco, good cash money waits on no man!"

The trail boss stopped and turned his horse around. "Tell you what, Mr. Cattle Buyer Man. You figure out what forty-four dollars a head amounts to, bring me cash, and then we'll do business."

"I'm afraid I'd need a bill of sale and a brand inspection first. Also, I'd never carry that much cash. It would be pretty stupid of me, wouldn't it?"

"Yeah," Waco said, looking amused, "I guess it would be. All right, how far is it to Dodge City?"

"As the crow flies, not more than ten miles."

"Then you better start counting cattle. When you're finished, me and a couple of the boys will ride in with you while the others will push on to a bed ground south of town."

"What about the brands?" Nash dared to ask.

"We got a lot of cattle we bought from small homesteads and outfits comin' up the trail. Some of them people couldn't read nor write. You take this herd as it is, or I'll find a new buyer. Shouldn't be hard, given the prices we're talking about."

Waco frowned. "Have we got a deal or not? Yes or no. I won't dicker."

"All right," Nash said. "I'll count and we'll deal at forty a head."

"No paperwork or questions asked."

"I—"

"Has to be that way, Mr. Cattle Buyer. You choose."

"It's a deal!"

"Boys," Waco said, "help this gentleman with the count. This is payday!"

The outlaws surrounded Nash and escorted him into the herd, where he stood up in his buggy and did a fine job of pretending to tally for the next full hour.

"All right," he called at last. "We have a count!"

"What is it!" Waco yelled.

"I got 2,350."

"That's seven head short!"

"Very well," Nash said, knowing that generosity cost him nothing, "we'll call it 2,355. At forty dollars a head, that amounts to . . . $94,200."

That really set them to whooping and hollering. Alvin Nash sat down in his buggy and grinned thinking, Laugh now, you murdering varmints. But before sundown tomorrow, you'll all be in jail and facing a hangman's noose.

He turned his rig around and headed back to Dodge City, knowing that Waco and some of his hardcases would be following close behind. Nash had made his living reading people's minds and smelling their greed. And this bunch, he thought, was evil and extremely greedy.

CHAPTER

1 5

Matt had paid a boy to watch for Alvin Nash's return and now the kid rushed into his office all out of breath. "Mr. Nash is on his way back and he's bringing in four cowboys!"

"Thanks," Matt said, slipping a few extra coins into the boy's pocket. "How far south are they?"

"Not more'n a mile or two!"

"Not a word of this to anyone now."

"No, sir!" The excited kid glanced over at Festus, who was lying on the cell bunk. "How's your butt feelin' today, Deputy Haggen?"

"Better," Festus replied, looking embarrassed. "Run along and keep your mouth buttoned."

When the kid was gone, Matt glanced at his pocket watch. "Festus, I expect they are trying to get to the bank before closing time."

Festus crawled off the bunk, stretched, and shuffled out of the jail cell. "Is that where we oughta arrest 'em?"

"It depends on whether they stick together or not," Matt replied. "Hopefully, Waco will be the only one at the bank while his friends belly up in a saloon. I've already told Mr. Brodkin what to expect at his bank.''

"I'll bet he wasn't too happy about that.''

"No,'' Matt said, "he wasn't and I can't say that I blame him much. Festus, why don't you go over there right now and have Brodkin let you hide behind the counter. When Nash brings Waco in for the sale money, you shouldn't have much trouble getting the drop on him.''

"I can do 'er,'' Festus promised. "But first, I'll run off any bank customers in there so there's less chance of 'em getting in the way.''

"Good idea. I'll follow the other three and catch them by surprise. If all goes well, we'll have half the bunch without firing a single shot.''

"Well,'' Festus said, "that all sounds real good, but don't you think you ought to deputize some help when you try to arrest them three other fellers? Matthew, these boys are likely to open fire rather than hand over their weapons.''

"There's no time for that now,'' Matt replied. "Between you and Alvin Nash, you shouldn't have any trouble disarming Waco. I'm not too worried about the other three so long as I can sneak up behind them without being recognized.''

"I sure wish—''

"Festus, you're not moving very fast so you'd better get started.''

"Yes sir.'' Festus pulled on his hat and went hobbling out the door. He was in a world of hurt but tried not to show it as he made his way gingerly across the busy street.

"Howdy, Festus!''

Festus groaned because it was Barney, the telegraph operator who liked nothing better than to hear his own squeaky voice.

"Hiya, Barney. Sorry, but I sure ain't got no time to jaw now.''

"What's your big hurry? Late for your nap, or something?''

"That's not funny. I'm headed for the bank.''

"Then I'll just mosey along with you. I'm trying to find Doc. He got a telegram from his sister, Agnes. She's comin' in on the next train. Can you believe that? I sure never expected that Doc would send for no sister!"

Festus stopped in front of the bank. He had to get rid of Barney and he had to do it without raising the man's suspicions: because, if Barney so much as suspected that trouble was on its way to Dodge City, he'd be shouting the news all over town and creating a panic. "Look, Doc is probably at his office and—"

"No, he ain't," Barney said. "Festus, I already checked."

"Then try the Long Branch."

"Ain't there either. Maybe he's inside the bank."

"Naw," Festus said. "Try the Delmonico."

"Too early for Doc to have his supper."

Festus was trying to stay calm, but he was getting upset with this foolishness. Waco and his gang were on their way and here he was wasting time on Barney. "I don't know where Doc is! Go off somewhere and around."

"Geez, Festus, you take a little old slug in the butt and you sure get proddy! I was just trying to be sociable and I figured you'd want to know about Doc's sister."

"I'm sorry," Festus said, "it's just that I'm in a hurry."

Barney nodded. "Well, you shouldn't ought to hurry when you got a bullet wound in the butt. I'll walk over to the bank with you. I didn't think that you and Marshal Dillon got paid this early in the month."

"I didn't," Festus replied, realizing that there was no way he could tell Barney not to go to the bank.

When they went inside there were only two customers, but one of them was that awful Bessy Fife and she was giving a red-faced clerk the dickens for a charge that she didn't think she ought to pay. Right in the middle of her tirade, however, she spotted Festus.

"Well, if it ain't Deputy Haggen!" she declared, focusing her wrath on a favorite target. "I do declare and to think that I was feeling sorry for you 'cause you got shot in the bee-hind!''

Festus despised this woman, but he was desperate to oblige and get her, along with the other customer and Barney, out of the bank before Waco and Alvin Nash arrived.

"Mrs. Fife," he said, summoning up the last of his patience, "I'm sure glad to see you, too. And thanks for your kind concern."

The woman grinned with wicked intent. "Deputy, I wasn't as concerned about you as I was for poor Dr. Gentry. Imagine having to bandage your skinny bee-hind!"

She tittered and Festus seethed.

"Anybody seen Doc Adams?" Barney asked when he stopped laughing. "His sister, Agnes, is coming in on the next train to take care of him."

"Well, I do declare!" Bessy exclaimed. "I heard she was real ugly. Festus, maybe you ought to call on Agnes—I expect it'd be your only chance to ever get married."

More gales of laughter. Festus looked past the clerk and saw the banker, Mr. Brodkin, scowling at him with obvious disapproval. That look told Festus that he was about out of time.

"The bank is closing!" he shouted, grabbing Bessy by the arm and trying to steer her outside.

"You let go of me!" she cried. "Festus, what is the matter with you today!"

"The bank is closing," he said stubbornly.

Bessy and Barney both glanced up at the wall clock, which said four-thirty. Bessy threw off Festus's hand and stomped her big feet down hard. "This bank still has another half hour to be open! Isn't that right, Mr. Brodkin?"

The banker also looked up at the clock. "Ah . . . yes, yes, it is, Mrs. Fife. But we have some important transactions to take care of after closing and it . . . ah, would help if everyone gave us a few extra minutes by leaving early."

"Well, I do declare!" Bessy cried in outrage. "First you overcharge me by sixteen cents and now this insult. Whatever is this bank coming to!"

Festus wanted to coldcock the old battle-ax and drag her bloated body out on the sidewalk, but he knew it would cost him his job. Furthermore, if his roundhouse punch missed, Bessy was big and tough enough to give him a hard scrap and Festus knew that he was not in tolerable fighting condition.

Festus was desperately trying to think of a way to get Bessy, Barney, and the other customer out of the bank when he happened to glance outside and see Alvin Nash accompanied by Waco and three other outlaws rein in before the bank. Nash climbed down from his carriage and the Texans dismounted and tied their horses to the hitching rail. Words were spoken and then the cowboys hurried off to wet their whistles in one of the nearby saloons just as Matthew had predicted.

"Excuse me!" Festus shouted. "But I . . . I got to see Mr. Brodkin right now!"

Festus practically broke down the little gate leading back to the banker's office. He hit the floor and rolled under a desk to hide just as Nash and Waco entered the lobby.

"What is the matter with you!" Bessy cried, trying to peer over the teller's cage.

"Shhh!" Festus hissed.

"Well, Mr. Nash, how are you today!" Brodkin called, trying to save the moment as he rushed forward into the lobby. "And Mrs. Fife, good-bye and have a good day."

Festus could well imagine the scene that was taking place in the bank's lobby. The banker was attempting to shut Bessy and Barney up somehow before they alarmed Waco.

"Mr. Brodkin! Has everyone gone crazy!" Bessy shouted. "First Deputy Haggen tries to throw me out the door and now you. What is going on!"

"Yeah," Barney said, standing up on his tiptoes and peering over the teller's cage. "Festus, what are you doing hiding under that desk! Has everyone gone crazy!"

Festus knew the game was up. He yanked his six-gun out of its holster and stood up just in time to see Waco jump behind Bessy and put a stranglehold around her neck as he drew his own six-gun.

"You set me up!" the outlaw screamed at Nash. "You set me up for a trap!"

Nash swallowed. "I—"

"Shut up or I'll kill you! Deputy, throw down your gun and get out here or I shoot everyone right now!"

Festus knew that he had no choice or Waco would turn the bank lobby into a slaughterhouse. "All right. All right," he called, climbing to his feet then pitching his six-gun onto the desktop. "There's no need to kill a bunch of innocent people. No need for that at all."

Bessy was turning purple from the stranglehold. She fought until Waco viciously whacked her across the back of her skull with the barrel of his pistol. Festus saw her knees buckle, but she didn't fall.

"I mean business!" Waco bellowed. "Get out here, Deputy!"

"Yes, sir," Festus said, hurrying back into the lobby and wondering how they were going to get out of this mess alive.

"Don't shoot us, please," Barney pleaded. "You can have my watch. You can rob this bank and take all my savings. You can do anything, but please don't kill us, Mister!"

"Good idea about robbing the bank," Waco said, gun now leveled at Festus. "Deputy, you get down on the floor. Bank teller?"

"Yes, sir!"

"Empty the drawers of cash, then empty the vault, too!"

"It's locked," Brodkin said. "He can't open it."

"Then *you* open it or you're a dead man!"

Waco turned his gun on the banker and Brodkin began to tremble. "Yes, sir!"

Nash, momentarily forgotten, reached inside his sleeve for his hideout derringer. He tried to take aim on Waco's head, but Bessy Fife was so big and his weapon so inaccurate that the gambler must have realized he'd stand a good chance of killing Bessy. And, while he was trying to get a better shot, Waco brought his gun around and shot the retired riverboat gambler in the chest. The derringer spilled from Nash's fingers and clattered to the floor as he collapsed.

Bessy screamed and fainted. Barney hit the floor and covered his own head, looking like a turtle trying desperately to form a shell. Brodkin and the other customer made a rush for the front door and that was when Festus attacked.

He threw himself into Bessy, ramming her so hard that both she and Waco crashed back into the wall. The woman dropped like a boulder, and before the Texan could recover, Festus scooped up Nash's spilled derringer, raised it, and fired both barrels point-blank into Waco's upper body. The trail boss slammed up against the teller's cage, eyes bulging with a flash of amazement before he slumped, dead, striking the floor.

Brodkin and the other customer burst outside screaming and Barney wasn't far behind them. Festus knelt beside Nash knowing there was little that he could do for or say to the courageous old gambler.

"I'm sorry," he whispered to the dying man.

"Don't be," Nash wheezed. "This is a good way to die. It don't hurt much."

"You shouldn't—"

"It was . . . was worth the risk!" Nash gasped a moment before he shuddered in Festus's arms and died.

Bessy was on the floor moaning and hollering as if her throat had been cut, but Festus didn't give her another moment of his time. Instead, he dashed outside and looked up and down the street. He saw the three Texas outlaws along with a lot of other people come pouring out of saloons to see what the gunfire was about. And then he saw Matthew.

Festus wasn't sure what to do in that split second, but he knew that if the three Texan killers recognized him, there was going to be a lot of bullets flying up and down Front Street, and some of them were bound to hit innocent bystanders. So Festus jumped back inside the bank.

"Bessy, it's over! Stop your wailin'!" he shouted at the hysterical woman.

But she wouldn't stop, so Festus jumped back to the doorway just in time to see Matthew rush up behind the three outlaws. Matthew pistol-whipped the first one, knocked the second one out cold with a thundering left hook to the jaw, and had no choice but to shoot and kill the last one, whose gun had already cleared its holster.

It was over. Old Alvin Nash and two Texan outlaws were dead and the other two were lying in the street knocked senseless and headed for jail. Everyone was shouting and carrying on like a bunch of wild animals.

"Quiet!" Matthew thundered. "You folks need to calm down!"

"Calm down?" Barney cried. "Why, I was almost murdered in the bank and you're telling us to calm down!"

Matt grabbed the telegraph operator by the shirtfront and shook him like a puppy. "That's right," he thundered. "And, if you don't, I'll put you in the same cell as these two killers we're arresting!"

Barney shut up and so did all the others. Matthew looked over at Festus and asked, "Is everyone all right at the bank?"

"Mr. Nash was killed by Waco and then I shot him dead."

Matt sighed heavily. "All right, a couple of you people grab these outlaws and carry them over to the jail. Take the dead one to Mr. Crump, the undertaker. Festus, go along to the office and make sure this pair is locked up good and tight."

"Where you goin', Matthew?"

"I'm going to get Alvin," he said, not even bothering to mention Waco. "And then I'm going out to round up the rest of this bunch."

"I'm coming with you."

"All right."

"I'll come, too," Jerome Gentry said, stepping forward. "You're going to need more help."

"I'll deputize you," Matt told the doctor. He surveyed the curious and excited crowd. "Anyone else want to be deputized?"

To the town's credit, at least a dozen men stepped forward, but Matt picked only the ones that were sober.

"Everyone can go back to their business now," he said, starting for the bank.

He was intercepted by Kitty. "Matt, are you all right?"

"Yes, but Alvin Nash is dead."

Kitty shook her head. Like everyone else, she'd thought a great deal of the old gambler. "He'll be missed."

"I know," Matt replied. "Does he have any family that you are aware of?"

"He had a boy, but he fell in the battle at Vicksburg."

"What about the boy's mother?"

"She died of fever many years ago. Mr. Nash only talked about her when he had far too much to drink."

Matt met Doc at the bank and said, "There's nothing you can do here, but it's nice you came."

"Of course I came!" Doc snapped. "I've been coming every time I heard gunfire for years!"

"I've got to go out and arrest the others," Matt said. "I don't suppose that young cowboy has come out of his coma yet?"

"Not yet," Doc said.

"I don't think it matters as far as Judge Brooker will be concerned," Matt said. "This bunch is as guilty as sin. When we butcher a couple of those cattle that had their brands altered and turn the hides inside out, we'll have all the proof we need to send this bunch to prison . . . if not the gallows."

"You take care of yourself when you go out to arrest the others," Doc warned. "They might have heard the gunshots."

"If they did, they'll just think it was some cowboy letting off steam. Doc, don't worry so much. I've got some men deputized and we'll have no trouble bringing in the rest."

"Be careful anyway," Doc repeated. "Murderers and cattle rustlers know what awaits them when they go before a judge. They might prefer to die with guns in their fists."

"If that's their choice, we can well accommodate them," Matt grimly replied as he went to pay his last respects to a valued old friend and formerly the best poker, checkers and horseshoe player in all of Dodge City.

CHAPTER

16

It was sundown by the time that Matt had his posse deputized and everyone was ready to ride. Doc had agreed to watch over the new prisoners and Gentry had strapped his medical bag behind the saddle of a borrowed horse just in case there was a gunfight.

"We'll be coming into their camp just after dark and there are only four of them," Matt explained as they rode across the tracks toward the stolen herd of Texas Longhorns several miles south of town.

"What if they open fire then?" Gentry asked.

"It's my hope that they won't realize who we are until I give the order to throw up their hands. However, if they go for their weapons, you have my permission to open fire . . . but be real sure who you are firing at! We don't want to be blindly shooting each other. Any questions?"

"Do you really think they'll put up a fight?" one of the newly deputized men named Burt Hadley asked. "I sure hope they're smarter than that, Marshal."

"It's not a matter of being smart," Matt told him, "but of being desperate. These men will probably hang or at least face a very long prison sentence. Given those choices, they may well decide to put up a fight, or at least try to escape.''

''If they get away in the dark, what then?''

''We can't let that happen,'' Matt said. ''There are so many other cattle herds and cowboys out on these bed grounds that we might never be able to find them again.''

Burt shook his head. ''Are you sayin' we should shoot 'em in the back if they try to run?''

''I'm saying that they're murderers and thieves and it's my responsibility as marshal to arrest all four of them. If they resist or try to escape, they will have to be stopped. Is that clear?''

''I guess so,'' Burt said, not sounding very sure.

''Festus,'' Matt said, ''other than Nash, you're the only one that has seen this bunch. That being the case, I'd like you to circle around the herd. If they run, it will be toward Texas and you'll be in their path and in position to stop and arrest them. Burt, go with Festus.''

''If you don't mind, Marshal, I'd rather stay with you.''

Matt did mind. He didn't know Burt very well, but the man had always seemed steady. He'd arrived in Dodge about two years before and had a good feed-store business and a nice family.

''All right,'' Matt said. ''Dr. Gentry, you ride with Festus. Burt, Mike and I will give you fifteen minutes, which ought to be plenty of time to get in position before we ride into camp.''

''Matthew,'' Festus said, ''I sure wish you'd let me ride with you into that den of thieves. I'd feel—''

''You can't, Festus. They would recognize you right away and I'd lose the element of surprise.''

''Yes, sir, but—''

''Just do as I say,'' Matt told him, reining up about a mile from the camp. ''There's the Conestoga, so there's no chance of picking the wrong outfit. Now, you and Dr. Gentry ride on around to the south. With this large a herd, there'll be at least two night herders on first watch. The other pair are probably in camp eating or already bedded down and asleep.''

"Come on,'' Festus said, riding off.

Jerome followed the deputy. Like Festus, he wished that they could have all stayed with Marshal Dillon but he didn't question their leader's orders. He'd borrowed a six-gun and there was lots of moonlight so, unless something went completely amiss, this arrest should be easy and they'd soon be back in Dodge City with some new prisoners.

"We'd better put the spurs to these horses,'' Festus said. "I sure don't want to be late getting in position.''

"I don't see how you can stand to sit in a saddle, given that wound in your butt.''

"Well, Doc, '' Festus answered, "I stuffed a little pillow I got from Miss Kitty in the back of my pants as we was crossin' the tracks.''

"Good idea.''

Ten minutes later, Jerome and Festus were in position directly south of the herd. Every few miles, just like stars fallen across the prairie, he saw the bright campfires of other Texas trail herds. "Festus, do you see any of this outfit's riders?''

"I do. See that feller comin' through the herd yonder? He's ridin' a buckskin or a palomino. Anyway, it's either light brown or yeller. I can't tell which.''

"Now I see him. You think he sees us?''

"If he did, we'd know about it,'' Festus replied. "I've been told that these Texans don't allow anyone to ride in very close to their herds for fear that they might try to steal a few head. Cowboys have been shot for crossing into pistol range.''

"Well,'' Jerome said, "we aren't in pistol range, but we'd have no trouble emptying a saddle with a rifle from this distance.''

"I sure don't want to do that,'' Festus allowed. "If them boys don't surrender, we are gonna have to be awful careful where we point our guns.''

"Don't worry," Jerome assured his friend, "I won't panic and start any crazy shooting."

"I know that," Festus said. "I just wish we was the two backin' Matthew up instead of Burt and that other jumpy fella."

Matt Dillon was also wishing that he had Festus at his side. Not only was his deputy a cool customer in a gunfight, but he was quick and deadly. The same, however, could not be said for Burt and the other man whose name he'd already forgotten.

"Look!" Burt whispered. "Ain't that a night rider coming around the herd!"

"No," Matt whispered, alarmed that they were already imagining things, "but we ought to come upon them soon. Ride a little behind me and I'll do all the talking. My aim is to get in as close as possible before they realize who we are."

"Yeah, but . . ."

Matt reined his horse to a standstill. "Burt, why don't you and your friend ride on back a ways toward Dodge City?"

"Huh?"

"Just a ways," Matt said, suddenly deciding that this pair would be more liability than asset. "If they make a break and manage to get past me, you will both be waiting to make the arrest."

"Us?" the other man asked. "Arrest them?"

"It's not likely they'll do that, but if they do, you boys will be there to stop them."

"Why . . . why sure!" Burt said. "John, that makes sense, doesn't it!"

"I guess so."

"Go on then," Matt said impatiently. "Protect the town."

It didn't make much sense, but the two deputies were so relieved to get out of a possible gunfight that they didn't question Matt's reasoning.

"Good luck, Marshal!" Burt hissed as he wheeled his horse around. "You shouldn't have any trouble."

"That's right," Matt said tightly. "Thanks for your help, boys."

Matt felt better the moment the nervous pair rode away. Deputizing citizens was always risky; their frayed nerves coupled with inexperience could get a seasoned lawman killed.

Matt had a gun in his holster and another tucked in behind his belt. One could always misfire . . . but not both. He left the one in his holster and took the other one in hand, resting just in front of him and behind the saddle horn, where it could not be seen by anyone directly to the front.

Now he finally spotted a night rider. The Texan was riding a dark horse and was a short, squatty fellow with a big hat. Matt weighed the advantages and disadvantages of hailing the cowboy and decided to keep quiet as long as possible. He was within a hundred yards when the Texan first saw him.

"Hold up there!" the night rider called. "Who are you, and what do you want!"

Matt had been hoping that he'd be mistaken for either Waco or one of the cowboys who'd accompanied him into Dodge, but he should have known that wouldn't be the case because of his large size.

"I'm lost," he called out, putting a slur in his voice. "Say, fella, is this the . . . the Slash B outfit?"

"Heck no!"

"Well, it must be! I got a bottle of whiskey in my saddlebags for a fella ridin' for the Slash B! Forgot his name but . . . but ain't you him?"

There was a long pause, then, "You got *my* whiskey, do you?"

"Yes sir! Jest like I promised."

"Ride in slow so as not to spook these cattle. I been on the trail for months without a drink and I am good and thirsty!"

Matt dipped his chin to keep his face hidden in the

shadow of his hat brim: it was possible that this rider had been to Dodge City before and would recognize him.

"I ain't used to ridin' in among all these cattle. Makes me nervous, 'cause if I was to fall off, they'd trample me."

"Naw! These cattle won't hurt you!" the cowboy said, riding out to meet him. "You must be drunk already."

Matt tried to hiccup, but it didn't sound very authentic, so he just giggled a little and let the Texan ride in close.

"All right, where is that whiskey!"

Matt twisted around a little to the off side, as if reaching into his saddlebag, but instead of a bottle he brought the barrel of his pistol up fast, cracking the cowboy across the forehead. The Texan's startled shout died stillborn in his throat and he tumbled from his cow pony. Before he could rouse and have any chance of alerting his friends, Matt dismounted and whacked him again, this time across the back of the head. The cowboy quivered in the moonlight and then moved no more.

Matt disarmed the man and used his own rope to hogtie him securely. Then he remounted and rode on toward the Conestoga. It wasn't until he was in close that he saw the flickering fire and two other cowboys sitting beside the back wheel of the big wagon. When they saw him, both jumped to their feet and one yelled, "Who are you!"

"Marshal Matt Dillon. You're under arrest."

"What for! Where's Waco and—"

The cowboy who hadn't spoken went for his six-gun. Matt saw the move and raised his gun out and fired in one smooth but unhurried motion. His bullet struck the cowboy in the chest and Matt knew that he was a dead man. The other cowboy dove under the Conestoga. Matt had no chance for a shot at the man and he heard him yell, "It's Marshal Dillon! Run for it!"

Matt spurred his horse around the wagon trying to find his target, but the cowboy had bolted in among the cattle that were jumping to their feet and starting to bawl with alarm. Suddenly, from among their numbers, Matt saw the stab of gunfire and felt a slug strike his horse, causing its front legs to buckle. Before Matt could kick free of the falling animal, it landed on his right leg, pinning him to the earth a moment before the Longhorns bolted and someone screamed in the night.

"Stampede!"

Matt felt the very marrow of his bones turn to ice. He twisted around and saw that the big Conestoga was not more than fifty feet away. Slamming his free foot down hard in the seat of his saddle, he shoved with all his might and tore his pinned leg out from under the thrashing horse. He tried to jump up and run for the safety of the wagon, but his leg wouldn't support him. A huge Longhorn knocked him spinning and another stomped on his leg as he dragged himself under the wagon to avoid a maelstrom of flying horns and hooves. The earth shook and rolled as the herd thundered in all directions. Some of the crazed steers crashed against the heavy Conestoga wagon, bounced off, and raced on into the night. One huge beast got its horns entangled in the spokes and before it could tear free was trampled into the dirt, tearing out all the wagon spokes, snapping them like mere toothpicks.

Matt wanted to scream with worry and frustration. What had happened to Festus and Dr. Gentry? Had they been caught in the path of the onrushing herd and killed?

"Festus!" he shouted, knowing that his words were lost in the storm of flying hooves. "Festus!"

When Festus heard the first gunshot, he'd frozen in momentary fear and then he'd seen the Texas night herder racing his horse across the face of the what seemed like a monstrous killer wave of flying horns and hooves. One moment the cowboy was trying to turn the stampede and the next moment he was going down under the deadly wave of onrushing Longhorns.

"Let's get out of here!" Gentry shouted.

"I got to find Matt!"

"You can't help him now! Let's go!"

With the horrifying image of that night rider and his

horse being swallowed alive, Festus knew that the doctor made tall sense. His horse was so terrified that it was already spinning and racing for its life. Festus forgot about the pain in his backside and grabbed his saddle horn, hoping that the crazed animal did not jam a forefoot into a badger or prairie-dog hole and fall. If it did, that would be the end.

Gentry was just ahead of him, riding like he was being chased by the hounds of hell. Festus overtook him and they could almost feel the hot breath of the lead steers as this herd swept across the grazing grounds south of town. The stampede exploded into another herd causing it to also stampede.

Oh dear Lord, Festus thought, we're going to have a sea of crazy cattle running all the way down to the Canadian River before they quit. And, if these Longhorns don't kill us, the Texans sure will, come tomorrow.

CHAPTER

17

Three days had passed since the shoot-out and stampede and the Texas cowboys were still out on the range trying to gather and sort Longhorns into their proper herds. Besides all the extra work and aggravation, a chuck wagon belonging to the Spear S Ranch had been demolished and two cow ponies had been so badly injured that they needed to be destroyed. Worse yet, Matt's leg had suffered a severe contusion and he was forced to use a cane in order to limp around town.

"You're lucky just to be alive," Doc Adams said as he poured himself another cup of coffee after changing Festus's bandages and examining Matt's swollen and discolored leg. "My gawd, you two are quite a pair!"

"Doc," Festus said, "I reckon Matthew and I have enough troubles without you remindin' us of 'em."

"Well, you better understand that if Matthew were up for reelection, he'd be out on his ear. All the businesses in Dodge City are goin' broke waiting for cattle to be sold so the cowboys can get paid and spend their money. Why,

I've even had people comin' to *me* trying to borrow enough to tide them over!''

"I've been told that the herds are almost sorted out," Matt said. "I expect the money will start to flow soon."

"It better," Doc said. "I'm just glad that I'm retired and not trying to collect from anyone."

"My main concern is to get evidence that will send our prisoners away for a long time . . . if they don't hang." Matt added, loud enough for the outlaws to hear, "Those boys don't want to cooperate and you know how angry that makes Judge Brooker."

"I sure do," Doc said. "The last time it happened, the judge got so mad he ordered that bunch to be hanged that same day! Must have been a hundred people saw them kicking and dancing on the gallows. If I were you, Marshal, I'd make sure that the gallows are ready, because there won't be any waiting around once the judge arrives back in Dodge City."

"You're right," Matt said, busily jotting down a note that would be interpreted by the Texans as a gallows reminder. "I'd also better make sure that Percy Crump has three pine caskets ready."

"Wait a minute!" one of the prisoners shouted. "We didn't kill anyone! It was Waco that did all the trigger work."

Matt shook his head, climbed to his feet, and grabbed his cane. He hobbled over to the cell and said, "You don't really expect that Judge Brooker is going to believe that you fellas just watched Waco murder and steal cattle by himself, do you?"

"Well," another cowboy, with a bandage on his face and panic in his eyes, said, "none of us *killed* anybody!"

"But you're cattle rustlers and thieves," Matt said in a tight voice. "We'll probably never know how many small outfits you attacked and how many men you buried on the cattle trails, but I'll bet it was more than a few!"

The clear leader of the bunch was named Floyd Tate,

and up until now, he'd kept the others silent. "Listen, Marshal," he said, "maybe we can cut a deal."

"What kind of a deal?"

"In exchange for confessions, names, and numbers, we don't swing."

"I can't promise you anything," Matt said. "Only that Judge Brooker would take a full confession into consideration and it might make the difference between prison and the hangman's noose."

"You ain't offering us much," Tate said, bitterness thick in his voice. "Maybe we'll just take our chances with a trial. You ain't got any proof we killed men or rustled cattle."

"Is that what you think?" Matt asked. "Tate, we've got a young cowboy that is willing to testify that you attacked his outfit, killed his family, and stole his herd."

"What cowboy!"

"The one that got away after you ambushed the Rocking R outfit. He was riding a black gelding with white stockings. Remember?"

"Damn," the one name Joe whispered. "He couldn't know that unless—"

"Shut up!" Tate hissed.

"Joe," Matt said, almost smelling the Texan's rank fear, "if I were you, I'd think real hard about a confession."

"If he tries, I'll kill him with my own two hands," Tate warned. "Marshal, you don't have any cowboy. If you did, we'd have seen him here gawkin' at us and tellin' you we were the ones. I think you're runnin' a bluff."

"What about my deputy?" Matt asked. "Festus, are these the ones that tried to kill you last week when you met them down south?"

"They sure are, Matthew. In fact, all three of them was shootin' at me when I lit out of their camp."

"There you go," Matt said, looking Tate in the eye. "Attempted murder of a lawman alone will put you away for a long while. And when we butcher a few head of your stock and find that their brands have been altered, that's even more evidence. I expect that Judge Brooker will keep the town's undertaker, Percy Crump, busy.''

"Floyd," Joe pleaded, "they got us cold! Let's try and cut a deal!"

"Yeah," Bill Grimes, a bowlegged cowboy with only half of his left ear, agreed, "there ain't no point in hangin' if we got a chance to save our hides!"

"What if the marshal is bluffing!" Tate demanded.

"Now that," Matt said, "is a stupid thing to say, given what I've just told you."

Tate swallowed hard and expelled a deep breath. "I want something in return."

"No promises. No deals."

"Marshal, all I want is your word that you'll ask the judge to keep us off the gallows because we cooperated!" There was desperation in Tate's face and pleading in his voice when he added, "That's the least you can do!"

Matt twisted around on his cane and looked at Festus and Doc. "What do you think?"

"I dunno," Doc answered. "You must realize how mad everyone in Dodge is about that bank-robbery attempt and now all the herds being stampeded."

"Yeah," Matt said, "I know."

"And," Doc continued, shaking his head, "we've seen it often enough to know that there's nothing that satisfies the people in Dodge City like a good hanging party. It would bring all the cowboys in and be real good for business. Remember how the Ladies' Aid Society sold lemonade and cookies and made almost two hundred dollars the last time we hanged a bunch like this?"

"That's right," Matt said, "and the volunteer fire department sold those little sausages and made a lot of money."

"What kind of people are you up here in Kansas!" Joe croaked, eyes round with terror.

"Oh, we're nice enough folks," Doc replied, "but we're not opposed to profiting off a little entertainment."

"That's right," Matt said. "Festus, how would you feel

about me asking Judge Brooker to spare their lives in return for full confessions?''

Festus hobbled over to Matt's side and studied the three desperate prisoners. ''Well,'' he answered, ''I just don't know. Seems to me that Waco was by far the worst.''

''That's right!'' Joe cried. ''He was givin' all the orders and he's dead!''

Festus shook his head. ''You boys is old enough to know what you were doin'. And Matthew is right when he says that Judge Brooker is gonna go hard on you after all the evidence is starin' him in the face.''

''Try, dammit!'' Joe yelled, tears filling his eyes. ''All we're asking for is not to hang!''

''Matthew, I'd sort of like to know the whole story.''

''All right,'' Matt said, eyes boring into the prisoners. ''But I'll need a written confession signed by all three of you. I'll take your signed confessions to Judge Brooker and recommend that you get prison rather than the gallows. But what he decides is out of my hands.''

''Fair enough,'' Tate gritted. ''I can't write, but Joe and Bill can. I'll sign what they write with my X.''

''Doc,'' Matt called, ''there's paper and pen on my desk. Bring them over, will you?''

''Sure, but I think you are being too easy on these fellas. The whole town is gonna be real upset if we don't have a necktie party. To my mind, they deserve to hang!''

''Don't listen to him, Marshal,'' Joe pleaded. ''Everybody deserves a second chance.''

''How many chances did you give to the cowboys whose cattle you stole after you ambushed and shot them?'' Matt challenged.

When he received no answer, Matt took the writing materials from a grim-faced Doc and shoved them through the bars, adding, ''I want *everything*. Every outfit you buried and—don't forget—we'll find out their brands when those cattle Waco was going to sell are slaughtered. I'll demand a full report, and every altered brand had better be in that confession or I'll recommend you three hang!''

Matt turned around and made his way back to his desk, not at all certain that he had done right by giving his promise to these three killers and cattle rustlers. But now he and Festus wouldn't have to have cattle butchered so they could look for brands. They also didn't need the testimony of that young cowboy, who might never regain consciousness, although Doc Gentry said he was showing hopeful signs. And as for what Judge Brooker would decide, well, it was a close call. Clearly, these three deserved the gallows, but that was entirely up to the judge. Matt was glad that he'd have no part in the decision.

"Matt," Doc said, "I'd better get back to the house. I'm feeling kind of weak and worn today."

"Are you getting enough rest?"

"Sure I am!" Doc snapped. "But I'm tired all the time now. I'm old! That's the problem and it's a condition that you'll finally understand . . . if you have the good fortune to live to be my age."

"Take it easy, Doc. I was only asking."

"Yeah," Doc grumbled, "well, I'm getting fed up with people telling me that I look tired and unwell. After a while those kinds of questions start to work on your mind."

"I'm sorry, Doc."

Doc muttered something more and shuffled out the door, looking bent, as if he were carrying the weight of the world on his thin shoulders.

"Matthew, he sure doesn't look very good," Festus observed. "I think it's a good thing that his sister is a-comin' to Dodge City to take care of him."

"We'll see," Matt answered, keeping an eye on the cell and watching the three prisoners as they huddled over the paper where Joe struggled to write out their confessions.

Later that afternoon, Matt took the signed confessions over to the courthouse and left them with a clerk with the orders that they were to be given to Judge Brooker the moment he arrived back in town. According to the three prisoners, they'd only rustled two other herds beside the Rocking R and killed no one. Matt doubted this was true but supposed he'd never find out.

Deke Peters, the legal clerk, said, "Marshal, I don't know what kind of deal you made with your prisoners, but Judge Brooker will probably go ahead and hang them."

"I didn't make any deal," Matt said.

"People in this town are sure upset," Deke continued. "Businesses are in rough shape. There's no cattle sales and it—"

"Look," Matt growled. "I know this has postponed the cattle sales but the money will start to flow soon."

"It had better," Deke said, looking glum. "My brother's saddle shop is about to go under. He was just hanging on anyway waiting for the cowboys, and now you and Festus go and scatter them herds. Doesn't make any sense to me or anyone else."

"Deke," Matt said, feeling anger knot in his belly, "just . . . just give these confessions to the judge."

"Sure, but I hope he sentences them three to hang anyway. Be good for business, you know. The charities . . ."

Matt didn't listen to any more and headed outside. He was on his way back to the office when he saw Kitty waving at him. "Matt, I need a word with you!"

"Can't it wait?" he asked. "It's time for Festus to go eat and you know how crabby he gets when he's hungry."

"What I've got to say will only take a minute."

"I suspect you want to chew me out about no cowboys and no business just like everyone else in town."

"No, it's about Dr. Gentry."

Matt frowned. "What about him?"

"Well," Kitty said, "it's hard to explain."

"Try."

"All right. He's got my girls all upset. In fact, I've had to break up two fights and a screaming match in just the last couple of days."

"What's wrong?"

"He's *seeing* them," Kitty said, folding her arms across her chest.

172

"Are they sick?"

"Yeah, you could say that. They are *love*sick. Matt, Jerome Gentry has my girls fighting for his favors, and I'm not talking about that Chickasaw Cure that he's been selling by the bottle."

"Kitty, I'm not feeling up to snuff and I'm in no mood for guessing games. What, exactly, are you talking about?"

"I'm talking about the fact that they're going over to his medicine wagon on the pretext of feeling bad and they are coming back with blushes on their faces! Matt, they won't tell me what is happening, but it's pretty obvious."

"What?"

"Dr. Gentry is . . . is giving them a . . . I don't know! A *love* potion!"

Matt blinked and almost laughed outright. "Kitty, you're not making sense."

"Nothing about that man or my girls is making sense!" Kitty cried. "I can't get my girls to pay any attention to any man other than that smooth-talking doctor! They're all mooning over him like lovesick calves!"

Matt heaved a sigh. "There is no law that prohibits a man from being attractive to your girls."

"Oh, he's doing more than that! He's taking advantage of them. Dr. Gentry has at least three of them ready to kill for his attentions."

"Talk to them," Matt told her. "They're your girls, so make them . . ."

"Make them what?" Kitty demanded. "Matt, they're all swooning over Dr. Gentry! And you know that he's going to be breaking their hearts!"

"What do you expect me to do? Your girls are grown women and they're certainly not . . ." He hesitated.

"Not what?"

"Well"—he blushed—"let's just say that they're not a bunch of nuns. Okay?"

"So that gives Dr. Gentry the right to use them!"

"If they choose to be used . . . then yes! What are you asking me to do, tell them that they can't visit him? That kissing Dr. Gentry on . . . or worse, is bad for their hearts? Kitty, be reasonable!''

She stomped her foot on the boardwalk, clearly infuriated. ''I can see that this conversation has been a complete waste of time, Matthew! I had thought that you would understand.''

''Well, I do understand, but there is nothing illegal about a man enjoying more than one woman at a time.''

Kitty whirled and headed back for the Long Branch Saloon, leaving Matt wondering what would happen next.

''Marshal! I need to speak with you a moment!''

It was Lathrop, the storekeeper, and from the doleful expression on his face, Matt knew that he was going to get an earful.

''What!''

''We need some business in this town, Marshal! Do you have any idea what is going on? Well, I'll tell you! This town is dying for cattle money. How could you put us in this kind of a fix? We pay your salary!''

Matt limped away, so angry that he dared not reply to the man. He had not gotten twenty yards when Barney overtook him.

''Marshal, I got some news.''

''If it's good, I'll hear it,'' Matt snapped. ''But if it's bad, save it for later.''

''It's about Doc.''

''Which one?''

''Old Doc Adams. His sister is arriving on the next train! I just got a telegram from her at the train stop in Newton! She'll be here today!''

''Well,'' Matt said, shaking his head, ''I don't know if that is good news or bad. We'll just have to wait and see. Have you told Doc yet?''

''No.''

''Then do it,'' Matt advised. ''It'd be nice if he wasn't the last one in Dodge City to know.''

CHAPTER

18

"Matthew, you don't look too happy," Festus observed. "In fact, you look downright unhappy."

"I am, but so is everyone else in Dodge. Why, even Kitty is upset . . . not only with the lack of business, but with me."

"Why?"

Matt told his deputy about their disagreement concerning Dr. Gentry and finished with, "I can understand why Kitty is upset about no cowboys to spend money, but what am I supposed to do about Dr. Gentry and her lovesick girls?"

Festus scratched the two-day growth of whiskers on his prominent jaw. "Well, Matthew, that there Dr. Gentry ought to be warned that he could get in big trouble again with Kitty's girls. I reckon a few of them, if they get jealous enough, could finish him off with a knife or bullet . . . shoot, they could even use poison. I was readin' in one of them dime novels how this old gal got real fed up with—"

"I'll keep that thought in mind," Matt interrupted, looking flustered. "Maybe the next time I see Doc Gentry, I'll take him aside and tell him about your dime novel.''

"Well, Matthew, these things can and do happen! But I sure wouldn't know what to say to Doc Gentry.''

"Me neither," Matt confessed. "The last time I tried, I wound up making a complete fool of myself by jumping to the wrong conclusion about him and Mrs. Nelson. By the way, have you heard anything about her husband?''

"I ran into Ma Smalley over in front of her boarding-house this morning," Festus answered. "We got to talking and Mr. Nelson's name came up. She saw him yesterday and said he looks real bad.''

"I'm sorry to hear that. Harvey Nelson is a fine man. One of the best in Dodge City.''

"Yer right, Matthew. And I was just thinkin' how good it is to have Dr. Gentry practicing medicine, given our current infirmities and all the trouble we been a-havin'. Don't know what we'd have done with Doc Adams retiring.''

"That's true," Matt agreed. "This town would be in a fix and that's another reason why I hate to confront Gentry. If he should get angry and leave because I wrongly offended him, I'd really be in hot water with the mayor and city council.''

Matt limped over to his desk. His leg throbbed and he sure hoped the pain and the swelling subsided soon: when the trail-weary and thirsty Texans started arriving in Dodge City with cash in their pockets, he would need to be on his feet night and day patrolling the saloons, dance halls, and red-light district across the tracks where muggings, fights, and killings were still commonplace among people that neither asked nor gave any quarter.

"Hey, Marshal," Floyd Tate called from the cell. "When is that judge comin' to town?''

"Any day now.''

"Who'd you give that confession to?''

"That's none of your concern," Matt snapped with irritation. "But the judge will get it as soon as he arrives.''

"You think he'll hang us?" Joe asked.

"I don't know," Matt replied. "But worrying about it won't help."

"Easy enough for you to say, Marshal Dillon. You ain't the one that might soon be the guest of honor at a necktie party."

"Festus," Matt said, ignoring the prisoner, "why don't you go and get something to eat. Then make the rounds and be back in about two hours and I'll have my supper."

"I'll do it. Rest that leg. Might help to put it up on your desk. I'll help you."

"No thanks." Matt quickly declined the offer. "If I got it up there, I might play hell getting it back down. Oh, by the way, I just heard that Doc's sister is coming in on the train today. You might want to keep a lookout for her."

"My oh my!" Festus beamed. "She sure didn't waste any time gettin' to Kansas! Wonder what she looks like."

"I have no idea. I just hope that she's more of a help than a hindrance to Doc. He needs someone to cheer him up and convince him not to retire."

"I dunno." Festus shook his head doubtfully. "Old Doc, he sounds to me like he's pretty well made up his mind to polish the seat of a rockin' chair full-time."

"That will kill him faster than his heart. Doc will go crazy sitting around all day."

"More likely," Festus said with a wink as he put his hand on the doorknob, "he'll drive *us* crazy!"

For the first time that day Matt actually smiled. "You're right. He does enjoy coming over here and drinking our coffee and then trying to get your goat."

"Oh," Festus said as he was going out the door, "I let old Doc *think* he's rubbin' my fur the wrong way, but he don't bother me . . . much."

Once outside, Festus stretched and scratched, then hobbled down the street. His buttocks were still paining him, but he thought it was important that the citizens they were sworn to protect did not realize both he and Matthew were lame. So he forced himself to walk straight and upright and even helped steer poor Louie Pheeters toward his room.

"Dagnabit, Louie, you smell like a brewery again today!"

"That's good, ain't it?" the little drunk asked with a lopsided grin. "Why, Deputy Haggen, you do say—hic—the nicest things! Wish—hic—I could say you smell good."

"Aw, get out of here," Festus growled, prodding Louie along. "How come you don't sober up once in a while and try to make somethin' of your sorry self?"

Louie stopped, wobbled around full circle, and gazed up at Festus with his red, watery eyes. "I *am* something! I'm the best old drunk in Dodge City! There's been—hic—others—hic—that tried to be a better drunk than me"—he burped—"but I beat 'em all hands down!"

"Get on out of here," Festus said, suppressing a smile, "before I throw you in jail with them murderin' Texas cattle rustlers."

"Give us all a bottle each and I'll drink 'em—hic—under the . . . the cell bunk!"

Festus shook his head and walked on to get a bite to eat. Louie was harmless and even entertaining, but he was probably killing himself with far too much cheap liquor. No one knew his past because he rarely talked about himself. Some said he had once been a successful accountant in Baltimore but had fallen on hard times, embezzled company funds, and was sentenced to a long stint in prison. Festus didn't know about that, nor could anyone figure out where Louie got enough money to drink on every day. Sure, he did a few odd jobs like sweeping out the saloons and emptying spittoons, but that was rewarded with a few morning beers rather than cash.

Louie Pheeters was a mystery man, but then, so were a lot of other people that passed through Dodge City. Unlike back in Festus's boyhood hill country, the people here were a restless bunch, often moving along the railroad lines from one town and job to the next.

Just before reaching the restaurant, Festus saw Dr. Gentry with one of Kitty's girls, Miss Gloria LaFaire, hanging all over his arm. She was a raven-haired beauty and her low-cut-at-the-neck red satin dress left little to the imagination.

"How you doin', Deputy Haggen!" Jerome called with that wide grin displaying perfect white teeth. "I'll be by later to check your bandage. How is Marshal Dillon's leg treating him?"

"Not too good," Festus replied, tipping his hat to Gloria, who looked him up and down and then tittered like a pretty bird.

"In that case, I'll prescribe him some of my special Chickasaw Cure," Jerome announced. "It helped you with the pain, didn't it?"

"Sure did," Festus answered, nodding his head vigorously. "But I was seein' double and it gave me a hangover."

Gloria giggled and danged if she didn't burp. That made Festus suspect that she was also taking the Cure.

"Well," Jerome replied, "the Cure might have been a tad stronger than usual. That can be rectified."

"Can be what?"

"Fixed," Jerome explained. "Would you like to join us for a round of drinks at the Long Branch?"

"No thank you, Doc. I gotta get somethin' to eat and then meet the train that's comin' in bringin' Doc's sister, Agnes."

"Yeah, the telegraph operator told me about that," Gentry said. "I expect she's going to be a considerable comfort to Dr. Adams."

"Are you buyin' him out?"

"I don't know. He's hard to deal with and I'm not sure what's in my future."

"We sure hope you stay here in Dodge City," Festus said, unable to keep his eyes off Gloria, who cast the doctor a sloe-eyed look and added, "That's right, honey, we *all* want you to stay close."

"Well, Festus," Jerome said, looking a bit embarrassed

179

because of Gloria's comment, "we'll see you later. Enjoy your supper."

"I will," Festus replied, thinking how much more he'd have enjoyed it with Miss Gloria sitting across his table. Some men just had all the luck when it came to women.

Festus devoured his usual meat loaf and potatoes, coffee and apple pie, consulted his pocket watch, paid his for his meal, then headed for the train station. He was looking forward to meeting Agnes and he sure hoped she wasn't anything like old Agnes Alder, Bessy Fife's best friend and a woman he thoroughly despised.

"Howdy, Deputy," the train depot manager called. "Are you here to greet Doc's sister, Miss Adams, and welcome her to Dodge City?"

"I am." Festus smoothed the front of his shirt and picked some of his supper off it with a dirty fingernail. "I hope she's goin' to enjoy her stay!"

"So do I, but you never know."

"Know what?"

"Well, a woman that has lived all her life back East probably ain't going to take to the West. It's mighty different here in Kansas and this is still a pretty raw cattle town. She'll hear the cowboys raisin' hell and see them fallin' all over themselves drunk and probably decide to leave."

"I hope not," Festus said, looking all around. "Where's Doc?"

"I have no idea. Maybe in bed feeling sorry for himself or drinking at the Long Branch. Who can say what that old reprobate is doing?"

"Old what?"

"You know, old geezer." The man grinned apologetically. "I don't mean to put Doc down, Festus, but he's become a bear to get along with these past few years, especially since he contracted his heart problems. And now that folks in Dodge got another choice in doctors, it's no surprise to me that they've all switched to Dr. Gentry."

"Well," Festus said, feeling the need to defend his old friend, "maybe that's just a mite shortsighted."

"What do you mean?"

"I mean that it's Doc Adams that has been savin' lives for as long as I can recall! He's the one that has been called out in the dead of a freezin' winter night to help someone that probably ain't got the money to pay him even for his medicine."

The train depot manager looked a bit sheepish. "Well," he said, "I hadn't exactly thought of it that way, but you're right."

"Sure I am! And what if Doc Gentry decides to move on to the next town? What are we gonna do for a doc then?"

"You think he'd do that? Why, he's making a fortune on his Chickasaw Cure alone!"

"Sure," Festus argued, "but Dr. Gentry could do the same in a bigger town, like Denver or Santa Fe. Might even do a whole lot better."

"I dunno," the man said dubiously. "He seems to be enjoyin' Kitty's girls an awful lot, too! That man is—"

Festus was spared any more conjecture by the shrill whistle of a steam locomotive. It blasted three or four long, mournful wails and then puffed into the depot, shaking the platform's heavy timbers.

Festus looked around, hoping to see Doc, but he still hadn't arrived, causing him to think, It's a darn good thing I came or the poor old gal wouldn't have a soul to welcome her to Dodge City. Dagnab Doc, anyway!

Miss Agnes Adams was the last one off the train and Festus identified her the moment her dainty little foot touched down on Dodge soil. She was petite, less than five feet tall, and silver-haired, with a pretty but nervous smile. The depot manager offered his hand and then pointed toward Festus, amid all the steam and the train's deep huffing and chuffing.

A moment later the deputy was sweeping off his crumpled old hat and bowing slightly as he shouted over the train's engine, "Welcome to Dodge City, Ma'am!"

"Thank you! Can we leave this noise behind?"

"I'll have her baggage sent over to Doc's place," the depot manager yelled.

Festus offered the woman the crook of his arm and they hurried off toward town, with Festus saying, "I hope you had a good trip, Miss Adams."

"Oh, I did indeed! How interesting these dirty frontier towns are! Is there no place for men such as yourself to bathe or wash their clothing?"

Festus gulped. "Well, Ma'am, the wind blows a lot of dirt around in the streets and most work hereabouts requires a man to get dirty."

"But you're a lawman, not a miner or freighter."

Festus tried to slap some food off his shirtfront, but Miss Adams didn't seem to notice. "Has it been a while since you seen Doc Adams?"

"Years. Why, I'm not even sure that I'd recognize Galen anymore. Has he aged gracefully?"

"I don't know, Ma'am. You can be the judge."

"I'm sure that he hasn't," she decided out loud. "Galen was always very smart, but a rebel and a man of immoral and intemperate habits."

Festus didn't ask what that meant, but he thought she was probably talking about Doc's love of saloons, women, dance, and whiskey.

"What is his house like?" she asked.

"It's pretty nice. Front part of it is used as an office and examining room. Doc keeps another room farther back for patients too sick or shot up to move."

"Dear oh dear! That won't do after I move in. It wouldn't be at all proper."

" 'Proper'?" Festus asked. "Miss, I meant that he kept the spare bedroom for his worst-hurt and sickest patients."

"I understood you, sir. But that *must* change."

"But that's the way that Doc has always had things."

"Yes," she said, "but now his life is about to change and improve. For example, I'm going to insist that he take proper care of himself. He must eat properly, drink at least two gallons of water each day for his circulation, and—"

"Water? Doc never drinks no water."

"I must say that your grammar is utterly horrid!"

Festus wasn't sure exactly what Miss Adams was referring to, but he knew when he was being insulted. "Ma'am, I may wear my meals on my shirt but I can read and write . . . I'm not all ignorant."

"No," she said, offering him a condescending smile, "I'm sure that you are . . . are quite normal in most respects. Now, where is Galen's residence?"

"You mean his house?"

"That's right."

"We're almost there," Festus answered, noting how people were emerging from businesses up and down Front Street to stare. Thanks to Barney at the telegraph office, everyone in Dodge knew that Doc's sister was on that today's train and were curious to see what she looked like so they could get in on the latest gossip.

"Here we are." Festus pointed at the window with Doc's painted name. "I got a key."

"Why?"

The blunt question caught him off guard, but he recovered to answer, "Matthew—I mean Marshal Dillon and I both have keys so that when someone is bleedin' real bad in the night, we can get inside without waitin' for Doc to wake up and come to the door. He's a heavy sleeper, especially after a long evening at the Long Branch."

"What's that?"

Festus could tell that he'd said the wrong thing. "Well it's just a little waterin' hole, is all. Lots of real friendly folks."

"It's a whiskey den, isn't it!" she demanded. "Is that where Galen spends his evenings?"

Festus got the door open and almost charged down the hallway into Doc's rear living quarters, which were an unsightly mess, with clothes tossed on the floor and two empty whiskey bottles on the dresser. "I'm sure Doc has a bedroom all fixed up and waitin' for you, Ma'am, but I'm not sure which.''

"Never you mind," she told him, retreating with a look of shock on her face. "Where is Galen!"

"I—"

"Either you take me directly to him or I'll be forced to find him on my own." She placed her hands on her hips. "Now, which is it going to be?"

"I'll take you," Festus agreed, fearing she might blunder into one of the more . . . well, colorful saloons.

"Then let's go," Agnes ordered. "I don't mind telling you that I am sorely disappointed that Galen did not think enough of me to meet my train or have this . . . this place cleaned for my arrival."

"He probably got his dates mixed up," Festus said, wanting to avoid what had all the indications of a train wreck.

"*You* managed to know when I was arriving! Why shouldn't Galen?"

"Ma'am," Festus said, starting back down the hallway and wishing he'd have gone from his supper directly back to the office, "I've known Doc for a lot of years and he just isn't very good keeping appointments. He's the best doctor you could ask for in an emergency, but . . . well, not so good at this kind of stuff."

"You mean he is disorganized."

"I guess so."

"I'll change that."

"He's also sick and tired," Festus said, trying to hide his building annoyance. "Doc has saved a lot of lives in Dodge City, but it's taken its toll on his health."

"I may take him back to the East as soon as he is strong enough to travel. We could sell this pigsty and return to much nicer and more civilized surroundings."

"Doc loves it here in Dodge City. We'd hoped you would too."

"Not likely!"

Festus emerged back on the sidewalk feeling bruised and irritable, like Matthew.

"Now," she demanded, "where is this Long Branch whiskey parlor?"

"Right this way," Festus replied, dreading what was probably going to happen next.

CHAPTER

19

Festus was worried. "If you haven't been in a saloon before, Miss Adams, maybe you ought to just wait outside here for a minute while I go get Doc."

"Are there other women inside?"

"Yeah, but—"

"Then move!"

Festus took a deep breath and went inside, hoping that Doc was at the Delmonico Restaurant. No such luck. The minute they stepped inside, Festus saw Doc Adams sitting with Miss Kitty, Doc Gentry, and Miss Gloria LaFaire. They were drinking and laughing and having a high old time. Festus knew that was about to end.

"Galen!"

Doc's head snapped around like the popper on a bull-whip. A cigar was punched in the corner of his mouth and it drooped like the tail of a whipped dog.

"Agnes?"

"Galen, how could you treat me this way! Do you know how worried I've been over your health and welfare? How

I haven't slept a wink since I got your telegram! How . . . how upset I've been!''

Doc studiously removed his cigar and squinted across the now silent saloon. ''Well,'' he finally said, ''you're still upset, but a few drinks would do you wonders. Come on over here and meet my good friends and my colleague Dr. Gentry.''

Festus held his breath as the proper little woman marched over to their table, nose tilted to the chandeliers and chin quivering with indignation. Agnes Adams looked mad enough to kill her brother.

''Smoking!'' she cried when she reached Doc's table of friends. ''Smoking and drinking the devil's poison and you with a bad heart! No wonder you look so awful!''

''Well, Agnes, you don't look so good yourself.'' Doc squinted toward the entrance, found Festus, and demanded, ''Why the hell did you bring my sister here!''

''She gave me no choice, Doc!''

Kitty stood up, forcing a big smile, ''Miss Agnes, allow me to introduce myself and our friends.''

Agnes raked the saloon owner up and down with her hot accusing eyes and cried, ''You . . . you hussy!''

Kitty blinked but never said a word. Gloria, however, did. She came to her feet and screeched, ''Why, you old biddy, how dare you talk to Miss Kitty thataway! She *owns* this joint!''

Agnes balled her little fists up and walloped Gloria right in the nose, hard enough to set it bleeding.

''Ouch!'' Gloria cried, staggering and then hauling back her own fist.

Dr. Gentry and Kitty managed to get between the women and then Doc pushed to his feet, came around the table, and grabbed his sister by the arm. ''Agnes,'' he said with surprising gentleness, ''I can see that this has been a mistake and that I am to blame. You don't belong in this establishment, nor do you belong in the great American West. But don't worry, I'll buy you a ticket on the next eastbound train.''

Agnes broke down in tears. She crumpled at the waist, covered her face in her white-gloved hands, and sobbed. She was still sobbing when Doc led her outside and down the boardwalk.

For several minutes everyone stood quiet, then Festus could feel the tension slowly drain away. "Miss Kitty, I'm real sorry, but she was bound and determined to find Doc. I was afraid she'd go lookin' in some bad places."

"It's all right," Kitty assured him. "Festus, why don't you come in and have a drink on the house. I think we could all use a few."

"I'd like to take up your offer, Miss Kitty. I surely would, but I have to get back so Matthew can get his supper."

"Sure. But don't worry about it so much."

"You shore ain't no hussy," Festus said, trying desperately to repair his damage. "You shore didn't deserve to be talked to thataway."

"It's all right. Go on now." Kitty turned to the bar and called, "Sam, drinks on the house! And let's get some music. Where's my piano man!"

Festus caught the shine of tears in Kitty's eyes and it sure made him feel awful. Miss Kitty was about as fine a woman as you could find anywhere. And maybe she'd never be in no high-society circles, but there weren't any of them in Dodge City anyway, thanks be to gawd.

When Festus got back to the office, he told Matthew about what had happened. "I sure messed up good," he confessed, shaking his head when the story was completed. "I ought to be horsewhipped."

"No, you shouldn't, Festus. It's nobody's fault. I expect that the reason that poor little woman was so hard on Kitty and Doc is that she is beside herself with worry and wrung out from lack of sleep."

"I don't know about that, Matthew. She's mighty disapproving."

"Then it's better that she get on the train like Doc says. But that doesn't solve his problem."

"No, sir, it does not."

"Look," Matt said. "I think I'll go over to the Long Branch and see if I can cheer up Miss Kitty."

"She'd like that. I feel almost as bad as she does, I reckon."

"I'm sorry, but this will all pass." Matt grabbed his hat and headed for the saloon.

When he stepped inside the Long Branch, Matt could feel that the mood was low-down despite loud piano music. Kitty was struggling hard to maintain a smile on her pretty face, but Matt knew her well enough to see right through her mask.

"Hello," he said. "Mind if I join you?"

Kitty got up from the table and came over to take his arm. He felt her shudder and heard her take a deep, calming breath before she said, "Matt, why don't we find our own table?"

"I'd like that."

"Sam, two beers. No . . . on second thought, bring a bottle and a couple glasses."

"Comin' right up!"

When they sat down together, Matt leaned close.

"Festus told me what happened. I'm sorry, Kitty. My guess is that Doc's sister is just wrung out and beside herself."

"I know and I'm all right."

"Are you?"

"I'll be fine. But I feel sorry for Doc. Matt, you should have seen his face when that woman called out his name. Doc turned about two shades of white. The last thing that he needs is his self-righteous sister telling him he's awful."

"Doc won't stand for that."

"He might," Kitty argued. "I've never seen Doc so low as he's been lately. That woman could finish off what little spirit he has left."

"Then I'll help put her on the train tomorrow," Matt

promised. "In fact, I'll take up a collection to put her up for the night in the hotel rather than at Doc's place."

"Might be a wise idea." Kitty waited until Sam brought them a bottle. When she poured, Matt heard the bottle dance on the rim of his glass because she was trembling so badly. "Kitty, what's wrong? Why are you so upset?"

"She . . . she called me a . . . hussy. I haven't been called that in a lot of years."

"Forget it!"

"I'm a saloon owner," Kitty told him. "I employ girls and I keep them safe and in line. You know that. I run a good house and there are no scarlet women here. My girls are good girls. They dance, they entertain, they help the men enjoy themselves, but that is all . . . at least on my time. If one of my girls steals or takes money for her—"

"Kitty, you don't need to convince me of anything and you don't need Agnes Adams's approval, either. You've done a lot of good in Dodge and I know how much you care for your girls and how many you've helped on the other side of the tracks when they were sick or in bad trouble."

"Well," Kitty said, wiping a fresh tear from her eyes, "I have tried to do good. But there are times when I can feel women like Agnes looking at me like I was a . . . I dunno, something very dirty and ugly."

"Ignore them! You're a beautiful woman—beautiful inside and out."

"I was hoping you'd tell me that." Kitty sniffled, but she also managed a genuine smile. "Matt, you haven't told me I was beautiful in a long, long time!"

"I apologize. You ought to be told regularly. If not by me, then by others."

" 'Others' don't count." Kitty placed her hand on his. "Could you come by my room later this evening when you're off duty? I could use a strong shoulder to lean on tonight."

"Of course. But right now I'd better make my rounds and see what is going on. I think I heard some cowboys

190

gallop up as I was coming over here and I expect they're paying a visit to the Lady Gay Dance Hall and Saloon. I've had trouble there every year when the cowboys arrive and I mean to give them a stern and early warning. Who knows? Maybe if I do that, no one will be killed there this season.''

"Don't count on it," Kitty advised. "That is a rough crowd and you know Eli loves nothing better than to smash faces with his big fists."

"I know."

Matt patted Kitty on the arm instead of kissing her, because everyone was watching. He pushed himself to his feet, trying not to grimace.

"Matt, where's your cane?"

"I left it at the office. I can't very well cross the tracks with a cane in my hand, now can I? How impressive would that look to those wild cowboys?"

"Not very," Kitty had to admit. "But—"

"I'll be all right," he said. "You be all right, too, and I'll see you later."

Kitty gave him a happy smile. "That's a promise?"

"It is," Matt told her before leaving.

The Lady Gay Dance Hall and Saloon had always been the most notorious establishment on the south side of the railroad tracks. Its owner, Eli Keeler, was a former buffalo hunter and bone picker. Large, profane, and fierce, Eli had a shock of wild red hair, massive, scarred eyebrows, and a jaw as prominent and impregnable as a slab of granite. He possessed knuckle-busted fists the size of hams and he liked to brag that he had once been a New York prizefighter whose career ended only because he was so feared that no one would toe the mark with him anymore.

He liked to taunt and challenge Matt to a fistfight because they were about the same size, but Matt always declined. In truth, he secretly doubted that he or any other man in Kansas could whip Eli Keeler with fists alone. And so it was always a trial to enter the Lady Gay and order everyone to keep the peace. Keeler would rant and rave, and once or twice Matt had actually been forced to arrest the giant at gunpoint and keep him locked up until he was sober.

There were a dozen cow ponies tied up at the hitching rail in front of Eli's saloon when Matt arrived and he could hear a lot of wild shouting and cursing inside. Nothing against the law concerning that. In Dodge City, it was understood that there was a double standard. Establishments on the north side of the railroad tracks were expected to operate differently than those on the south. No prostitution being the main difference, but also a much cleaner and more honest standard of conduct. It was here, on the south side of the tracks, that things could quickly get out of hand.

When the Texans arrived flush with cash, it was not at all uncommon to have a shooting nearly every night. Doc Adams had spent a lot of time south of the railroad tracks at places like the Lady Gay and many was the night he'd returned across the tracks to inform Percy Crump that his undertaking services were immediately required.

"Say now," Eli boomed across the crowded saloon, "if it isn't Marshal Dillon come to pay his respects to the Lady Gay!"

There was a hush of silence, but it only lasted a moment and then the revelry continued. Matt shouldered his way over to the bar and said, "Eli, I see that you got the first customers up from Texas in tonight."

"Sure! They need to sow their wild oats a few days and nights before they cross the tracks into your neighborhood."

"I'd appreciate it if you'd try to keep the bloodshed to a minimum this season," Matt said, noting how Keeler had imported several new prostitutes and that some of the Texans were already staggering drunk. "If I hear gunfire coming from here, I'll be making arrests."

"Now, Marshal." Keeler leaned his elbows on his bar and made a face like he'd bitten into a lemon. "You know that we take care of our own troubles on this side of the tracks. So why don't you just stay up north and baby-sit Miss Kitty and her kind?''

Matt knew he was being baited and chose to ignore the insult. ''Your saloon and dance hall is inside the city limits and I've sworn to uphold the law here on both sides of the tracks. Last year there were a lot of complaints about cowboys being mugged after leaving your saloon. I won't tolerate it anymore.''

''You sound out of sorts,'' Keeler replied. ''I heard that you got hurt. Something about your horse having to be destroyed and you havin' a bad leg. Too, too bad! Maybe you ought to think about retiring, like old Doc Adams.''

''And maybe you ought to listen to what I'm telling you,'' Matt replied. ''Cross me and I'll have you in jail and before Judge Brooker, who doesn't look any more favorably on your shenanigans than I do.''

''Who needs the judge to settle our differences, Marshal?'' Keeler clenched his big fists. ''We could settle them right here and now . . . once and for all.''

''You'd like that, wouldn't you?'' Matt said. ''Cross me and I'll split your thick skull with the barrel of my pistol. After jailing you, I'll close down this den of thieves.''

''Aren't you coming up for reelection?'' Keeler asked.

''Not for another six months.''

''Well, I got a feeling that given how you and Haggen made such a mess out of the south-range stampede and caused so much hardship among the merchants and their families, you might be smart to start looking for another job.''

''Don't count on me leaving, Eli. I expect to be around for a good long while.''

''Too bad. Can I pour you a drink?''

''No thanks.''

''Then you'd best be on your way, Marshal. People in here spend money or leave.''

''You've been warned,'' Matt said, turning to go.

Suddenly a big man slammed into his injured leg and he stifled a cry as he fell. Before he could get up, a fight broke out and another combatant crashed into him. Matt took a wild punch to his forehead and surged to his feet, knowing that the fight was staged so that he would be beaten senseless. Afterward, the assailants would disappear and Eli Keeler would claim his innocence.

A mug of beer sailed past Matt's head and he drove an uppercut into the soft belly of the man who'd just missed. Someone struck him in the kidneys and his knees again, but he stood his ground and managed to drive an elbow into his assailant's face, cracking his nose.

Eli Keeler came around the end of his bar with a vicious look on his face and Matt knew that he was about to be sledgehammered by one of the saloon owner's infamous fists. Ducking an overhand from Keeler, he stepped in close and slammed his knee up into the big man's groin. Keeler's mouth flew open and Matt caught him with a powerful left cross that landed just below the ear. Keeler staggered, cursed, spat in his palms, and started to attack again, but Matt drew his six-gun and stabbed the barrel into the man's right eye.

"Ahhh!" Keeler howled as Matt fired his gun into the ceiling and shouted, "Everybody freeze!"

Keeler screamed in agony, "Marshal, you poked out my eye!"

"Maybe," Matt said, retreating toward the door. "Yeah, and the next time you try and set me up for a beating, I'll *shoot* your other eye out!"

Matt left the saloon wondering if he should ask Dr. Gentry to come and take care of Eli's eye. He decided not to bother. Either it was out and nothing could be done, or it would heal on its own.

He crossed the tracks and was nearing his office when Ma Smalley intercepted him. "Marshal, what's wrong!"

Matt halted, bruised leg throbbing and on fire. "What do you mean?"

"There's blood on your face."

Matt reached up and touched his forehead, then looked

at the smear of blood on his fingers. "Can't be too bad if I didn't even feel it."

"It's a nasty cut. You had better have Doc take a look at it. But first, I came to tell you the young cowboy that Doc has had me taking care of came around."

"He did?"

"Yep," Ma said. "One minute he was out like usual and the next he was sittin' up in bed yammerin' like a jaybird. His name is James Ridley. He comes from a ranch down near Del Rio and he told me that him and his people were ambushed and he was the only one to get away alive."

Matt nodded with grim satisfaction. "I wonder if he can identify the men in my jail cell."

"I expect not," Ma said. "The boy says it all happened so fast he didn't have time to see faces."

"Too bad."

"You'd better find Dr. Gentry," Ma fretted. "That's a nasty cut. What happened?"

"Eli Keeler set me up at the Lady Gay."

"You ought to let the whole bunch of 'em kill themselves off. The world would be a lot better place if they did. Kill them whores, too!"

"I can't let that happen," Matt told her. "And thanks for tellin' me about James Ridley."

"I hope that bunch in your jail hang even if that boy can't identify 'em," Ma said. "There's too much Texas trash in Dodge City."

"Most of the cowboys are good men," Matt said. "Maybe a bit too wild, but they've been without for months coming up the trail and they're just a little too excited."

"Excited, hell! They all ought to be horsewhipped and sent back home to their mamas!"

Matt disagreed but knew that you never won an argument with Ma Smalley, so there was no use in wasting your breath. He'd get his head patched up and then go see Ridley. Maybe things would break their way and he'd have more than enough evidence for Judge Brooker to hang the three in his jail, if that was what he ruled to be fair justice.

195

CHAPTER

20

The following Monday's trial was short but not sweet. One of Waco's cattle was slaughtered and the hide proved without a doubt that it was a Rocking R Ranch steer. With that much evidence against them, Floyd Tate, Joe Mensinger, and Bill Grimes pleaded guilty of cattle rustling, but the charge of murder, for which hard evidence was lacking, was dropped. The three Texas cattle rustlers were sentenced to a term of twenty-five years in the federal penitentiary.

Both Matt and Festus were more than pleased when a federal officer of the law showed up the very next day after the sentence and hauled them off in handcuffs and leg irons.

"I saw Doc today," Festus said.

"Which Doc?" Matt asked.

"Why, old Doc Adams. And danged if he wasn't lookin' pretty spry."

Matt hadn't seen his friend in several days but he'd been planning a visit, so he climbed out of his office chair, pulled on his hat, and said, "I think I'll mosey on over there and see how he and his sister are doing."

"I expected her to be gone back East by now."

"Well," Matt said, "maybe Agnes settled down once she had come rest and saw that Doc wasn't quite as degenerate as she'd imagined."

"As what?"

"Degenerate. It means . . . well, sort of corrupt or dissipated."

"You shore can use them their ten-dollar words, Matthew!" Festus crowed. "Danged if I don't wish I could speak like you and Doc. But . . . but I never thought Doc was generated."

"*De*generate," Matt corrected.

"Whatever. All he does anymore is smoke and drink." Festus winked. "Matthew, I've known *preachers* that'd do worse behind the barn or up in the hayloft when the full moon was a-shinin'."

"Maybe so," Matt said, ignoring his deputy's remark and lecherous grin. "I'll be back soon. I understand that the Texans have collected all of James Ridley's cattle herd and helped him get them sold. They've also taken up a collection for him and I understand it's now up to eight hundred dollars. That and his cattle money ought to help Ridley ease his losses."

"I was talking to that young fella and he sure misses his pa and brothers. He sent his ma and sisters a letter that Doc Adams wrote for him a-tellin' 'em the bad news but that he'd be home soon."

"Everyone feels bad for James," Matt agreed. "If I'd been Judge Brooker, I'd have probably hanged those three, but that is not my decision. I'm just glad that they've gone to prison."

Festus grabbed his own hat. "I'm going to make the rounds across the tracks now, Matthew. Dr. Gentry was supposed to take the bandage off Eli Keeler's eye and find out if it was blind or not."

"If it is," Matt said, expression turning grim, "I've heard that he has sworn to kill me."

"I've heard the same. Want me to arrest him if his eye was poked out?"

"No," Matt said, "we can't do that on a threat. Keeler already has too much sympathy from the rougher element across the tracks. Arresting him would just add fuel to the fire and there's already enough hard cases over there who want a piece of my hide."

"Well," Festus vowed, "they're goin' to have to go through Deputy Haggen to git it!"

"Thanks," Matt said with sincere appreciation. "And be careful. To some of those people, all lawman are to be hated and feared."

"I'll be careful," Festus promised. "Say good-bye for me to young James, if he's on his way back to Del Rio."

"I'll do it."

Matt headed over to see the Texas cowboy. James Ridley was with several other cowboys all about to ride out of Dodge for Texas. When he saw Matt, he grinned and said, "Marshal, I'm glad you happened by. I sure want to thank you for everything. Thank Festus for me, too, will ya?"

"I'll do it. Be careful. You're carrying a lot of money."

"Not so much. Mr. Brodkin gave me a check to cash down in Del Rio. It's not worth anything to anyone else with my name on it, so I don't have to worry. Besides, I've got a lot of protection."

Matt glanced at the half-dozen young Texans that had befriended Ridley and were going to escort him back to his cattle ranch way down near the Rio Grande River. "Yeah, I can see that you are in good company. I'm sorry this turned out so bad, James."

The kid's smile died. He was thin and pale, but looked fit enough to ride. "Me, too. But I got some younger brothers and other kinfolks. And I got enough money to pay off the ranch and restock it. I'll be back to see you in a couple years and treat you all to a steak dinner at the Delmonico Restaurant. Finest money can buy."

"I'll hold you to that," Matt said.

"Doc!" The kid looked past Matt and he was grinning.

"I was hoping you'd come to say good-bye."

Doc Adams and Agnes joined them and danged if they weren't also smiling. Matt could see that Festus had been right. . . . Doc looked rested and healthy.

"Son," Doc said, "I almost killed you with chloroform on my operating table. I wasn't thinking right and—"

"Doc," the kid from the Rocking R Ranch interrupted, "we all make mistakes now and then. I've heard how many lives you've saved. Some of 'em Texas cowboys like myself. And I know that you've often done it without pay or maybe even thanks. So I'm the one that owes you, not the other way 'round. Here's a hundred dollars cash money for your services along with my thanks."

Doc was clearly moved and his hand closed around the bills, but then he shook his head. "I thank you for paying me, but I want you to take the money back."

"No, sir!" James Ridley said, backing up and then mounting his fine-looking black gelding. "Doc, you keep that money in exchange for all the cowboys you fixed that couldn't pay you. And if you want to do me a favor, don't retire. You're too fine a doctor, with too many folks yet to save."

Doc didn't have time to argue because the kid and his friends were suddenly wheeling their cow ponies and galloping down the street, whooping and hollering like Comanche Indians. They shot across the tracks and disappeared in a dust cloud.

"Galen," Agnes announced, "I liked what that young man said and I think he's right. You are still too young and valuable to retire."

"Aw," Doc said, "Dr. Gentry can handle things. I've agreed to sell him my practice."

"I don't think that's wise, Galen."

Doc's eyes flashed. "Well, Agnes, what you think is wise or not wise doesn't matter very much in Dodge City."

"Hey!" Matt interrupted. "No fighting."

"We've always fought and always will fight," Agnes

declared, her eyes dancing and her chin jutting out with defiance.

"Galen is the stubbornest man I ever knew."

"And you're the stubbornest woman, Agnes!"

"Listen." Matt pushed between what looked to him like a pair of fighting bantam roosters. "I think the main thing is that you've recovered your health, Doc. Maybe battling with Miss Agnes is exactly what you needed to regain your old cantankerous and fighting spirit!"

" 'Cantankerous'!"

"That's right. And I also agree with her that you shouldn't retire. Dodge City is growing and there's room for two good doctors. Besides, young Dr. Gentry is a little . . ."

Matt wasn't prepared to finish what he had in mind to say.

"A little what?" Agnes demanded.

"Well, I just think he's not quite ready to settle down and plant his roots in one town for all that long."

"Matt, I just told you that he was buying me out!"

"With what?" Matt asked. "The proceeds from his Chickasaw Cure?"

"*And* all the fees he's been collecting for his services." Doc heaved a deep sigh. "On a saner subject, we were both with Harvey Nelson when he passed away night before last. The man had suffered a great deal and we were giving him laudanum by the bottle there at the last."

"I'm sorry to hear that. What is his widow going to do?"

"She's selling out and leaving for Denver. I heard that she has some relatives there."

"Might be for the best," Matt said with a shake of his head.

Doc used his forefinger to rasp his bristly mustache. "I got some other bad news."

"And that is?"

"Eli Keeler is blind in that right eye and he's sworn to kill you."

"Maybe it's just talk."

"We both know better than that," Doc replied. "Agnes, why don't you go back to the house and get supper ready?"

"Absolutely not! I want to know what can be done about this threat."

"It doesn't concern you!"

"Yes, it does."

"See! See," Doc cried in exasperation. "This is the stubbornest woman in the world."

"Look," Matt said, dredging up a grin. "I can handle Keeler if he comes gunning for me."

"But he won't 'come gunning' for you," Doc argued. "You know as well as I do that he'll hire some gunslick to ambush you on the street. Matt, you've got to arrest that man before he carries out his threat."

"I can't arrest Keeler for a threat and I'll not make him the biggest hero south of the tracks, which is what he'd most enjoy. No, Doc, the best thing to do is ignore Keeler and hope that he comes to his senses."

"You put his eye out! He's a brawler and the thing he's most proud of is that he can whip any man. But he can't do that one-eyed. He won't be able to see a fist or a club coming in on that side and he knows his reign of fighting supremacy is over. My guess is that he hates you with a passion for that."

"I never meant to blind that eye," Matt said, "but I don't feel bad about it, either. He was going to have me stomped and beaten in his saloon. Maybe even killed."

"He ought to be run out of our town," Agnes declared.

" 'Our' town?" Doc inquired with raised eyebrows. "What's this 'our town' business?"

"Well," Agnes stammered defensively, "as long as I'm here, it is part my town. Isn't that right, Marshal Dillon?"

"That's right, Miss Adams. As a resident, even a new one, it's yours as much as anyone's."

"I don't know why you're always siding with Agnes and against me!" Doc stormed. "After all that we've been through and I've done for you, I'd expect better."

Before Matt could reply, Doc stomped off, leaving him

alone with Agnes outside the livery. "Given his bad heart, I sure hate to upset your brother."

"Ha! 'Upset' is his happiest state of mind, Marshal Dillon. I found that out a long time ago and was determined to get his old juices flowing again. And I think I've succeeded quite admirably. Don't you?"

"Yes, ma'am!"

"Well, we are correct that he ought not to retire, Marshal. I saw that right away. However, it does seem that his former clients have all deserted him."

"Not all."

"You're right," she agreed. "But most. I have met that young Dr. Gentry. He's quite the handsome dandy, isn't he?"

"Yes, he is."

"I've also heard gossip that he is a rogue."

"What do you mean?"

She scoffed, tilted her head far back, and glared up at him. "Don't play ignorant with me, young man! I've seen his type before. He is not only a rogue but a rascal, a rapscallion, and a knave!"

Matt struggled to suppress a grin. "He's not that bad, is he?"

"Bad? Of course not! He's probably wonderful, but he is also a scoundrel of the first order. I've only been here a few weeks, but my ears aren't plugged with tree sap, you know."

"I'm sure that they're not."

"Oh, I've heard plenty about the handsome and debonair Dr. Jerome Gentry, who claims to be part Chickasaw Indian. That is pure hooey, if you ask me!"

"Why do you say that?"

"He's Italian! Or Sicilian. Or perhaps Latin. Yes, most likely Latin, with that fine profile so very much like Nero or Julius Caesar. I'm sure of it!"

"I don't know about that, but he does attract women," Matt said, "and he isn't fearful."

"Except perhaps of the truth!"

Matt didn't know what to say, so he tipped his hat and smiled. "You have a good day, Miss Adams."

"And you watch out for that horrible Eli Keeler and his hired gunman!"

"I will," Matt promised.

Half a block away, he stopped and debated heading across the tracks just to check on Festus. But that might send the signal that he didn't think his deputy could handle Keeler or his rough crowd. So he made the north-side rounds and returned to his office to pace back and forth, trying not to worry about what was going on at the Lady Gay.

CHAPTER

2 1

The full moon was shining bright and the heavens were glittering with stars when Matt stopped outside Jerome's colorful medicine wagon. He hesitated for a moment, listening to the giggles and hilarious laughter inside and then he pounded on the wagon's door.

"Go away!" Jerome shouted. "I'm closed for business."

"It's Marshal Dillon. Open up!"

"Damn!" came a whispered response. Then: "Betsy, would you please let go! It's the marshal!"

"Oh, let him come back later. I'm not finished yet!"

"Gentry, I'm running out of patience. Open up!"

"Right with you, Marshal! Betsy, stop it!"

More giggles and ribald laughter.

Matt shook his head and counted to ten, trying to control his anger. "Gentry, don't you ever get any rest!"

"Why sure! I was—stop it, Betsy!"

Matt banged on the door again and it finally opened. Gentry was fumbling with his belt and Betsy was wearing very little to fumble with.

"Something wrong, Marshal? A shooting?"

"No."

"Then someone got knifed or beaten in a fight. Probably on the south side of the tracks, huh?"

"No."

"Poison?"

"Gentry, this is between you and me. Betsy, Kitty wants to see you."

"But this is my night off!"

"Well," Matt answered, "from what Kitty tells me, you've been taking a lot of nights off and she's not too happy."

"Oh," Betsy whined, "all right. I'll go talk to her."

Jerome shrugged his shoulders. "Maybe we can get together sometime tomorrow, Honey."

"I'll be back later tonight, Darling."

"Marshal, hang on a second while I grab my shirt."

Matt nodded and struggled to ignore the passionate farewell that followed between the two young lovers. "Come on, come on!"

"Right with you, Marshal!"

"I'll be waiting over by the corral."

Jerome joined him a few minutes later. He was still only half-dressed and pulling on his shirt. "What is it?"

"We need to talk about you and the Long Branch girls. Miss Kitty says that you've created quite a problem."

Jerome stopped dressing. "What, exactly, do you mean?"

"Well, the other day Festus saw you with Miss Gloria and tonight it's Betsy. Who knows who you'll have in this wagon tomorrow night or the next."

Jerome's smile died. "Marshal, is romancing women a crime in Dodge City?"

"Of course not."

"Then is kissing on . . . you know, more involved acts of affection illegal in your town?"

"Dammit, Gentry, you know it isn't!"

"Then what's the problem?"

"You're creating a problem by seducing half of Kitty's saloon girls!"

"Not half. No," Jerome said, shaking his head. "Not nearly half. I don't mean to sound unkind, but there are a couple of girls in her place that are pretty homely. I've seen bloodhounds with better faces."

"Well, too many!" Matt was getting frustrated. He sure didn't feel like this was part of his job duties, but he owed it to Kitty at least to have a talk with this man.

"Listen, Marshal Dillon, I just happen to enjoy women."

"Obviously. And because of it, Rita Clancy is dead and Kitty says her girls are fighting like cats. I am not a prude, but I won't allow you to keep this up."

Jerome placed his hands on his hips. "Are you actually ordering me not to see Kitty's girls?"

"No, but . . ."

"Then what?"

"Can't you just settle for one!"

"Why?"

"Because I'm asking you. Because Kitty is asking you, and because if you don't, there could be more bloodshed."

"I think you're exaggerating more than a little. Gloria and I had a . . . falling-out. Betsy is the one that I'm most interested in right now."

"Why don't you try and make her your *only* girlfriend for a while and give the others a break?"

Jerome slowly buttoned up his white silk shirt. "Listen," he said, "maybe I've worn out my welcome here in Dodge City and need to move on."

"That's not necessary."

"Not yet it isn't," Jerome replied, "but it probably will become necessary sooner or later. Marshal, believe it or not, I like and admire you, Festus, Kitty, and Doc. I like Dodge City and almost all of its people. I haven't felt as much at home in quite a while and I don't want to ruin things."

"This town needs you, Doctor. I'm the one responsible for sending that telegram and I'm still glad that you came because of it."

"Thanks, but things have changed, haven't they?"

"What do you mean?"

Jerome shrugged. "Well, for starters, I am partly responsible for Rita Clancy's death. I can't get over that and it haunts me."

"You didn't kill the woman, her husband did."

Jerome wasn't listening. "And I've also ruined Doc Adams's medical practice."

"That's not true."

"Sure it is! He was severely depressed and I turned on the charm. I saw that he had rafts of patients that I could steal and I stole them. But Doc is feeling a lot better about himself lately. I think it has quite a bit to do with that cowboy, James Ridley, recovering. Dr. Adams is a fine physician and he still has a number of good years."

"He needs help," Matt said. "Maybe you need to try and tone down the charm and redirect some patients back to Doc, but there's business enough for the both of you in Dodge City."

"Marshal, that's debatable. The way I see it, I took advantage and caused Rita to die. Sure, along the way I saved a few lives . . . George Bates and maybe even that cowboy and a couple of others."

"That's right, and—"

Jerome didn't let him finish. "But I think I've about used up my welcome here and—look out!"

Jerome threw himself at Matt just as the double barrels of a shotgun sprayed fire and lead across the moonlit stable yard. Matt felt himself being struck by pellets and heard Jerome cry out as he took even more of the blast. They both went down and rolled into the deep shadows beside the barn. Matt desperately struggled to unholster his gun as the assassin reloaded.

"Marshal, I . . . I think I'm dying!"

Matt tore his six-gun free. It required all of his strength to lift and aim the weapon at the dark figure that was snapping the breech of the shotgun shut in preparation for a second, lethal blast. Warm, slick blood made it almost impossible for Matt to grip the butt of his Colt revolver. He had to use both hands to steady his aim as the assassin approached, squinting into the shadows. Matt fired once, twice, then a third time, seeing the man stop, stagger, then crash over backward. The marshal shot him once more just to make sure that he was dead.

"Help!" he bellowed. "Help!"

Betsy was the first one to reach their side but she was nearly hysterical. "What can I do!"

"Find Doc Adams and Festus!" Matt pushed himself to his hands and knees and struggled to drag Jerome out into the moonlight.

"Oh my goodness!" Betsy screamed when she saw the doctor's bloody face and clothes.

Matt shot her a threatening look. "Get Doc!"

"Hang on," he pleaded. "Don't die on us!"

Jerome managed a weak smile. "Was it another jealous lover?"

"I don't know," Matt grated. "I'm going to try to pick you up and carry you to Doc's office. Just . . . just hang on!"

Matt wasn't sure how badly he'd been shot himself and he certainly wasn't sure if he had the strength to lift and carry Gentry, but he gave it his best try. When the wounded man cried out in pain, Matt started to lower him back to the ground.

"No, it's all right," Jerome grated. "I'm probably bleeding to death. Got to . . . to get to Doc!"

Matt had reached the same grim conclusion. Picking the doctor up as gently as possible, he began to hurry up the street toward Doc Adams's office. He felt like he was running in quicksand and he was staggering when several men took Jerome out of his arms and then helped him continue on to Doc's office.

"Get them both in here!" Doc shouted. "Hurry! Easy now, they aren't sides of beef!" He took one look at Jerome and swallowed hard. "What happened!"

"We were shotgunned," Matt answered.

Jerome had lost consciousness. Doc used a precious minute to examine Matt, then said, "You're going to be okay. I'm going to have to stop Dr. Gentry's hemorrhaging or he'll die in a few minutes."

"Take care of him, Doc! I can wait."

"Agnes, get some bandages and see if you can bandage Matt up a little while I take care of Gentry!"

Matt didn't remember much that happened during the next few hours. He heard Gentry cry out several times and he could hear Festus shouting as he cleared the room of everyone except himself, Kitty, Doc, and Agnes.

"Who did it!" Festus asked someone, anyone, outside.

"There's a dead man down by the livery yard!" a man yelled. "That's where they were ambushed!"

Kitty and Agnes worked together getting Matt's shirt off and bandaging wounds while Doc worked frantically on Jerome.

"Is Gentry going to live?" Matt asked over and over, his voice sounding distant and hollow, as if he were lost in a deep, dark well. "Kitty, will he live!"

"I . . . I don't know."

Festus charged up the street, and when he reached the livery, he saw the assassin's body and rolled it over. Needing better light, he grabbed the corpse and dragged it over to the medicine wagon, the door of which was hanging wide open. He jumped up into the wagon and grabbed the burning candle, then held it over the body's face.

"Cleve Harkins," he whispered, letting the candle fall and extinguish itself in the dirt. "Eli Keeler's henchman!"

Festus knew Harkins only too well. The man was Keeler's most trusted friend and a known gunfighter from Montana. Festus and Matthew had questioned him a number of times about murders, but they'd never had enough evidence to arrest him. It was said that Cleve Harkins did most of his work for hire in Arizona, New Mexico, and Colorado, but there was no bounty on his head or warrants for his arrest in Kansas.

A shotgun was still clenched in his hands. Festus tore it

free and saw that it had been reloaded. "Getting shot to death was too way damned good for you," he muttered as he searched the man's coat pockets and extracted extra shells.

He turned and stared across the tracks at the Lady Gay Saloon, then fingered his deputy badge. Festus wasn't sure if there was enough evidence to arrest Eli Keeler or not, but, by damned, he was going to try.

"Festus!" Barney cried, running across the tracks. "What happened!"

"I'd say that Eli Keeler sent Cleve to ambush Matthew. Both he and Doc Gentry were hit. I'm going across the tracks."

"Holy smokes! Festus, you better wait to get some help!"

Festus clenched the big shotgun until his knuckles turned white. "They kin try, but I'm goin' to do my duty or see the devil dance this night!"

Then he was striding across the tracks, moving swiftly toward Keeler's place. There were at least a dozen shadowy men gathered in front of the Lady Gay, but none of them as big enough to be Keeler. Festus pointed the menacing barrels of the shotgun in their direction. "I'm Deputy Festus Haggen, and if any of you try to stop me, I'll blow you to hell!"

Not surprising, the crowd parted and then Festus was barging into the saloon where the only man left inside was towering behind his bar.

"Keeler," Festus shouted, "you're under arrest!"

"What for!" The giant leered, then took a long pull on a bottle of whiskey.

"The attempted murder of Marshal Matthew Dillon and Dr. Jerome Gentry. Throw your hands up and git out here!"

"You got no evidence against me!"

Festus raised the shotgun and pointed it at Keeler, knowing he could not miss from twenty feet. "This is all the evidence I need. Git your hands up or I'll blow your head off!"

Keeler slowly emptied his bottle, then raised his hands and slowly came around to face Festus. He planted his feet a yard apart in the dirty sawdust and said, "You're making a bad mistake, Deputy! I'll have your badge for false arrest. I'll sue the city and they'll toss you out of office. Without a badge to hide behind, you're nothing. You'll be pushing up clods on Boot Hill by this time next week."

"Are you threatenin' me?" Festus asked, squinting one eye. "Is that what yer doin'!"

"I'm giving you the chance to leave my place alive," Keeler growled. "And then I'm giving you the chance to get out of town while you still can. Without Dillon's backing"—he reached for his pistol—"you're nothing but a dirty—"

Festus brought the shotgun's walnut stock up in a short, vicious arc that terminated at the point of Keeler's granite chin. The big man slammed against his bar, overturning a line of bottles and glasses. The blow would have knocked any ordinary man unconscious, but Keeler merely shook his head, then lunged forward with outstretched hands. Festus ducked and punched the barrel in his gut, yelling, "Freeze or I'll blow out yer innards!"

With an insane bellow, Keeler grabbed Festus by the throat. His thumbs probed for the windpipe with practiced skill while his thick fingers positioned themselves to snap the vulnerable cervical spine. Just as the giant began to crush the life out of Festus, he pulled his triggers.

The saloon rocked with the muffled explosion as Keeler's massive body was thrown backward, striking and overturning his bar in a shower of glass, whiskey, and beer.

"I guess maybe you thought I was bluffin'," Festus choked as he struggled for air. He quickly reloaded, then pivoted toward the crowded doorway, where men stood gawking.

"You boys heard me try to arrest him! Eli is dead and so is Harkins. Any more trouble and I'll be back with this shotgun!"

"What about this place!" a man dared to ask.

"Drinks on the house till it's all gone!" Festus blurted without thinking.

Nothing more needed to be said and the stampede was on. It was all that Festus could do to work his way back outside, where he staggered over to a house Watering trough, ducked his head in the cold water, and tried to collect his scattered wits. He twisted around to see a riot taking place as men fought to collect Keeler's cheap casks and bottles of whiskey and beer. Eli Keeler's massive body was somewhere underfoot, but no one seemed to care or even notice.

Festus figured that the whole rotten bunch would be blind drunk in an hour and someone would likely torch the saloon and dance hall. He heard whores screaming and a couple of gunshots.

"You kin all kill yourselves fer all I care," he said in a tortured voice as he trudged back across the tracks.

"Deputy Haggen, what happened over there!" Barney shouted.

"You don't want to know," Festus answered as he trudged across Front Street and barged into Doc's office, dreading what he expected to discover.

"They're still alive," Betsy said, throwing her arms around Festus's neck and sobbing. "But Jerome is hurt real bad!"

Festus could see Doc, Kitty, and Agnes still working feverishly to save Dr. Gentry. "Yew better come outside and wait," he told the weeping woman as he led her onto the sidewalk, closing and then stationing himself beside the door to keep any other intruders from getting in Doc Adams's way.

There was a knot of Kitty's girls standing together, and when Betsy told them about Jerome, they started to wailing and carrying on something awful, making Festus wonder if anyone would ever cry for him if he were all shot to pieces.

"Is the marshal dead!" Lathrop shouted. "Deputy, what is going on!"

Festus took a deep breath and told them straight out that

Dr. Gentry was fighting for his life but that Matthew wasn't hurt so bad. "All we can do is pray for 'em," he ended. "It's in Doc's and God's good hands now."

"Look!" someone cried. "Across the tracks!"

Everyone turned and Festus saw that the Lady Gay was already being sacked and torched. He guessed that he should probably go over there and try to establish law and order. But his heart wasn't in it right now. Not with Matt and Gentry all shot up and bleeding so bad.

So he just watched that evil place go up in flames like a funeral pyre, and listened to the Long Branch girls cry and carry on.

CHAPTER

22

M att recovered quickly, but Jerome had taken the brunt of the shotgun blast and it was three months before he regained most of his strength. However, he never would recover his dashing good looks: the shotgun pellets meant for Matt had left scars on his handsome face.

"Your life is going to be different now," Doc Adams told him one sunny afternoon in July. "Jerome, you might as well accept the fact that women aren't going to be falling all over you anymore."

Jerome studied his face in the mirror. The top of his left ear was missing and there were several prominent scars along his cheek and neck. He knew that he was lucky just to be alive, and that had it not been for the quick work of Doc Adams, he'd have bled to death. Furthermore, had even one of the large pieces of shot struck him directly in the head or throat, he would have been killed instantly. As it was, he'd nearly lost his right arm and only Doc's skill as a surgeon had saved it from amputation.

"This white streak across the crown of my skull where

the hair used to be black makes me look like a stinkin' skunk," he said with a scowl.

"It shows character," Doc replied. "Just consider yourself lucky to have a full head of hair . . . unlike some of us."

"I owe you my life, Doc."

"And Matt owes you his life. He's also saved my hide more than once, so I guess we are all tied together . . . sort of like blood brothers. Huh?"

"I guess." Jerome tried to smile but couldn't manage it while looking at his face. "The Long Branch girls aren't coming around anymore. Can't blame them."

"They're fickle," Doc snorted. Then he winked and added, "Besides, it's *me* that they're really crazy about. Women like old doctors for reasons I haven't figured out but don't question. Why, just yesterday Gloria told me again that I am handsome. Maybe I'll have her move in and take care of me in my dotage."

Jerome did finally manage to smile, but his spirits were very low. "Doc, why did Agnes go back east? I thought you made a great team."

"Oh, we did," Doc agreed, his expression turning serious. "And after we got used to each other, we became friends for the first time in our lives. But Agnes got homesick and I think she came out here in order to save me. When she saw that I'd be fine on my own again, Agnes couldn't wait to leave. The wild Texas cowboys were a trial and kept her nerves on edge."

Jerome expelled a deep breath. "I've decided not to buy your practice, Doc."

"That's good, because I've decided not to sell it for a while."

"I might be leaving Dodge City."

"What's the matter?" Doc asked. "Have you run out of the Chickasaw Cure?"

"I can always make more," he replied. "But you've stolen all your clients back. I'd starve here."

"No, you wouldn't," Doc told him. "There's enough business for us both."

"Maybe, but I'd like to see Denver and Santa Fe. I might be back, but I might not."

"You know you'd be welcome."

"Thanks. Thanks for saving my life."

"Thanks for restoring my confidence," Doc replied. "You never once criticized me for almost killing that cowboy or any other mistakes."

"No one is perfect," Jerome said, again studying his scarred face in the mirror, "and nothing stays the same."

"Maybe that's good," Doc suggested. "Oh, and by the way, I understand there is a very pretty lady asking about you."

"Betsy?"

"Nope." Doc brushed at his mustache. "I think this one arrived on the train yesterday from Wichita."

"Samantha!" Jerome exclaimed, closing his eyes and remembering her lovely face.

"Yes," Doc said. "I suppose word of what happened to you and Matt finally reached Wichita."

Jerome again studied his scarred face and then suddenly turned away. "Doc, do me a favor, would you?"

"Sure."

"Tell Samantha to go away."

"Are you crazy! I've seen this woman. She's beautiful."

"Yes," Jerome agreed, "she is. And that's part of the problem, because I'm—"

There was a knock at the door and then Matt and Festus both came stomping down the hallway. Matt grinned and said, "So, Gentry, are you ready to meet Miss Wilcox?"

"No, I'm not."

"How come!" Festus demanded. "If there was a woman as pretty as Miss Wilcox come a-callin' on me, I'd even take a bath!"

"I . . . I'm not feeling up to company," Jerome said lamely. "Please tell her to go away."

"I don't think she's willing to do that," Matt replied.

216

He cleared his throat. "Doc, I told her how you saved my life and about what it cost you."

"But you couldn't really describe how I look now, could you, Marshal?"

"I did, but it didn't seem to matter."

"It *would* matter!" Jerome insisted. "Please tell her I don't want to see her."

"You're going to have to tell me yourself," Samantha said, entering the room.

Jerome spun around so that she couldn't see his face. "Go away!"

Doc motioned to Matt and Festus that they should leave the pair alone.

"Jerome? I divorced my husband and don't tell me I made a big mistake."

"Listen," he whispered, "I'm proud of you for leaving but—"

"Turn around," she said, gently placing her hand on his shoulder.

"I . . . I can't."

"Then we will both have to stand right here until one of us drops."

Jerome lowered his hands and clenched them at his side. Slowly, he turned and their eyes met. "Samantha," he choked, "look at me now."

Her blue eyes filled with tears and she raised her hand to cradle his face. "Jerome, I see a hero. I see the man that I fell in love with and couldn't forget. What do you see, Jerome? Tell me the truth."

"I see the one woman I could love forever."

Samantha came into his arms and then they were both crying, hugging, and kissing.

"Well, lookee here!" Festus called a few minutes later when the pair stepped outside, linked arm in arm. "I guess maybe things is gonna work out all right after all!"

Doc and Matt were grinning like a couple of fools, but Jerome hardly noticed as he escorted Samantha down the street.

"Hey," Festus called, "where you lovebirds a-goin'!"

Jerome stopped and turned. The sun was bright on his face and he suddenly felt very, very good. He looked sideways at Samantha and then called back to Festus, "This lovely woman says she wants a *complete and thorough* examination in my medicine wagon. Marshal Dillon, do you have any objections this time?"

"No, Doc, I don't believe I do," Matt said, cheeks reddening in a blush that caused his two friends to burst out laughing.

"So," Samantha said as they continued on, "do you suppose that you'll ever settle down and become a one-woman man?"

"My darling," Jerome replied as he opened the door to his medicine wagon and helped her inside, "I'm betting our futures on it!"